DOUBLE PHOENIX

by Marilinne Cooper

Copyright© 2014 by Marilinne Cooper
All rights reserved
Second edition copyright© 2019
by Marilinne Cooper

This is a work of fiction. Names, characters, places and incidents are either the product of the author's imagination or are used fictitiously. Any resemblance to actual persons, living or dead, business establishments or events is entirely coincidental.

CHAPTER ONE

"Hello? Is anybody here?"

The screen door was unlocked and the front door to the West Jordan Inn stood open. Although the reception area was cozy, no pleasant, gray–haired innkeeper's wife sat behind the cluttered desk ready to welcome Hunter and Miles to northern Vermont.

"Hello?" Hunter poked his head through an archway off to the right. "Wow. Nice barroom. Awesome stained–glass window."

Miles peered up a steep flight of carpeted steps. "Maybe someone is upstairs."

Hunter crossed the room to a swinging wooden door on the opposite side of the room. As he pushed against it with his shoulder, it suddenly crashed open from the other side. "Ow. Shit."

"Oh, I'm sorry. I didn't realize anyone was here." Sarah hastily dropped her armload of tablecloths onto the front desk. "Are you all right?"

"I'm fine. Just hit my funny bone, I think." A smile began deepening the creases of his tanned face. He rubbed his elbow while scrutinizing the slim, striking woman standing beside him.

She was wearing a faded red T–shirt and a pair of blue denim shorts which seemed to emphasize the bareness of her endless legs. Her dark hair was pulled back in a thick braid reaching almost her to her waist. A look of impatience crossed her face when the two men exchanged glances and then burst out laughing.

"You're just not what we expected," Hunter explained.

"Well, what can I do for you? We're not really open yet. The lounge opens at 4:00, the dining room at 5:30. We do have a few basic rooms upstairs–"

"Really? So we could crash here for the –"

"Actually, I think we're lost." Sarah looked at the other man who had finally spoken. Shorter than his companion, his deep complexion and full head of dark curly hair gave him a Mediterranean appearance. "We're trying to get to East Jordan, but judging from the fact that this is the West Jordan Inn, I'm guessing we missed it." While he talked, he kept turning to look out the window, peering nervously at his car.

It was Sarah's turn to laugh. "By about twenty miles, I'd say. East Jordan is on the other side of Jordan Center, down Route 216 past Jordan Falls. But there isn't any place to stay, unless you have friends there."

"I don't know. Do we have friends there, Miles?"

"I guess we won't know if they're friends until we find them and meet them. Oh, looks like she's up." In a swift motion, he darted outside, leaped across the porch and opened the back door of the car.

Through the office window, Sarah could see him lift a coffee–colored infant from a car seat and then kiss her beautiful little face. The breeze ruffled her soft golden curls as he bounced her on his arm to soothe her crying.

"Where are you guys travelling from?" Sarah asked curiously.

"Today? Boston. Yesterday? London. The day before that? Nigeria."

She turned to gape at the tall man beside her, noticing this time that his sun–lightened chestnut hair was caught at the nape of his neck in a ponytail that extended several inches down his back. Because of his height, the two silver earring studs he wore in one ear were right at her eye level. They caught her attention for a second before the screen door slammed again.

"There we go. See Hunter over there with the pretty lady?"

The baby's face broke into a one–toothed smile at the sight of her other traveling companion.

"Hi, Kashi, sweetie! So I think we ought to get a room here for the night, man," Hunter said. "You can make some calls from here, see what you can figure out. Besides, jet lag is catching up with me fast all of the sudden."

"Well, like I said, the rooms are pretty simple, you might want to check them out first." Rummaging in the top desk drawer, Sarah pulled out a couple of old–fashioned keys and led the odd trio up the stairs.

"Is there a bathtub?" Miles asked. "I'd love to give Kashi a real bath. She's never been in anything bigger than a wash basin."

"There's one in the shared bathroom in the hall, but you'll have it all to yourselves. No one else is staying here right now."

"Just think, Miles, a hot bath! How long has it been since you had one of those?"

"I can't remember. Probably a year. How about you?"

"I don't know. I certainly never had one in India. Probably Shanghai. No, I take it back, I did have one on that coffee plantation outside of Nairobi."

Miles laughed. "I bet you did."

Sarah looked over her shoulder in disbelief, but they didn't seem to be joking. She opened the door to a room and stood back so they could see in.

"Hey, welcome to America!" Hunter immediately walked into the room and threw himself down on one of the twin beds covered in colorful patchwork quilts. "This is downright cozy," he remarked, surveying the wide pine floorboards scattered with handmade rag rugs and the long Victorian window draped in lace curtains.

"Cozy? It's palatial!" Passing the baby to Hunter, Miles pulled open the bottom drawer of an antique white dresser and set it on the floor. "We can put a pillow in here for Kashi and we'll be all set."

Sarah tried to keep from laughing as she handed him the old–fashioned metal key. "If you need anything, come down and find one of us. Tyler's in the kitchen and I'll probably be out setting up the dining room and bar."

As she turned to go, she was once again struck by the beauty of the infant who was sitting on Hunter's chest. She was watching Sarah with round brown eyes, while she gripped Hunter's forefingers in her chubby hands. "Come on down and tell me about your travels later on. And I'm sure Tyler will be fascinated to meet you both."

"What's your name?" Hunter called from the bed.

"Oh, sorry." She came back into the room and extended her hand. Miles, who was still standing, shook it warmly. "I'm Sarah. Sarah Scupper."

"I'm Miles. And he's Hunter. And that's Kashi. Is there a phone here somewhere I can use?"

"Sure. There's a pay phone down in the lounge."

Sarah was struck again by the contrast in the two friends. Despite his pleasant manner, Miles seemed very tense and anxious under the surface. Hunter, on the other hand, appeared as laid–back and relaxed as an old farm cat.

"Miles, why don't you just hang out for a few minutes and get your head together before you start calling?" Hunter suggested. "We've just travelled ten thousand miles. We're here now, man. What's another hour or two?"

As Miles hesitated uncertainly, Sarah slipped out of the room and back down the stairs. It was nearly four and she still had to put the tablecloths back on the tables in the dining room and change her clothes. But she found herself curiously attracted to these strangers and their mysterious mission to northern Vermont.

And maybe some stimulating international conversation would help Tyler get out of the funk he had been in lately.

In the kitchen, Tyler Mackenzie held his bleeding finger under the faucet and swore as he looked at the bloody knife next to a pile of chopped onions. These days he was having more and more trouble keeping focused on the mindless tasks of prepping food for the restaurant. His thoughts were constantly wandering off, vacillating between places he had been and places he wanted to go to. Places he could write interesting magazine articles about. Articles that would help him find his way back into the world of investigative journalism, the world he had abandoned over a year ago. Cooking had been one of his hobbies at that time; now the main challenge was how to keep it from being a draining drudgery that sucked the creativity out of him.

He could not remember the impulsive, passionate way he had felt when he had agreed to leave New York and move in with Sarah.

When he lost his job, it had seemed like a sensible, as well as romantic, thing to do. He and Sarah had been lovers for years, but had always been forced to spend months at a time apart from each other because of the nature of his work. They certainly had had their ups and downs; more than once Sarah had ended their relationship, unable to cope with never knowing where in the world he might be or the uncertainty of when she would see him again. He had felt that he owed it to her to try this experiment in living and working together.

Life without a deadline...it had been peacefully pleasant at first. For a while he had been able to suppress his natural restlessness and enjoy the new, relaxed nature of his existence. Even their lovemaking became leisurely – it was no longer a desperate attempt to consume as much of each other as possible before they had to separate again.

But as winter became spring, he found himself more and more dissatisfied with what he had become. Sarah, on the other hand, had settled right into their present way of life. She was still so happy to have him right there with her, helping out at the inn. So happy to not have to be alone anymore. So he tried not to complain.

When she announced that she had stopped using birth control because she wanted to have a baby, he couldn't contain himself any longer.

"What if I don't want to have a baby? Don't you think we ought to talk about this first?"

"Tyler, I don't have much time left if I want to try and do this."

"What are you talking about? You're not dying, are you?"

"My childbearing years are almost over. I'm thirty–nine. Even my eggs aren't as fertile as they used to be. If I'm going to do this, I have to do it now. I mean, WE have to do it now."

She seemed so determined that he stopped arguing with her about it. He couldn't tell her that he didn't even want to live here anymore, let alone be a father. But then even sex, the last exciting frontier in this humdrum small town existence, even sex lost its passion as Sarah decided what days of the month they should do it and what days they shouldn't, how often and even what positions they should use.

So far she hadn't gotten pregnant. But Tyler found himself seething with anger at how untruthful his life had become, how unfaithful to his own principles and desires he was being. He knew he could not go on like this much longer. At some moment in the near future the smoldering volcano he had become was going to erupt and the tenuous peace between them would be destroyed by the molten lava of his own fiery feelings.

By the time Sarah entered the lounge to set up the bar, Miles was already standing by the pay phone, desperately flipping through the pages of the phone book. Finally he threw it down in disgust.

"Anything I can help with?" Sarah called out to him as she dumped a five gallon bucket of ice into the sink.

Dejectedly Miles sat down on the nearest bar stool and leaned his elbows on the bar. "It's just a wild goose chase and I must be the goose. Traveled halfway around the world trying to track down a couple of names and a post office box number. I'm not a private detective, I'm a marine biologist who's just spent two years in the third world."

"Are you looking for a private investigator?"

"No, but I may need one." Miles smoothed a crumpled piece of paper on the bar. "I'm looking for Victor Nesbitt. Or his wife Jillian Richardson. They used to have a theater school in London. Now they have a post office box in East Jordan, Vermont."

"Really? But hold on a second. I think there's someone here who might be able to help you out." Not missing a beat in her routine of setting up the bar, Sarah poked her head through the swinging door to the kitchen. "Tyler! There's someone out here who needs a private investigator."

Before Miles could protest, Tyler came through the doors, wiping his hands on a white apron that was slung low around his waist. Miles' first impression was that this man was not a cook by profession. His lanky, well–proportioned build and startlingly handsome face instantly brought to mind movies or modeling. He had an ageless appearance, although some gray was beginning to show in his thick, wavy, bronze hair, which oddly enough, was nearly a match for the shade of his eyes. His intelligent and inquisitive expression was belied by the slightly angry set of his mouth.

"What's up, Sarah?" He sounded faintly impatient.

"This man here, who happens to be our guest for the evening, has travelled all the way from Nigeria to find someone in East Jordan and all he has is a post office box number. I thought you might have some helpful suggestions for him." Picking up a tray of glasses, she entered the dining room, leaving them alone.

Miles looked a bit flustered as Tyler extended a hand to him. "Tyler Mackenzie. I'm an investigative journalist by profession, although you probably wouldn't have guessed that from my attire."

"Miles Romano, but look, I'm really not interested in hiring somebody –"

Tyler brushed the idea aside with a wave of his hand. "And I'm not interested in your money. As Sarah knows, my brain needs a little more tweaking than it gets back there in the kitchen. Helping you with your problem might help me with mine."

With a well–practiced motion, he reached over the bar and squirted himself a glass full of water from a hose. "Want something?"

"Not now, thanks."

Tyler settled himself on the stool next to Miles and quickly took in his tired eyes, sun–bleached T–shirt and well–worn boots. "Nigeria, huh? What were you doing there?"

"Peace Corps. I spent the last two years in a small village on a river helping establish a fish hatchery." Miles fidgeted anxiously with an ashtray on the bar. "But don't get me started on that subject. What I'm trying to do right now is find this guy and his wife over in East Jordan who aren't listed in the phone book or with the information operator and have only a post office box as an address."

"Well, that shouldn't be too hard." There was hint of disappointment in Tyler's tone. "From what I recall, East Jordan isn't even a crossroads, it's just a thirty–mile–an–hour zone on the highway. You probably just have to knock on a few doors and ask."

"I don't know. I think these people are pretty new in town. A few months ago they were running a theater school in London. Then this thing happened and they closed it down without leaving a forwarding address. I had to bribe their old landlord yesterday to get that much from him. Apparently he insisted on knowing where to forward their bills."

"So what about 'this thing' that happened?"

Miles sighed and looked away. "Maybe I will have a beer. Is it too early to get one?"

With another experienced stretch, Tyler leaned over the bar and opened a refrigerated cooler. "Sam Adams okay?"

Tyler was silent as Miles drank a few ounces of beer, obviously trying to put off speaking for as long as possible. Finally, he put the bottle down and began speaking quickly. "Okay, here's the story. About the same time I went into the Peace Corps, a good friend of mine left for this theater school in London."

"Male or female?"

"All right, she was my girlfriend, or she had been when we were in college. When I decided to go overseas, she decided that she better do something to fill up the void I left in her life." A shadow of grin passed briefly across his face. "Rather than stay at home and mope, she decided to do a junior year abroad studying acting in England. She liked it so much, she quit college and stayed on."

"So is she who you're trying to find in East Jordan?"

Miles frowned. "I wish. Yeah, I guess, that is sort of what I'm trying to do." His expression cleared a little and he went on. "Anyway, she used to write to me regularly, I mean, it wasn't like we we're still trying to carry on a relationship or anything. It was understood that we didn't expect to stay together, that if one of us met somebody else, well, that's how life goes. So when Emma's letters stopped coming, that was my immediate thought. But when she continued not answering my letters, I became worried. So I sent one to Victor Nesbitt, the director of the school, asking him to forward it to Emma, in case she wasn't there anymore."

He stopped for a moment as a couple of regular patrons came in through the door, talking and laughing loudly. Sarah appeared almost immediately, greeting them warmly and serving up their usual drinks without asking.

The sight of customers reminded Tyler of the kitchen responsibilities that awaited him and he urged Miles to continue.

"So anyway, in the meantime my last letter to Emma came back to me with the word 'Deceased' written across her name." Overcome by emotion, Miles closed his eyes for a moment.

"Deceased?"

Miles nodded. "And then my letter to Victor Nesbitt returned as well. 'Moved, no forwarding address.' So by that time I was starting to feel like I had entered the Twilight Zone. Next time I got into town, I tried telephoning the school but all I got was a recording saying the phone had been disconnected. I tried Emma's sister in Buffalo, but she hadn't heard anything from Emma in months. I didn't tell her about the 'deceased' letter – no need for her to worry as well."

"What about Emma's parents?"

Miles shook his head. "Both dead. So the best idea I could come up with was to stop in London on my way back from Nigeria. My time was almost up anyway."

He was interrupted again, this time by the appearance of Hunter carrying Kashi on his shoulders. "There he is. I told you we'd find him here." Hunter lowered the infant down into Miles's arms. "I'm fading, man. I can't keep my eyes open. Let me just snooze for a couple of hours and then I'll watch her for you, okay?"

Tyler looked bemusedly at the scene taking place in front of him. A long–haired man in a tie–dyed T–shirt, khaki shorts and plastic European sandals was passing a baby to Miles, a beautiful brown–skinned baby with golden ringlets, who was wearing only a white tee and tiny hoops in her ears.

"There's my girl! Where's your diaper?" Miles patted her bare bottom affectionately.

"It was wet. I guess the others are still in the car. Look, I'll see you in a while, okay?" Hunter loped back out through the door that led to the lobby.

"So who's this?" Tyler asked curiously.

"This is Kashi. She's mine. I mean, I've more or less adopted her." Miles laughed a little. "Yeah, my life is more complicated than you might think."

"She's Nigerian."

"Well, half–Nigerian." Miles inspected the cardboard coaster his beer was sitting on and then held it out to Kashi. She grabbed for it with a chubby fist and then immediately began chewing on the edge of it. "Hmm. Guess it won't hurt her."

A group of women wearing matching bowling shirts entered the bar. Almost instantly they had surrounded Miles and Kashi, oohing and aahing over the unusual event of seeing a baby in the bar.

"Her father was another Peace Corps volunteer," Miles informed Tyler after the excitement had died down and the bowling team had departed for a table. "Her mother was a sixteen–year–old girl from a very poor village. When he found out she was pregnant with his child, he freaked and ran. The girl's family was beside themselves with anger, and the whole village started to become very anti–American. The girl was upset because she had hoped her baby would be able to have a fine life as a U.S. citizen. Instead the baby was destined to be an outcast in her own society."

"So you said you would bring her to the United States."

Well, in order to do that with the least amount of red tape, I signed the birth certificate saying I was the baby's father. So technically she's really my daughter, not even my adopted one."

"Phew, what a big responsibility." Tyler shook his head, trying not to think about Sarah's plans for his own future.

"My original fantasy had involved Emma as the other parent. So that was another reason why we went to London on the way home." Depression seemed to sweep over him suddenly and he downed the rest of his beer quickly. Kashi continued chewing contentedly on her coaster. "But like I said, the best we could get was a forwarding address from the landlord. And the hint of some scandal that forced them to close the school down. Turns out it had been closed since last March, almost six months ago."

"Scandal?" Tyler glanced at his watch and knew he had to get back to the kitchen.

"Something about a tragic accident while the directors were yachting on the Mediterranean. I couldn't get any details about it or any proof that Emma might really be dead. And that's why I'm here."

Tyler stood up. "That's quite a story. I've got to get back to work, but let me think about what I can do to help you. Maybe we can drive over to East Jordan in the morning."

"And I better get a diaper on this little butt." Miles pried the coaster out of Kashi's hand and then slipped his finger into her mouth to remove the bits of soggy cardboard she was chewing on.

One more question was burning inside Tyler. "So who's the guy you're traveling with? How does he fit into the picture?"

"Hunter? Just a friend. A world traveler on his way back home. We met on the bus to town one day. He seemed excited by the fact that I was actually living and working with the Nigerian people so I offered him a place to stay for a while. Then this thing with Emma came up and then the thing with Kashi and he just kind of moved in permanently and helped out. He's been great with Kashi on this trip. I couldn't have done it without him."

They agreed to talk later on in the evening after the dinner hours were over. Tyler made his way back to the kitchen feeling rather dazed. He couldn't understand why two men had such interest in caring for a baby that wasn't even theirs. He couldn't imagine making such a commitment himself and the realization troubled him immensely.

As Miles started to leave the bar, Sarah called after him. "I just remembered something," she said rather breathlessly as she caught up with him at the door. "There was a play over in Jordan Center a few weeks ago put on by a group I'd never heard of before. Let me ask a few people here if they recall it. Or if I can find an old copy of the local paper, I'm sure there would be something about it. I'll let you know."

By the time Miles returned from the car, juggling a box of diapers, a suitcase and the baby, she was gesturing for him to come back into the lounge.

"Here it is. Look." In one hand she held a newspaper that was folded back to display a large ad. It advertised a production of "Wait Until Dark" playing at the Jordan Center Community House. The performance dates were two weeks past. It had been put on by the Double Phoenix Theatre Workshop of East Jordan. There was even a phone number to call for more information.

"It's worth a try," she said, slipping the folded newspaper under his arm. "Good luck." With a smile at Kashi, she moved swiftly back into the other room.

It was nearly nine o'clock when Sarah looked up to see Hunter sitting at the bar with Kashi asleep in his arms. His freshly washed hair made wet patches on the shoulders of a clean, but wrinkled T–shirt. "Is it too late to get something to eat?" he asked.

"Is Miles coming down also?" She handed him a menu.

When he shook his head, a few drops of water from his hair fell on Kashi's back. "No. Sometimes he's just so incredibly obsessive. He called the phone number that was in the newspaper you gave him, the one for the theater company. He must have spoken to somebody there because the next thing I knew he said he was going off for a few hours. God, I'm starving! Can you just bring a bowl of soup to start with?"

As Sarah laid a place setting for him, Hunter carried Kashi across the room to where a couch created a cozy corner with a fireplace. After placing her gently on one of the cushions, he went on with his conversation as though he'd never stopped.

"I mean, the man hasn't slept in days! But he said he would sleep better if he knew the answer to the question that had been bothering him for months. Do you have any dark beer on tap? If not, I'll take whatever kind you've got in a bottle. The darker the better. Did Miles tell you what's going on?"

"No, but Tyler filled me in." It had been a busy night, but in the few minutes of conversation they had managed to snatch in the kitchen, Tyler had told her the story Miles had related to him.

"Well, all I can say is, that I hope getting some answers changes his state of mind. The dude has been in a mood." Hunter laughed at his own choice of words. "Miles said your husband is a private investigator."

"He's not really my husband, I mean, we're not married," Sarah answered a bit absentmindedly, as she added up a couple of dinner tabs. "And really he's just a journalist who fancies himself as a detective. But he's generally pretty good at it."

"And he's a pretty good cook too if he made this," Hunter said as he sampled the Mexican corn chowder. "Why don't I try the curried chicken stir–fry special? Ah,

America is such an eclectic country. But it still feels weird being back."

Sarah wrote down his order and ripped the carbon copy off. "How long have you been gone for?"

"Almost eighteen months. If it wasn't for Miles needing my help, I probably wouldn't be back now." He shrugged. "But I don't really care."

Picking up a tray of dirty dishes, Sarah went into the kitchen. Tyler was already scrubbing down the stove. "Can you squeeze in one more order for stir–fry?"

"I guess so," he grumbled. "Did that guy from Nigeria ever come back down from his room? I wanted to get out there to talk to him."

When she told him that Miles had gone off to look for the Double Phoenix Theater Company, he stopped working to stare at her. "Where'd he come up with that name?"

"I told him about it. I remembered reading about them in the paper and I thought it might be a place for him to start. Apparently it was a good choice."

"Apparently." Tyler slammed a frying pan down on the cast iron stove and lit the burner under it.

"What are you mad about? Did I do something wrong?" As she put the dirty dishes in the dishwasher, she stole a glance over her shoulder at him.

"Wrong? Not at all. Sounds like you did just right." But his petulant tone and the frown on his face told her otherwise.

"Then what's your problem?"

"What problem? Who's got a problem?" All she could see was his back as he stood motionless in front of the open refrigerator. When he did not turn around after several interminable seconds, she abruptly stopped filling the dishwasher and went back out to the bar.

She did not understand what was happening between them. Tyler had become so tense and introverted lately. It wasn't like him not to express what he was feeling.

The last of the dining room customers were filing out the door. She could see they had left a pile of cash on their table to cover their bill. In the bar, a man and a woman still sat at a table in the corner, holding hands, deeply engrossed in conversation. Three carpenters who were regular customers sat at the far corner of the bar, discussing a diagram that one of them had drawn on a napkin. It was a quiet night for the middle of the week in early September.

Her eyes travelled the length of the bar to where Hunter was finishing his soup. He was certainly an interesting character. She could not begin to guess his age, but she would venture that he was well under thirty.

The kitchen door flew open interrupting her thoughts. Tyler left a steaming plate of food on the end of the bar and disappeared immediately.

"That was fast," Hunter commented as Sarah placed the colorful meal in front of him. "Mmmm, the spices smell great. Reminds me of India."

Before Sarah could even reply, Tyler came bursting through the swinging door again. His apron was gone and he had one arm into a denim jacket. "I'm going out," he announced flatly. "Mind if I take the car?" Without waiting for an answer, he added, "Don't wait up for me."

Sarah stared after him as he slammed the outside door. Then she frowned and bit her lip.

"He seems rather wound up."

"Very unusual behavior. He's never gone off like that before." She flushed with guilt, feeling sure it had something to do with her. "He's seemed kind of discontented lately."

"Can't imagine why. Seems like he's got just about everything a man could want up here. A beautiful place to live, a gorgeous girlfriend, a thriving business–"

"Oh, we don't own the business. We just manage it for the owner who doesn't live here anymore." Sarah cleared away the dishes from the last empty table in the dining room and then counted up the cash that had been left to pay the bill. There was an extra twenty–five percent as a generous tip. "It's not a bad living, but we do work our tails off. How about you? What do you do for money?"

Hunter grinned suggestively. "Just about anything that pays well enough. I haven't had to work much for the last few years. I came into a nice sum of money that I used for travelling. Now that it's just about gone, I've got to think about finishing college."

Finishing college. So he was probably even younger than he looked. "Where did you go to school?" Sarah asked distractedly. She was beginning to realize that Tyler's abrupt departure had upset her more than just a little.

"UC Berkeley. California is the only place for Californians to go to college. Doesn't cost us anything, you know."

"So you're still a long way from home then."

Hunter shrugged. "I don't even think in those terms anymore. Home is wherever I am at the moment."

Sarah still had work to finish so she left Hunter with another dark beer and went back into the dining room to close it down. But all the mindless tasks she had to do could not keep her from wondering where Tyler had gone and what was on his mind.

On her way to the front office, she passed by Kashi curled up peacefully on the couch. She couldn't resist reaching out to touch her. There was nothing as soft as a baby's skin. Kashi's felt a little cool however, and Sarah looked around for something to cover her with. The closest thing at hand was her old black cardigan that hung on the back of the chair at the front desk.

Tucking it over the little bare legs, Sarah wondered if this was how it would be when she and Tyler finally had a baby of their own. Would she let it sleep on the couch in the bar all night? What would they do with it when it was awake? She had never really thought through the day–to–day realities of how having a baby would change their lives.

A blast of cool air and a burst of laughter made her look up at the group of people coming in the door. New customers; the night was not over yet.

It was well past twelve when Sarah finally locked the side door to the lounge. Hunter had long since gone upstairs with Kashi, Miles still hadn't returned and neither had Tyler. She felt odd, sort of nervous and out of synch, as though something important was about to happen. She could not imagine what. Fixing herself a midnight margarita, she closed down the bar and went upstairs to bed.

Sarah felt as though she were pinned down under the covers and she couldn't figure out why. Opening her eyes, she saw that it was morning and also saw the reason she couldn't move. Tyler was stretched out on top of the quilt. He had never undressed, he was still even wearing his jacket. His clothes reeked of cigarettes and beer, smells she had never associated with Tyler. She saw that he had been coherent enough to kick off his shoes.

Early as it was, she found she was not interested in sleeping anymore. Wrapping a silk robe around herself, she remembered that there were guests in the inn; she should go downstairs to make a pot of coffee for them.

Through the window in the lobby, she was surprised to see Hunter sitting on the porch swing, rocking it gently with his bare feet. As she moved closer she could see that he was feeding Kashi a bottle of milk or formula. When she opened the door she could hear him singing softly. She recognized the words to an old Grateful Dead song that had probably been recorded when Hunter himself was a baby.

"Good morning," she whispered, not sure if he was trying to put Kashi back to sleep. If he was, he was not succeeding. Kashi's golden eyes were wide open, taking in every new sight and sound of the Vermont morning. She wore a pink sweatshirt with the Tower of London on it and a pair of tiny matching sweatpants. "I hope Miles appreciates what a good friend you are."

"Yeah, I hope so too."

Hunter looked up, a frown creasing his brow. His expression softened for a moment as he appraised her appearance, moving from her sleepy gray eyes down to the curves of her body that were outlined beneath the thin silk.

Instinctively, Sarah adjusted the wrap of her robe and tightened the belt. "What's wrong?"

"Oh, nothing." His eyes met hers for a second and then looked away. "Except that Miles never came back last night."

CHAPTER TWO

Tyler stood in the shower with his eyes closed, letting the hot water rinse away the shampoo in his hair along with the smells and sounds of the previous evening. He didn't really feel that hung over. Some coffee, breakfast, a little fresh air... he would be fine.

Hung over. It was a funny expression. What really hung over him was a cloud of apprehension. He was worried about how Sarah was going take it when he told her he had decided that he had to go, that he couldn't stay here any longer. Last night, in the false security induced by too much alcohol, it had seemed like such an easy thing to do. Just say goodbye, pack up and go. But alone in bed this morning he had realized that if he said goodbye to Sarah, it would probably be for good. And he was not sure if he was really ready for that.

By the time he found his way downstairs, he had nearly lost all the resolve he had fired up the night before. He was surprised to find Sarah in the kitchen actually cooking breakfast.

"Brunch," she corrected him with a nod at the clock. It was nearly eleven. "Anxiety needs to be fed."

"Anxiety?" Tyler asked as he poured himself a cup of coffee.

"Miles never came back last night from his trip to East Jordan. Hunter is starting to get a little worried, to say the least." Sarah carefully lifted an omelet out of a pan and slid it onto a plate.

"Well, maybe he found his old girlfriend there, still alive, and spent the night. Wanna make me one of those?" He kissed the back of her neck as she worked.

"You would think he would have called or come back by now. It's just hard to believe, you know, with the baby and all..."

"Oh, come on, these guys are lot younger than us. You must have had some fairly irresponsible reactions in your twenties, didn't you?"

Sarah shrugged. "What do you think a six–month–old baby from Africa eats?" She looked around the kitchen.

"Here." Tyler tossed her a banana. "Mash this up."

Sarah's grin of approval made him feel nervous again. "Did you try calling that number in the paper that you gave him last night?" he went on. "Maybe Hunter can reach him that way."

"That's a good idea. Why don't you help him do that?"

Tyler decided to ignore the fact that Sarah's suggestion sounded a little calculated. It took several minutes for him and Hunter to find the newspaper in the bedroom upstairs, which was now strewn with dirty clothes tossed out of backpacks and suitcases.

While Hunter ate his omelet and Sarah tried to feed Kashi the mashed banana, Tyler called the Double Phoenix Theatre Company.

"Damn, it's a recording," he announced.

"Thank you for calling Double Phoenix. Auditions for 'The Abdication' will be held Tuesday and Wednesday, September 2nd and 3rd, from five to eight PM, and Thursday afternoon from two to five. Directions to our workshop are as follows: Take Route 216 East out of Jordan Falls for three miles until you reach Quarry Road. Take a right. After two miles, Quarry Road becomes a dirt road. Go another half mile until you see our mailbox on the left. As you come up our driveway, you will see a big barn on your right where the auditions will be held. Thanks again for calling."

Tyler hung up and turned to Hunter, frowning. "What time did Miles leave last night?"

"Around eight. Why?"

"He must have gotten there right as the auditions were ending." Tyler repeated the contents of the recorded message. "*If* he got there. Maybe we ought to call the police, see if there were any accidents."

Hunter shook his head, his mouth full. "No, let's not do that yet, man. The cops can be such a drag."

Feeling a little lightheaded from hunger, Tyler picked up the unmashed half of Kashi's banana and devoured it. Sarah was not having much success getting Kashi to eat. Every time Sarah put a tiny bit of food into her mouth, Kashi's little tongue pushed it back out.

"Has she eaten solid food before?" she asked Hunter.

"Just porridge. Don't worry. It's just new to her. She'll get used to it." His plate empty, Hunter sat back in his chair and tugged on his ponytail thoughtfully. "So I guess I ought to figure out a way to get over to this Double Phoenix place this afternoon and find out if Miles was there last night."

"I'll take you," Tyler volunteered. "I'm curious myself what the outcome is to the story he told me yesterday. But first, I have to eat."

It was nearly two o'clock by the time they set off. Sarah had suggested that she take care of Kashi while they went. After much discussion, they decided she would not be able to get her work done, as well as some of Tyler's kitchen prep, if she had to look after a baby also. The reality of what that implied made her feel rather disgruntled as she stood on the porch watching Hunter and Tyler drive away.

Mothers have solved that same problem since the beginning of time, she told herself as she went back inside. I'm sure I can figure it out.

"This must be it."

Tyler turned the car into a narrow, gravel driveway. The trees on either side had grown together, creating the feeling of a long dark tunnel, which opened at the other end into wide expanses of green lawn and pastures. An old barn to one side showed signs of serious renovation and reconstruction. There was fresh, unpainted trim on the window frames and the roof looked newly shingled.

On a hill opposite the barn stood a large white farmhouse. A circle of rather rundown cottages nestled close to the edge of the woods behind it.

"Odd place for a motel," Hunter commented.

"Doesn't look like it did much business. But, you never know, it might have thrived back in the thirties and forties."

About ten cars were parked on a patch of ground that had been designated as a parking lot. Tyler squeezed Sarah's Subaru between a van with Indiana plates and a old Volkswagen Beetle from Texas. "I don't suppose you see Miles's rental car here."

Hunter shook his head. "Wow, somebody's got some money. Check out that Maseratti over there." He pointed to the flashy red sports car parked slightly apart from the others.

"Like Magnum used to drive." Tyler opened the door and stretched his legs.

"Who?"

"Sorry. Just a TV show that was probably before your time."

"I remember the show, I just don't remember what he drove." Getting out of the car, Hunter shifted Kashi from one arm to the other. "I need to get one of those slings the women use in Africa to carry their babies around in, he remarked as they walked towards the barn.

"Hey, this is America. Get a backpack. It's more ergonomically correct." Tyler found it unusual that on such a bright fall day, there were no signs of life outdoors at the Double Phoenix Workshop. "Everybody must be at the auditions."

He turned the handle of a newly constructed door, which had been set into the old–fashioned, sliding barn doors, and then stepped aside, letting Hunter enter first.

"Wow, who would've guessed..."

Tyler's eyes took a little longer to adjust to the darkness than Hunter's. Hunter had already climbed a small stairway that led to the top of what looked like a set of wooden bleachers. From there he had a good view of how the barn had been gutted from top to bottom and transformed into a theater.

Tyler found the eclectic mix of people scattered across the descending rows of steps more interesting than the reconstruction of the building. At the very top in the last row sat an extremely thin man whose most notable feature was a frizzy halo of hair in an unnatural shade of red. His yellow silk shirt emblazoned with black stars was tucked into a pair of faded blue jeans with fashionably ragged holes that exposed his bony knees. The expression of disdainful amusement on his narrow face was at odds with the way he chewed nervously on an unlit cigarette.

A few steps below him, a couple of overweight young women sat together whispering. Both of them had raven–black hair; one wore hers cropped and spiky, the other long and kinked. The short–haired one sported a diamond stud in her nose, while her companion had several rings on a pair of hands that displayed long, manicured purple nails. They both were dressed in several layers of shapeless black.

"Okay, would you mind reading that scene again? Just the last page this time." The owner of the loud commanding voice sat front and center. All Tyler could see of him was his silver gray hair pulled back in a short ponytail, but something about the man's demeanor told him instantly that this was the director. "Begin with Christina's line *–'Do you know how many times my mother blew up like a whale–'.*"

Tyler's eyes gravitated along with everyone else's to the stage. Three women stood there with open scripts in their hands, but the one who began reading was so beautiful that the other two seemed like dull shadows in comparison. Her radiant face was framed by shiny golden hair that fell to her shoulders and hung a little too long on her forehead. She had large eyes and full lips and stood a head taller than the others. Her rich speaking voice filled the theater in a way that demanded your attention.

"Why don't you get up and scream?" she shouted at the meek woman to her left and although it was only an audition, every eye in the building was riveted to her larger–than–life performance.

"Why?" The other woman responded in a tiny, bird–like squeak.

"For the pain on your baby's birthday." The tall blond woman reading Christina's part leaned towards her and the smaller woman instinctively backed away.

"W–women have managed before."

"The creatures are so large. Those solid heads. And such a small place to come out of." The vulgar gesture she made between her legs created a ripple of snickers through the audience.

The director stood up. "Thank you. That will be enough. Regina, will you read the part of Ebba now?"

As a soft, pretty girl headed up to the stage, Hunter slid onto the seat next to Tyler. "This is pretty wild," he whispered. "But I wonder when we'll get a chance to talk to that guy."

Tyler had become so interested in the audition that he had almost forgotten their reason for coming. As they watched several more women read for the part of Ebba, he began to realize that the play was a very modern interpretation of the life of the infamous Queen Christina of Sweden.

Ten minutes more and Kashi began fussing loudly. After some dirty looks from a few people, Hunter mouthed, "I'll be outside," and slipped away. As he looked around again, Tyler noted that there were not very many men waiting to try out for parts. Perhaps the male roles were already cast.

Moments later, the director spoke to that very issue. "All right, ladies, thank you all very much. The cast list will be posted tomorrow, IF we find someone to play Azzolino." For the first time, he turned away from the stage, his eyes searching the rustic theater. "Any new men show up to audition today?"

One of the raven–tressed women jerked a thumb over her shoulder at Tyler and said loudly, "Here's a new one."

Tyler felt his face flush as he quickly stood up protesting. "No, I – uh –"

But every head in the barn was craning around to look at him. As he was about to explain, his eyes met those of the gorgeous blonde who had stopped at the edge of the stage area. When she regarded him with sultry interest, he found himself muttering, "Sure, what the hell," and moving down the aisle towards her.

"Hey, he's really cute, where'd he come from?" came a high–pitched, breathy comment out of somewhere on his right.

Someone pressed a script into his hand and murmured, "Read the highlighted lines," and then he was on stage, eye to eye with the blonde actress, who was the same height as he was.

I've been acting all my life, he told himself. Dozens of times he'd pretended to be someone he wasn't in order to get information for a story he was investigating. He was damned good at it. And those times he'd had to make up the words. This time he even had a script to tell him what to say.

He looked down at the highlighted words on the page in front of him and realized he had no idea who his character was even supposed to be.

"Who IS Azzolino?" he whispered to the blonde.

Her eyes narrowed suspiciously. "He's the Cardinal who confesses Christina when she comes to Rome. She falls in love with him. And he with her." With a small sigh, she turned her back on him to mask her disappointment at his ignorance.

Tyler cleared his throat and read in a loud, accusing voice, "This chapter says you're the harlot of the northern hemisphere."

Her head whipped around suddenly with a curious smile. "How picturesque."

"This chapter says you are a man in disguise." He pointed at his script.

She laughed in character. "And a harlot too. Some trick."

"Why did you never marry?"

"I was far too busy."

"Why did you give up the crown?"

"To devote myself to lust."

"Answer my questions!" Tyler's voice thundered through the building. He knew he held the breathless attention of everyone in attendance and suddenly he also knew that this was the answer. This was the release from the restless boredom of his current life. This was next.

At the end of the scene, there was a round of applause followed by a low buzz of excitement. The director was already out of his seat and met Tyler at the edge of the stage.

"Congratulations. The part's yours if you want it," he said in a tone that was heavy with layers of unspoken thoughts and feelings. He gave Tyler a warm smile, but the expression in his eyes was remote and icy. It was the first real look Tyler had of the man's face. Long and narrow with a nose to match, there was a haughty superiority about it that was strangely attractive. And very intimidating.

"Well, I – I really didn't come here to audition. But I find myself very intrigued by the idea. What kind of commitment is involved?"

"It's a very intensive month of rehearsal, afternoons and evenings. There will be few days off with a major role like Azzolino." The director began flipping through the pages of a calendar and then stopped abruptly and extended his hand. "I'm Victor Nesbitt, by the way. And you are...?"

"Tyler Mackenzie." Tyler shook his hand, noting how deceptively strong the grasp of the long, bony fingers was.

"Do you know anything about Double Phoenix? Why DID you come here, anyway?" The man rested his calendar on the edge of the stage and backed up a few steps to scrutinize Tyler.

Tyler suddenly felt very uncomfortable and afraid of blowing his chances here. Again he stuttered a little as began speaking. "I– I–I'm with someone who is looking for a friend. He needed a ride because his friend disappeared with their car."

"Who's he looking for?" a young, platinum–haired girl asked. Tyler suddenly realized that most of the people in the room had gathered behind the director and were listening in.

"A guy who was supposedly headed here last night. About 5'8" with curly brown hair, in his late twenties maybe. Name of Miles Romano."

Nobody spoke as Victor flipped through some pages of notes in the back of his calendar as though looking for the name. Finally he shook his head. "I don't recall anybody of that name auditioning last night. Do you, Jillian?" The woman he addressed was the tall blonde who was still on the stage with Tyler.

“No, I don't, luv.” British, Tyler realized. He hadn't noticed her accent when they had been reading the script.

“Oh, he didn't come to audition. I believe he actually had wanted to speak to you about one of your former students. An old girlfriend he was searching for. Someone named Emma.”

There were a few gasps and then an eerie silence descended on the group gathered in the first few rows of the theater.

“Well, in that case I certainly would have remembered him if he had been here.” Victor turned to address the others. “You may all go now. As I said before, the cast list will be posted tomorrow. For any of you who don't make it, there is plenty of other work that needs to be done to mount this production, all of which will enhance your understanding of and background in professional theater.” He turned back to Tyler. “Tyler, if you're really interested, I'd like you to stay for a few moments so I can talk to you alone.”

With an undertone of anticipation, the others in the theater collected their belongings and walked slowly out of the building. The tall blonde named Jillian was the only exception. She hovered at Victor's side until he murmured something in her ear.

“Okay. I'll see you at home in a few minutes then.” With a narrow look at Tyler, she picked up her script and headed up the center aisle.

Victor rested his back against the edge of the stage with his arms crossed in front of him, appraising Tyler. “Are you really interested in doing this?” he asked at last. “Because if you are, let me explain a few things to you. Double Phoenix is a theater workshop that offers classes and lodging to serious students of theater. Because we are just getting off the ground here, our enrollment is still quite small. Consequently we open our auditions to the public, although very few people have the time to make the commitment we require. Our students have classes every morning in voice production, movement and acting. We have afternoon and evening rehearsals and for those not involved in the current production, the afternoon is a stagecraft workshop where they create the sets and costumes and learn about lighting. Have you ever had any formal training in theatre?"

"No, not really. I did some acting in college but that was years ago." Tyler's mind was already racing ahead to how he would work things out.

"And what about the current commitments in your own life? Any trouble getting out of those?"

Tyler laughed a little. "My girlfriend's not going to be too happy about it. We run an inn together over in West Jordan. But she can manage without me for a couple of months. She did for years before I moved up here. I'm actually a journalist by profession."

"Really?" Victor scrutinized him silently again for a moment. "Well, I think you're a natural for this part and it'd be a damn shame if you couldn't do it. None of our current male students really have the maturity the role requires."

Tyler flushed a little. Although he was over forty, he never really thought of himself as "mature."

"There is one more topic I have to cover and I know this is going to sound like a strange request."

Tyler leaned one elbow on the stage. "What's that?"

Hunter and Kashi appeared at the back of the theater. Victor didn't seem to notice them as they began heading down the aisle.

"It's about Emma, the girl you say this man was looking for. Emma is a topic we don't bring up."

"And why is that?"

"Mainly because it still upsets my wife very much. We had to close our school in London because of the uproar caused by Emma's death."

Tyler tried to pretend he wasn't intrigued. With a warning look at Hunter, he shrugged his shoulders nonchalantly. "Doesn't matter to me. I never knew her. But I am curious why you chose northern Vermont to re–open your school. It's not exactly an area known for its high cultural appeal."

"We wanted a place where we could start fresh without that tragedy replaying itself every time we turned around. The story didn't make the headlines here that it made in England." Victor looked over his shoulder, suddenly aware of Hunter's presence.

"He's with me," Tyler explained. "Guess what, man? I'm taking a part in the play!"

"Really?" Hunter's green eyes were kaleidoscopes of changing emotion. "That's wild. Did you ask him about Miles?"

"He says Miles never made it here last night. And I guess his old girlfriend did die." As Tyler turned back to Victor, he did not notice Hunter beginning to protest. "How did she die?"

Victor was shuffling through a black leather bag and did not look up as he answered. "She drowned. Here's a copy of the script for you. First rehearsal is tomorrow night at seven. Now, if you'll excuse me, I have a lot of work to do."

He gathered up his notes and shoved them into the bag. But before he turned to go, he shot Tyler another piercing look from his cold eyes. "And as I said, the subject of Emma is closed. If you want to stay and work with us, don't bring it up again."

"Sure. No problem." Tyler suddenly realized that Victor was waiting for them to leave the theater before him. "Well, we'd better get going too. You probably want to close this place up."

"But..." Sputtering a little, Hunter tried to catch up with Tyler's quick pace. "Listen, there's something's wrong here. We have to talk. Ouch!" he protested as Kashi grabbed a handful of his hair tightly in his fist. "Kashi, let go!"

Tyler squinted painfully as they came out of the dark theatre into the bright afternoon sun. It had been another world inside. The sight of Sarah's Subaru station wagon brought back reality and responsibilities. He had five pounds of frozen shrimp to butterfly by four thirty. He had black bean soup to make. "My God, I can't believe I agreed to do this. Sarah is absolutely going to freak."

"Tyler, listen to me. That guy in there was lying." Hunter had finally managed to extract his hair from Kashi's fingers and brought her down off his shoulder.

"What do you mean? Lying about what?" Tyler leaned on the open door of the car and stared at him over the roof.

"About Miles. He was here last night."

"What? How do you know?" Tyler looked back at the barn, expecting Victor to come out the door any minute.

"Because while you were in there with him, I talked to a girl who came outside for a cigarette. She was one of the girls we saw auditioning. Not that wimpy little one who was on stage when we came in. The pretty one with the reddish hair."

Tyler remembered her. The two women in front of him had assured each other in spiteful whispers that Victor would choose her for Ebba because she looked right for the part.

"Anyway, I asked her if she'd been here last night and if she might have seen Miles. She told me right away that she remembered him. She said he showed up just as the auditions were over. Everyone was leaving the theater and she had stopped to light up and he asked her where he could find Victor Nesbitt. She said she remembered him because he she thought he was here to try out for a part and she knew how bummed the director was because not very many men had showed up. She told him Victor was inside and she saw him go in."

"Do you think Miles never found him?" Tyler found himself already wanting to believe that his "director" was not guilty of lying.

"Of course, he found him. That sleazy guy is lying!" Hunter pounded his fist on the top of the car. "I heard him tell you he that no one was allowed to discuss Emma. What kind of crap is that?"

"I don't know. But here he comes, get in the car."

Tyler got in and slammed the door, but Hunter stood his ground.

"What do you mean? Let's go confront him, ask him what's going on."

"It won't do any good. He'll still deny seeing him. Now get in." Tyler adjusted the rear view mirror so he could watch Victor heading across the field next to the barn.

"Look, I've got to find Miles." Reluctantly, Hunter got into the car. "And I don't want to call in the police."

"They wouldn't do anything for forty–eight hours anyway." Tyler watched Victor wipe his feet off at the bottom of the porch steps leading up to the big white farmhouse. "No, something weird is definitely going on here. And the best way to find out about it is to get right into it." He started up the engine and backed up on to the gravel road.

"What do you mean?"

"I mean, I'll be back here tomorrow night with a legitimate excuse for spending lots of time here talking to people. Now let's go home. Maybe Miles went on a bender after finding out that Emma drowned and slept it off on the side of the road and is back at the inn waiting for you."

"Maybe." Hunter's silence indicated that he didn't have much hope of that happening. "Shit," he said after a while. "What if we never find him?"

"Don't say that. We'll find him. I'm pretty good at that stuff, don't forget. And I'll be back there tomorrow, as long as Sarah doesn't kill me tonight when I tell her she's going to have to find somebody else to be her chef."

"That's right, man, I forgot about your job." Hunter stroked Kashi's curls thoughtfully as she slept with her head against his chest. "Well, hell, I guess I'm not going anywhere until Miles turns up. Sooner or later, he's got to come back for Kashi and I'm not going to travel alone with her."

"Where were you headed, anyway?" Tyler asked curiously.

"Back to California, I guess. I was going to drive as far as Ohio with Miles and then fly from there. I've been travelling for almost a year and a half now and my money's nearly gone. So it's probably time to go home and round up some more."

"Do you know how to cook?"

"Sure, I guess so. Why?"

"Because I know an innkeeper's who's going to be looking for a cook in about forty minutes."

Hunter laughed. "You mean your job? I don't know how to cook THAT well."

"I'll teach you. Tonight."

"Get serious."

"I am serious. It works. You take over for me, I can do this play and find out more about this weird thing with Emma and Miles, and best of all it would get me off the hook with Sarah." Tyler hooted with exhilaration at how easily he had solved his problems.

"It sounds crazy, but hey, what the hell. I'll try it." Hunter looked out the window at the beautiful countryside they were driving through. On one side of the road the rolling hills were thickly covered in maple trees, a few of which had already changed from their summer greenery to a brilliant autumn red. Black and white cows added their stark contrast to the grassy background of an open pasture on the other side of the road. "I guess if I could handle Bangkok for three weeks I can stand a little bit of northern Vermont for a while."

CHAPTER THREE

"You what?"

It had been an extremely busy couple of hours and Sarah hadn't questioned why Hunter was helping Tyler prepare dinners. But when she came into the kitchen to pick up an order and found Tyler explaining what particular jobs had to be done each day of the week, she began to get suspicious.

"Why are you showing Hunter how to work the kitchen?" she had asked a few minutes later. "You know we can't afford to hire anyone else."

With a knowing glance at Hunter, Tyler had taken Sarah by the arm and drawn her back out into the lounge. He had thought she would not show her true feelings in front of a room full of customers. But as he quietly recounted the afternoon's events, her eyes widened and her face lost its color.

"Look, it's something I really want to do, you know I've been going a little crazy lately–"

"How can you do this to me in the beginning of fall foliage season?" Sarah hissed at him.

"I think I'm covering my ass pretty well. Hunter said he was willing to stay on–"

"And you trusted the word of some young drifter who just showed up yesterday and has–" Sarah realized that several heads were turned in their direction and she stopped abruptly.

"We'll talk about this later, okay?" Tyler put his face in front of hers forcing her to look him in the eye.

Her mouth had hardened into a thin, angry line. "I don't think there's much to talk about," she whispered through clenched teeth. "If this is the way you show your commitment to me, you might as well pack your bags, buster."

"Sarah–"

She pulled away from him and stalked into the dining room where she knew he wouldn't dare follow her. "How are your dinners? Everything all right?" she said pleasantly to an elderly couple.

Her reaction had been a little stronger than he had expected, but only a little. He hoped he could pacify her in bed tonight.

"Are you out of your mind? You think I'd make love to you the way I feel right now?" Sarah whirled around to face him, her eyes flashing like steel daggers. "I don't understand how you think you can be so irresponsible and get away with it. I mean, here we are, as good as married, trying to have a baby and you pull a number like this on me. How can I trust your instincts if you think this is the way you should act towards me?"

"Oh, stop thinking about yourself for a minute!" Tyler was shouting back at her now, his anger fueled by her confrontational manner. "Do you care that I don't feel fulfilled by spending my life cooking in a small town inn? Do you realize how hard it has been for me to let go of my career to live here with you? And did you ever think that maybe I really am not ready to settle down and be a father? That I've only been going along with this egg game for you?"

Her face had paled at the beginning of his tirade but now her cheeks flushed and her eyes filled with tears. "If that's how you feel, then I guess it's over between us. You might as well move out."

"It's not over. I'm still as wild about you as I ever was. I just need some space to do something for myself for a little while." With a quick motion, he reached for her hand before she could pull it away.

"Yeah, that always worked for you, didn't it?" Sarah's tone was bitter and she wouldn't look at him.

"Two months off chasing down some story, two weeks of sex with Sarah in Vermont, and then off again for another two months."

"Sarah, I can't tell you how alive I felt, for the first time in months it seemed, up there on that stage. And if I'm over there I can pursue this weird angle on Miles. I haven't had a mystery to unravel in long time."

She did not speak for a moment and he wondered if she had finally seen his point of view. But when she turned to him at last, there was no sympathy in her expression and her tone was flat and practical.

"How long until this play is performed?"

"I think he said a month."

"And Hunter has agreed to stay here that long? What happens when Miles turns up? Or what if Miles never turns up?"

"Hunter will do fine. And he's hoping you will help take care of Kashi until – until whatever." There was a big question mark still looming over the situation, but he hoped mentioning Kashi would have the right effect on Sarah. But she went right on in that same businesslike voice.

"And how did you think you would get back and forth to rehearsal every afternoon and evening? I need to have a car here."

"Maybe I can get a ride with someone." He knew that was not a likely solution but he wasn't going to admit it now. "Or maybe I can stay over there sometimes. Most of the actors live there, there's probably some place I can stay."

"Well, maybe you ought to look into that. The way I feel right now, I'd rather not see you for a while." Slipping her hand out of his, she left the living room. A few seconds later he heard her bare feet padding down the stairs.

He moved to the top of the stairwell, straining to hear if she was going outside. The smell of cigarette smoke told him all he needed to know. Sarah never smoked unless she was really upset; he hadn't seen her light up a cigarette in a couple of years.

By the following afternoon they had agreed on two things. First, that Tyler would take the car that night and look into whether there was any place he could stay at Double Phoenix for the next month. Secondly, that, despite Hunter's apparent paranoia of the law, they had to report Miles's disappearance to the police.

"It's the easiest way to track a missing vehicle," Tyler explained when Hunter vehemently protested. "You're not wanted by the cops for something, are you? Is that why you've been travelling around the world?"

"Do you think I would set foot back in this country if I was?" Hunter shook his head. "No, it's just this Kashi thing. I don't know if Miles has this all straightened out legally and I'm afraid they might take her away, put her in some orphanage, or send her back to Nigeria."

They both looked across the room at Kashi. She was sitting in the wooden high chair that usually resided in a corner of the inn's dining room, waiting for some lucky baby's night out. She had a look of intense concentration on her face as her chubby fingers picked Cheerios off the tray and helped them find their way to her mouth. Sarah sat next to her with a phone book and the portable phone, calling names of possible babysitters.

"All right, we won't say anything about Kashi, but depending how far they look, they might find out about her." Tyler looked at his watch. "We'll have Sarah call. She knows all the local cops around here and besides I've got to run."

Tyler picked up his copy of "The Abdication." After his argument with Sarah, he'd stayed up for the next few hours reading the play and then had lain awake in bed for two more hours feeling very moved and impressed by the script. It was extremely well written. He especially liked how the author had displayed

Christina's inner sexual torment by having one woman play her feminine side and another woman play her masculine side in flashbacks from her past. He couldn't wait to get started working on his part.

Hunter followed him to the door. "Everything okay between you and Sarah?" he asked as they stepped outside in the afternoon sunshine. "I could hear you guys arguing last night."

"Okay? Not hardly. 'Civil' is what I would call our relationship at the moment." Tyler got into the car. "'Over' is how she would describe it." He fought off the wave of depression that threatened to suffocate his excitement. "But it's nothing. We've been through this before. It'll do me good to get out of here for a few weeks."

"Hey, I've seen a lot of the world in the last year." Hunter leaned his elbow on the top of the car. "So far this place ranks right up there with the best of them."

"Yeah, well, I bet you never spent a whole year doing the same thing over and over again in any of those places. You might change your mind." Tyler started the engine.

"Yeah, but you're a lot older than I am. You're supposed to be settling down by now."

Hunter's offhand remark stung deeper than he had probably intended. Tyler cleared his throat. "Well, I hope it all goes okay for you here after your crash course last night. You remember everything I showed you, right?"

Hunter laughed. "My short term memory's been destroyed by too many alternative substances. I don't remember a thing. But don't worry, man. I'll be fine." He slammed the car door and stepped back so Tyler could drive away.

The rearview mirror gave him a last glimpse of the long-haired stranger in whose care he was leaving his trusting dinner customers. He had to be crazy to be doing this. But who cared.

"You're here early."

Tyler looked around to see who was addressing him. He had barely walked away from his car in the small parking lot across from the theater barn. He still didn't see anyone for a moment until a head appeared over the side of the Ferrari convertible. It was the thin man with the frizzy hair who had been sitting in the back row the day before. In one hand he held a soft chamois rag; he wiped the other hand on his stylishly ragged jeans before extending it to Tyler. Tyler noticed the nails were long and extremely well–manicured.

"I'm Tracy Lane. I know who you are. We all know who you are." He delivered his lines dramatically and punctuated them with a theatrical laugh. "I'm the set and lighting designer. Unfortunately, in such a small company, that also means I have to build the sets and hang the lights. Back in London I didn't have to get my hands dirty AT ALL."

His flamboyant delivery strongly suggested his sexual preference. Tyler tried hard not to prejudge him. "So you were with Victor at his school in London?"

"I've been with Victor and Jillian for years." Tracy walked around the sports car and then knelt down to polish the hub cap on the other side.

"So then you must have known Emma, the girl who died." Tyler felt a twinge of excitement at the well of information that might be tapped here.

"Uh–uh–uh! You know that's a no–no. I heard Victor tell you so." Tracy wagged his finger at Tyler like an old schoolteacher.

Tyler wondered why he hadn't noticed that Tracy had still been in the theater when he and Victor had been talking. He tried to act nonchalant about the issue. "Well, I'm just curious, that's all. It sounds like an interesting story."

Tracy gave his stage laugh again. "Interesting isn't the word for it, sweetheart."

"So is polishing Victor's car part of your dirty job as set designer?" Tyler's words came out a bit more sarcastic than he had intended.

"Victor's car? Ha, that's rich. This is MY car. Puhleez. I do enough for Victor without getting down on my knees and polishing his hub caps!" As Tracy laughed at his own sexual innuendo, Tyler couldn't help but grin. And wonder how someone in Tracy's position could afford such an expensive car.

"Well, actually I came early to talk to Victor. I'm wondering if there's a place I can stay here for a few weeks." Tyler looked around the little courtyard of cottages, noticing again how quiet everything was.

"Everybody's eating right now. They have supper early so they can get in a full night's work. Victor and Jillian eat by themselves in their house–" Tracy indicated the large white farmhouse– "and they don't like to be disturbed. The others have their meals in that pavilion over there." He pointed to a building that looked like it might once have been just a roof and four stone pillars, but now had walls and windows.

"So what do you think? Are there any available rooms here or am I way off base even asking about this?" Looking down at the top of Tracy's head as he shined the silver chrome, Tyler noticed that the roots of his fluffy red hair were a much darker color than the rest of it.

"Well, Courtney just got expelled–"

"Expelled?" The word made Tyler think of high school principals.

"You know, sent away. Kicked out. But she shared a room with Phoebe and I don't think Phoebe would go for a male roommate."

"What does a person get kicked out for around here?" Tyler was very curious.

Tracy shrugged. "We'll never know. Big secret between her and Victor. Must've done something she wasn't supposed to." Tracy pulled an old–fashioned gold pocket watch out of his jeans. He held it out to check the time, but Tyler thought he was also showing off just how expensive it was. "Victor's probably done eating by now. Why don't you just give a little knock on his screen door? The worst that can happen is he'll tell you to go away."

But before Tyler had a chance to thank Tracy for his information, Victor came striding out of the house and headed purposefully across the lawn to the theater. He was dressed all in black again and with his silver hair and sharp profile he looked almost sinister. Tyler could not help thinking that he also looked very out of place against the verdant backdrop of the Vermont countryside.

"Well, there's goes your chance to talk to him before rehearsal," Tracy remarked, idly polishing one of the side mirrors.

"What's a man like Victor doing up here in the middle of nowhere?" Tyler asked curiously as he watched the director disappear into the theater building.

"Putting on plays for the poor ignorant masses. You ask too many questions."

"But couldn't they make a better living at this in a city somewhere?" Tyler persisted.

Tracy threw his head back again for a dramatic laugh. "You don't know anything about them at all, do you? Money is no object, as they say. Jillian is loaded. She comes from an extremely wealthy family. They do this because they are theatrical artists who must create plays for the same reason a painter has to paint or a writer has to write."

"Oh." The slamming of a screen door made them both look over at the farmhouse again. Jillian was standing on the porch holding a bowl of dog food over the head of a large Siberian husky. She was dressed like a classic ballet dancer in a high cut black leotard and white tights. Placing the food on the steps, she waited until the hairy white dog began eating and then hooked its collar to a heavy chain. As she stood with her hands on her hips watching the dog eat, Tyler could not help admiring her statuesque physique and athletic muscular definition.

"Is she a dancer too?" Tyler asked softly.

"Oh, they all dress like that for their movement classes. But she's the only one who looks so fabulous in tights. The rest of them put their clothes back on right away, but she's pretty uninhibited. As you'll find out."

The sound of voices from across the field broke the spell for all of them. Jillian went back inside, Tracy returned to his polishing, and Tyler headed toward the theater to join the others who were moving in that direction.

As he approached the group, he searched their faces for the red–haired girl that Hunter had spoken with about Miles. He was almost immediately distracted by a couple of women who introduced themselves as Frieda and Rochelle.

Frieda was dark and pretty and slightly plump in a way that suggested she ate too much junk food. The extra twenty pounds gave her a feminine softness that was missing from the other women in the group. Rochelle had a pale, waif–like appearance with long blond curls and the figure of a ten-year-old girl. They accompanied him into the theater with their ingenuous chatter and questions. He realized that despite their youthful airheadedness, it would probably be quite useful to cultivate a friendship with them.

He received quite the opposite reception from a short, slight young man named Gabriel whose outstanding feature was a very bad case of acne.

"Gabriel wanted to play Azzolino." Frieda turned her back to Gabriel so he couldn't see her whispering to Tyler. "But who could ever believe that Christina would fall in love with him?" She giggled behind her hand.

Rochelle leaned in conspiratorially. "He thinks that just because he's studied here with Victor for nine months he can act. But he's a lousy actor. Victor gave him the part of Charles, probably just because he feels sorry for him."

"Who are those two coming in?" Tyler indicated the two black–haired women who had sat in front of him at the audition.

"Oh, they're not as scary as they look," Frieda confided. "You'll like them when you get used to them. Cassandra is the one with the spiked hair. She plays Chris, Christina's masculine side in the flashbacks. Paloma is the assistant director and stage manager."

Tyler still did not see the redhead he was looking for. He climbed up on the stage to help a couple of men who were setting up chairs. Tony and Marcus, they said their names were, and Tyler added them to the bank of new names he was trying to memorize.

"People!" Victor said loudly. "Let's all take our places on the stage for the read–through. My wife's the only one missing and she'll be here momentarily."

As soon as they were all seated, Jillian appeared as if on cue, rushing breathlessly down the aisle. She still wore her leotard and tights but had tied a short red skirt around her waist to create the illusion of modesty. In a practiced motion, she stepped out of her Scandinavian clogs before climbing the steps to the stage.

"Sorry I'm late." As she joined the group on stage, the sense of camaraderie slipped away. Tyler realized that although the other actors all appeared to be friends, Jillian stood apart, alone and unapproachable.

"Okay, we're ready to begin. As you may have noticed, Courtney has been replaced by Frieda in the role of Ebba. Courtney had to leave us unexpectedly this morning. And despite our attempt to lure some local talent into this production, Tyler Mackenzie was the only member of the surrounding communities that suited a role better than one of our own students. But we did at least generate some interest in Double Phoenix with the auditions."

Tyler realized with a sinking stomach that Courtney must have been the red–haired girl that Hunter had talked to. He wondered if she had been alone when she saw Miles. He would have to ask her former roommate, Phoebe, if he could figure out which one she was.

"I'd like to read through the entire script without any interruptions. If you have any questions, please save them for the end. And let me just remind you that, despite the contemporary treatment of some topics, this is Europe in the seventeenth century. The year is 1655. It would be extremely helpful in your character preparation for any one of you to do some research on what life was like at that time of history. Okay, so Birgitto the dwarf enters first...."

"The baby's sound asleep upstairs," Jennifer the babysitter announced as she came into the kitchen from the front hall. "I've got to go, my mom says I have to be home by nine on school nights. You ought to get like one of those baby monitor things where you can hear the baby upstairs while you're down here."

"She's right about that," Sarah said to Hunter, as she fished in her apron pocket for some money to pay Jennifer. "I hope you don't mind ones." She counted several bills out into Jennifer's hand. "Thanks a lot, Jen. You were great with her. Can you come back tomorrow night?"

"I don't know, I have field hockey practice unless it rains."

"Oh." This babysitter scheduling wasn't something Sarah had bargained for in her deal with Tyler, but Hunter didn't know anybody in West Jordan yet. "Okay, well, we'll call you about the weekend." As she followed Jennifer out into the lounge, she called over her shoulder, "Hunter, don't let that lobster bisque come to a boil."

"Right." Sarah had to give him credit for how relaxed he was, jumping into the unknown waters of the inn's kitchen. He just took everything in stride, didn't freak out when he made a mistake or get nervous when the pressure was on. Very different from Tyler's hyper style. They were going to have to simplify the menu a little for the next month, but that was okay. Working with someone so laid back was actually making Sarah feel a little calmer about all the changes happening between her and Tyler.

Later, when the dining room had emptied and the remaining bar patrons were under control, Sarah placed a call to the local police station.

Then, before telling Hunter that a cop was on the way to take his statement, she slipped upstairs to make sure Kashi was all right. Kneeling down on the floor next to the dresser drawer that doubled as a makeshift crib, Sarah felt as though she were checking on a litter of puppies. Tomorrow they would have to look for a crib; she thought she had remembered seeing one in the attic.

"She's okay, I've already checked her a couple of times." Hunter had materialized at her side without a sound. "What a little beauty, huh?" He squatted down beside Sarah, his shoulder brushing hers. "You ever think about having one of your own?"

"All the time. Been actively trying even. Now it turns out Tyler isn't really interested in having kids at all." Feeling the tears forming in her eyes, Sarah stood up abruptly.

"Really? I can't wait to have a few of my own. I mean, I can wait. I'm not ready yet. But I really want to have kids someday."

In spite of herself, Sarah had to smile at his youthful exuberance. "Well, it's different for guys," she said as they headed back downstairs together. "You don't have to worry about getting too old, except that your joints might get a little too stiff to get down and play on the floor easily."

"A stiff joint, did you say? I wouldn't mind smoking one right now at all." As Hunter grinned at his own drug–related humor, Sarah could not help but laugh.

"Can't help you out there, buddy. You're on your own in that quest." Sarah had a feeling that Hunter would be able to sniff out the pot–smoking customers as easily as a trained police dog at the Miami airport. "But I think I'd hold off for a few minutes if I were you. The police are sending someone down to get some information from you about Miles."

"Right now?" Hunter froze in his tracks."You didn't mention Kashi, did you?" An edge of anxiety was working its way into his voice.

"I promised you I wouldn't, didn't I?" Sarah wondered if there wasn't something more to the story behind Kashi's adoption, or if she really was legally adopted at all. Sarah touched his arm reassuringly. "Besides, they said when an unmarried man disappears of his own free will, nobody gets too excited for a few days. But since they don't have a hell of a lot to do up this way they said they'd look into it."

"Not too excited, huh?" Hunter scowled for a second and then relaxed. "I guess you're right. I wouldn't want the police on my tail every time I took off for a weekend."

"You probably ought to go see if you can find a picture of him, you know, his passport or something."

Hunter shook his head. "I already looked. I think he had it with him. You know, I've thought about this, and I've decided if it comes to it, I'm going to say that Kashi is MY daughter. Will you go along with that?"

Their eyes met for a moment. Sarah was not sure what emotion she saw there. "Why shouldn't I?" she said, turning away and moving back behind the bar. "It's just as believable a story as the one Miles told."

"So which one is Phoebe?" Tyler turned to Frieda and spoke just loud enough to be heard over the noise of everyone standing up. Victor had given them a ten minute stretch break between the two acts of the play.

"Phoebe? She's the one sitting down there in the audience." She nodded towards a rather plain looking woman, with a mop of mousy curls, whose face was mostly hidden behind large glasses with thick lenses. "She does costumes and props. Why? Do you know her?" Frieda looked at him with an odd expression on her face.

"No. I just heard she was the one who lost a roommate and I'm going to be needing a place to stay."

"Oh." Frieda giggled. "Victor doesn't let men and women room together. Or even share the same cottage. You wouldn't want to stay with Phoebe anyway. She's a strange one."

"Really? Actually I do have something I need to ask her. Would you introduce me?"

With another curious look, Frieda led the way down the steps. Intently sketching on a pad, Phoebe started nervously when Frieda addressed her. The distortion of her thick glasses made her appear permanently wide–eyed and surprised.

After a few seconds of idle chat, which seem to make Phoebe uncomfortable, Tyler got right to the point. "I hear you were Courtney's roommate."

"That's right."

"Were you with her the other night when she saw a very tanned man with dark, curly hair go into the theater to talk to Victor?"

Phoebe shook her head. "I don't know anything about that," she replied, avoiding Tyler's gaze by concentrating on darkening a shadow on the costume sketch she was making.

As though sensing the direction of their conversation, Victor approached them through the milling crowd. "Phoebe, Jillian wants to speak to you. I think she stepped outside." Still keeping her head down,

Phoebe rose and slid out into the aisle. Tyler noted that her manner was almost subservient.

Victor turned to Tyler. "You're doing quite well," he said. "Any questions you came up with when you took your script home last night?"

"Only one. Is there any place I can stay here for the next month?" Tyler laughed a little, but Victor's aura of intensity seemed to squelch any humor he saw in the situation. "Sarah doesn't want me to leave her without a vehicle every night. I thought you might have a spare room here...?"

Victor frowned, deep in thought. "Your situation is somewhat different than everyone else's here, you know," he said finally. "They're all paying quite a lot of money for classes and workshops as well as room and board. But we really need you for this play."

"Maybe I can do something for you in exchange for lodging," Tyler began, but Victor was already shaking his head.

"We have more man power around here than we know what to do with and we already have a couple of work/study arrangements. But I'll tell you what. You can stay at the farmhouse with Jillian and me. We have a few spare bedrooms. We can write you off as our personal guest. And as long as you're going to be here, you might as well sit in on the acting and movement classes during the day. It can only improve your performance in the play."

Tyler was momentarily speechless. He had not pegged Victor as man of generosity or kindness. "You're sure? I wouldn't be imposing? Your wife won't mind?"

"If I tell her you're staying, she can't say anything about it. We're both quite busy all day anyway and I'm sure you will be too. As long as you respect our privacy at night, there shouldn't be a problem."

Even the director at home, Tyler thought. He didn't like the way the man spoke about his wife but that was none of his business. "Well, thank you. I'm overwhelmed by your offer."

"You're welcome. Not a problem. So I'll tell Jillian to make sure Phoebe has the guest room ready by...?"

Phoebe again. Costumer and maid? Maybe it was one of those work/study things. "Is tomorrow too soon?"

Officer Golden, the one-man night force of the West Jordan Police Department, had come and gone before Sarah had said goodnight to the last customers at the bar. He met with Hunter in the downstairs sitting room, took down the descriptions of Miles and the rental car, as well as directions to Double Phoenix, where Miles had gone on the night he disappeared. Hunter promised to get back to him with the name of the girl who said she had seen Miles outside the theater as soon as Tyler came home with the information.

"Well, that was pretty painless," Hunter remarked as he entered the lounge while Sarah was locking up. His relief was visible as he flopped down on a bar stool. "I hope they find him. I mean, shit. What if he's been lying hurt somewhere all this time? Or what if he's already dead?"

Sarah finished pouring herself a shot of tequila and looked up at him. "Don't think about it. Think about something else."

For a long instant their eyes locked in a gaze that went deeper than surface appraisal. Then, shaking her head, she tipped her chin up and downed the tequila in one gulp. Her face flushed as the tingling rush of warmth spread from her chest all the way to her fingertips and toes.

Hunter laughed. "You're something else, Sarah Scupper. I'll do another one of those with you."

"Nope, not until I finish closing down the bar. You can either sweep the floor or entertain me with stories of your travels." She had the odd sensation that she was feeling and acting several years younger than she really was.

"How about both? I may be beautiful, but I can still walk and chew gum at the same time."

She tossed him the broom and they made short work of shutting down the Night Heron lounge. When Tyler arrived half an hour later, they were both sprawled out on the couch in front of the fireplace, and Sarah was laughing uncontrollably at a story that Hunter was telling her about a customs checkpoint in Turkey.

Her smile faded a little at the sight of Tyler and his heart felt as though it was sinking into his stomach. He waved at them from the doorway and continued up the stairs, afraid that he might give away all of his insecurities if he stayed.

He was not sure he could stand it if their relationship was really over. For a second, he had a wild impulse to race back downstairs, throw himself down next to her and take back everything he had said the night before. But he would be lying and she would know it. There was no place to go now but forward.

CHAPTER FOUR

"Come, Azzolino! Let's get ourselves some good French wine, and when I've drunk enough, I'll tell you the story of my life!"

"I wish to hear the story of your life without wine!"

"Not even a little sacramental sip?"

"Your – shit. I can't ever remember this line." Tyler looked down at his manuscript. Jillian laughed as she stretched out on the ground and closed her eyes. "Your eternal soul is at stake and you laugh!"

"Not only do you know your own lines but you know mine too!" Tyler pried a rock out of the dirt as he spoke. Taking careful aim, he skipped it across the small pond at the bottom of the grassy embankment they were sitting on.

It hadn't taken long for the two of them to agree on running lines outside on such a perfect fall afternoon. Spending so many daylight hours in the darkened theater, Tyler found he lost track of the time, the weather and the rest of the world. But the brilliant sky and unusually warm temperatures could not be ignored today. The fast–paced, busy routine of Double Phoenix seemed suddenly not as important as it had earlier in the day. At the moment, Tyler could think of nothing more idyllic than memorizing his lines at the edge of a pond with a gifted and beautiful actress.

"Well, we did this play before, you know. In London." Jillian's straw–colored hair flared out around her head on the grass like the rays of the sun. Her long bangs had parted in the center of her forehead and Tyler saw now that they were not just fashionable; they concealed a two inch scar just below the hairline. He wanted to ask her where it had come from but he had to seize the other opportunity that had just befallen him.

"Did you really? Tell me about London. How big was your school there?"

"We had about fifty students. We usually had two major productions happening at a time, as well as one acts and workshops put on by the different class levels." Jillian propped herself up on one arm and stared out across the pond, apparently lost in memories.

"So why did you give all that up to come here?"

She gave him a crooked, Mona Lisa smile. "Why did a good–looking chap with a promising career like yourself do the same thing?"

It was a perfect comeback and Tyler became introspective for a few moments, thinking about the circumstances that had brought him to the northern edge of the United States, just a few dozen miles from the Canadian border. "I guess I did it for love. How about you?"

"We did it for love also, love of theater. We couldn't work in London anymore."

"Why not? Because of the Emma scandal?" He knew he was being pushy, but it seemed like the only way.

"I'd rather not talk about it. It's still very upsetting to me having to leave everything." She sat up and turned her back to him. He was close enough to count the pattern of knitted stitches in the Norwegian cardigan she wore over her leotard, close enough to sense a change in her breathing and to know she was about to shut him out.

"How did you and Victor meet?" he asked, hoping he was changing the subject.

"It was a long time ago, when I was in college." As he opened his mouth to speak, she held up her hand. "I'm a lot older than I look. We were working in a summer Shakespeare festival together in Canada many years ago. Look, we really ought to get back to these lines. Victor wants you off book for this scene by tonight."

Tyler usually felt very much in control with probing conversations like this one, but Jillian kept slipping through his fingers like water. He was suddenly desperate. "Why do you think Victor lied to the police the other night when they asked him about Miles Romano?"

"What?" She turned to stare at him, but her face displayed none of the emotion that he had just heard in her voice.

"I know Miles was here, somebody else spoke to him and told him where to find Victor. Why did Victor say he never saw him?" He knew he was overstepping his boundaries but he had to try.

There was only a split second pause before she replied, but it was enough to make him realize that she was covering something up. "Tyler, we really like you." The ubiquitous "we" again. "But if you can't respect our privacy, Victor will probably ask you to leave."

"Look, Jillian, I'm sorry, but the man has been missing for almost a week now. When he was last seen, he was on his way here to find out about how his ex–girlfriend died, who just happens to be the Emma we're not allowed to mention. He left his baby girl with a friend at the West Jordan Inn for a few hours while he came here. The friend and the baby are still waiting for him to come back."

Jillian's face seemed to be losing its color. She opened her mouth as though to speak and then slowly shut it. Finally she said, "I'm sorry, but I can't help you. I don't know anything about this."

Still moving very slowly, she stood up and walked to the water's edge. Kicking off one of her clogs, she tested the water temperature with her toe. And then, before Tyler realized what was happening, she had shed her sweater and her other shoe and was diving in.

"Jillian! Holy shit!" Tyler was instantly on his feet, but his adrenaline rush was quickly tempered as Jillian's head broke the surface and she struck out across the pond with strong, practiced strokes. In half a minute she climbed out on the other side, her black leotard and footless tights shining like a wet suit as the water ran off. The thin spandex clung to her body, leaving nothing to the imagination; her nipples were two hard pebbles that broke the smooth curves of the shimmering surface.

"Will you bring my things, Tyler?" she called, wringing the water out of her hair. "I guess I better head back to the house." Hugging her shoulders, she did a swift jog around the pond and up the hill towards the farmhouse.

"You're crazy, Jillian, you know that?" he shouted after her. But as he collected her clothing and books, he knew she was not crazy at all. It had been a swiftly calculated move that effectively took the attention away from their conversation and ended it at the same time.

One thing was obvious. She knew way more than she was saying. He had to find out more about Victor and Jillian and what had happened with Emma. And one well–placed phone call ought to do the trick.

It was a strange arrangement, living with Victor and Jillian, and Tyler was not altogether comfortable with it. A double bed took up most of the polished hardwood floor of his small room, which was wallpapered in an overpowering yellow floral print. A desk had been crammed in next to a dresser and a couple of nightstands completed the crowded decor. It was not a place he felt like hanging out, but it was all the privacy he had here.

From what he had glimpsed of it, Jillian and Victor shared a spacious room that took up one whole side of the building at the other end of the hall. At least one wall had been knocked out to create the airy, loft–like effect and from what he had seen of the furnishings they seemed to be mostly black and glass and steel – starkly modern in contrast to the rest of the old–fashioned farmhouse.

He ate his meals with them at the round wooden table in a country kitchen that would have made Martha Stewart sigh with contentment. Jillian seemed to do most of the cooking, but Phoebe did the cleaning up. He hadn't quite figured that one out yet.

The only other room he had access to was the living room. It was large and cluttered and had comfortable old couches and overstuffed chairs that had probably come with the house. Victor and Jillian retired to their bedroom fairly early each evening, so this was where Tyler spent most of his time. He was glad he had been invited to join in the classes during the day. Otherwise, he would have had way too much free time on his hands.

He hated to admit it, but the biggest difference between himself and the others here was that nobody drank. He'd always liked a good wine with dinner and a few cocktails afterwards, but after living with a bar in the house for a year he had developed a serious mental and physical dependency on alcohol. He hadn't realized how much so until he was suddenly deprived of it.

After a couple of days, he decided there was no reason he couldn't drink in moderation here. He talked Tracy into driving him into Jordan Center to pick up a bottle of aged whiskey, something he could keep in his room and sip away at slowly. When he discovered that Phoebe did the grocery shopping for Victor's household, he slipped her some money to buy him a six pack of imported beer and told her to keep the change. But the clandestineness left him with a feeling of guilt and depravity, as though he were a really sick man who was doing something very wrong.

He had called Sarah a couple of times, but their conversations had left him feeling bleaker rather than better. All she could talk about was how she and Hunter had gone to yard sales and secondhand stores to buy baby things for Kashi and how the baby backpack had made things so much easier to get their work done. They thought Kashi was sick because she had been crying all night, but it turned out she just had a new tooth coming in. Kashi was learning to drink juice from a sip cup, Kashi had pulled herself up on the bars of her crib, Kashi had a diaper rash.

Tyler was really not interested in what Kashi was doing and Sarah could not seem to care less about his acting career. He had never felt farther apart from her. He was trying to find out what had happened to Miles and he knew Sarah was secretly hoping that Miles would never turn up.

Finding Miles might be the only way he and Sarah could get back together again.

A trail of muddy footprints told him that Jillian had already disappeared upstairs. He left her script, her sweater and her clogs on the kitchen table and then darted quickly up to his room for his address book. The call he had to make now could not be made from Victor's telephone.

In the building where the students took their meals, there was a public telephone. It was late afternoon and Tyler hoped nobody would be around.

The room had an odd atmosphere to it. At one end was an enormous fireplace, which had obviously been part of the original outdoor pavilion before it had been walled up to create a dining room. Along the other side was a kitchen area with a large industrial stove, stainless steel sinks and wooden counters. Cassandra and Paloma were cooking dinner to the accompaniment of some tuneless heavy metal music that blared loudly from a portable cassette player. They did not see Tyler until he was standing in front of them.

"Can you turn it down just a little while I make a phone call?" he shouted.

Paloma stared at him blankly for a second and then said, "Sure." She reached for the volume button with a hand featuring long nails painted an extraordinarily dark shade of burgundy. Tyler noticed that the nails on her other hand were a shiny black that matched her hair.

"I'll only be a minute," he apologized.

"Just turn it off." Cassandra edged in front of Paloma with an annoyed gesture and popped the tape out. "I don't want to miss the next part of that song."

The room seemed very quiet after the deafening decibels of the cassette had been silenced. Tyler almost wished they'd left it on so that he would have a little more privacy for his call. But as he crossed the room to the pay phone, the two girls seemed to be pointedly ignoring his presence, already deep in discussion about the merits of the lead singer of some band.

Next to the telephone was a schedule for kitchen duty. It had to be just his luck that these two were cooking tonight. Consulting his address book, he punched in his calling card number and then a phone number in England.

"Lucy? How are you? I didn't wake you, did I? It's Tyler Mackenzie."

"Tyler! Where are you calling from? Are you here in London?" The sound of Lucy Brookstone's voice brought back memories from another era in his life, a more fast-paced, challenging time that almost hurt to recall.

"No, actually I'm calling from Vermont. It's where I live now."

"Vermont? Really? Who are you working for these days?"

Tyler did not want to tell her that his journalism days had come to a standstill. "Myself. Which means I'm not on an expense account and can't talk long. But I have a favor to ask you."

"Okay. What's up?" Lucy asked. Tyler was momentarily flustered, flooded with memories of the two weeks he had once spent working and living with Lucy. A freckle–faced, auburn–haired reporter who was all business and all heart, Lucy was eternally ready to help a colleague in need.

"I need you to look up some information for me." Using a quietly urgent tone, Tyler outlined the story as he knew it. "Find out whatever you can about this woman Emma's drowning – I'm sorry I don't even know her last name. If you need it, I can probably find out. But it happened last summer, I think. I'm sure if you search for articles on Jillian Fox and Victor Nesbit, you'll come up with something."

"You're not giving me much to work with here, Tyler." Lucy's laugh was a lovely bubbling sound that made Tyler grin in spite of himself. "But the story sounds vaguely familiar. I'll see what I can do. Can I email you what I find?"

"I'm not at home and I have nowhere to hook my computer up here. Why don't you fax it to me at the inn?" He gave her the number.

"Okay. You owe me one, sweetie."

Tyler remembered that Lucy was a great listener and he stifled a sudden urge to unload everything on her. "Thanks, Lucy. I'll call you soon for a long chat. You still living alone?"

"You know how it is. I'll probably never settle down. You're lucky you caught me in. Oh – I've got to go, I've got another call coming in."

Tyler felt moody and sentimental after he hung up. Talking to Lucy, reminded him how much he missed doing investigative work. He and Lucy had worked together on a story about illegal aliens who slaved for pennies in a sweatshop/factory that made a very well–known brand of jeans. It had been an exciting and satisfying experience, including the nights spent in Lucy's double bed.

"You know your lines for tonight, Tyler?"

He had been moving in a daze across the lawn and had not even noticed Gabriel falling in step with him. "Almost. How about you?"

"Actually I've been off book for three days now. You know, if you need help, I'll run lines with you."

Tyler was not sure why the acne–scarred actor was suddenly befriending him. "That's okay. Jillian and I worked this afternoon. And I don't really have any scenes with you, do I?"

"No, but I can play the parts opposite you. It would be useful for me too, since I'm your understudy."

Ah, there was the motive he'd been looking for. "Okay, maybe tomorrow, Gabe. I'd like to rest a little before rehearsal."

What he really wanted to do right now was pull out his laptop and do some writing. Writing always helped him organize his thoughts. And his thoughts felt very disorganized right now.

"Hunter?" Sarah walked into the empty kitchen balancing Kashi on her hip. "Where do you think he is?" she asked the baby. Kashi gnawed on a rubber pretzel and cooed.

Through the window in the outside door to the kitchen, she caught a glimpse of the back of Hunter's head. "I wonder what he's doing out there." It hadn't taken long for her to develop the habit of speaking all her thoughts aloud to Kashi.

As she turned the door handle, Hunter jerked his head to the right with a paranoid sideways glance. As Sarah and Kashi came through the door, his face slid into a wide grin.

"What are you doing?" Sarah asked him curiously. A second later she noted the joint in his hand and wondered why she hadn't recognized the smell of the smoke. "Oh."

"Want some?" His voice had an odd, thin quality to it as he held the smoke in and the joint out.

She shook her head. "No thanks. I haven't indulged in years. Don't forget you have to work in a couple of hours."

"Not a problem. I work better high." At Sarah's dubious look he added, "Well, it's more fun anyway."

"I just hope you don't screw up."

"I didn't yesterday, did I?"

Sarah realized that Hunter was telling her that he had been stoned while he was working last night. "You shithead." She punched him in the arm playfully. "Why didn't you tell me?"

"Just to prove my point. Sarah, what if he never comes back?"

She looked up, startled by his change in tone. His smile had been replaced by deep lines of worry.

"Miles. What if he's dead? What are we going to do?" His arms reached automatically for Kashi and her face lit up with delight as he lifted her in the air.

"Stop thinking that way, Hunter. You don't know that he's dead."

"Then why isn't he back here with his little sweetheart?" He stubbed the joint out on the side of the building and put the remainder in his shirt pocket. "You don't know Miles. He is one of the most responsible people on earth."

Sarah hugged herself as a cool wind whipped suddenly around the corner of the building. Autumn was asserting its presence today and it was hard not to feel as unsettled as the weather. "People change," she said quietly.

Hunter shook his head stubbornly. "Miles was like a rock of strength for those people in Nigeria. He's not the kind of guy who would say the hell with everybody, I'm driving to Las Vegas to gamble for a week. If he's not here, then something's really wrong."

His green eyes met hers over the top of Kashi's head. Surrogate parenting for the last several days had given them a closeness and connection that would normally take months or years to develop. "Sarah." His voice was almost a whisper now. "What will we do if he never comes back?"

Sarah had not realized the depth of his anxiety until now. His own sense of responsibility was suddenly threatening to undermine his carefree, unattached lifestyle. She tried to suppress the unexpected rush of emotion that overcame her.

"Let's just take it one day at a time the way we have been," she suggested quietly. "We've been doing just fine, haven't we?"

She fixed her gaze on the crystal blue color of the afternoon sky after she spoke, unable to meet his eyes. The truth was they were doing better than just fine, but the truth was more than she was ready to cope with right now.

The cool evening air felt good on his face as Tyler stepped out of the theater for a break. Nobody had turned on the outside lights yet and the darkness was nearly complete. He found it interesting how during the day, the theater seemed like a dark hole that shut out the brightness of the sun. At night, it was the opposite – a beacon of warmth and activity that chased away the black stillness outside.

This introspective mood followed him as he returned to the theater and took a seat in one of the back rows. Victor was on stage with Cassandra and Rochelle and Marcus, running one of the flashback scenes from Christina's childhood.

Tyler's eyes moved from face to face, noting the shining look in Rochelle's eyes and the rapt attention Marcus was paying. Even Cassandra had lost her usual disdainful air and was listening to Victor with an adoring expression.

He's like Svengali, Tyler thought, suddenly remembering the classic silent movie he had seen many years ago in college. It was the story of a magician/hypnotist who puts a girl under his spell and eventually seduces her, but all that he really remembered was Svengali's flashing eyes. Melodramatic in the style of the era, they seemed to magnetize and hypnotize in a frightening, evil way.

Victor had that same intensity. When he directed an actor in a role, his pale eyes drew the person in, captivating more than just their gaze. He might become, for just an instant, the part they were playing, he might speak a line the way he wanted it spoken. If you concentrated hard enough, it was as though he traded souls with you for a second and managed to leave a piece of himself inside you. Anyone he spoke to seemed to absorb his words as though they were gospel and he was treated with the adoration and respect that was usually reserved for spiritual teachers and gurus.

Although Tyler had experienced this phenomenon himself, he wasn't as easily fooled by it as Frieda or Cassandra. But he understood now why they all seemed to idolize Victor and why they lusted after the man's attention. He had a way of drawing a character out of you, touching places in your psyche that you never knew had existed. Tyler wondered what it would be like to have that kind of power over a group of people.

"Tyler?" A soft voice at his shoulder broke through his thoughts. Phoebe was staring at him, or maybe she wasn't staring. Her thick glasses always made it hard to tell where her eyes were really looking. "You had a phone call a little while ago. Sarah wants you to call her as soon as you can."

Glancing up at Victor on the stage a little fearfully, she held out a portable phone to him. As soon as he accepted, she retreated out of the theater.

Figuring he probably had at least ten or fifteen minutes before Victor would need him again, Tyler slipped out into the lobby and quickly dialed the number of the inn.

"Sarah? What's up?" He dispensed with any small talk, knowing that she had not called to chat in the middle of dinner hour.

"Two things. One is that you got a ten page fax today from someone named Lucy that I think you're going to find very interesting."

"Wow, that was quick." Tyler started racking his brains for how he was going to get his hands on the fax.

"I can mail you the fax if you want. But the other thing is more important. Just a second." He paced nervously as he heard her saying good–byes to customers and ringing money into the cash register. "Sorry." She sounded breathless when she returned.

"So what's the other thing?"

"It's really awful actually. Hunter is so worried, he can barely concentrate. But we're straight out here tonight, so he had to stay. But after work he has to go over to the police station in Jordan Center."

"Why? What happened?"

"A body has turned up and the police think it might be Miles."

CHAPTER FIVE

Sarah yawned. It was nearly one thirty in the morning and Hunter was not back yet. He didn't know his way around the back roads that well; she hoped he hadn't gotten lost on his way to or from the Jordan Center police station, or wherever else they had to take him. She had no idea where the morgue was, maybe at the hospital.

From the end of the hall she heard Kashi start to whimper. Although she always left the connecting door open between the apartment and the guest rooms, at that distance she did not think Kashi's crying would be loud enough to wake her from a sound sleep.

She crept quietly down the hall and poked her head around the edge of the door to Hunter's room. Kashi's eyes were closed but she was fussing and wiggling, her head wedged up into a corner of the crib. As soon as Sarah picked her up, however, she relaxed, laying her head against Sarah's shoulder and contentedly sucking her thumb.

So Sarah did what made the most sense; she tucked Kashi into the middle of the big queen size bed, snuggled in next to her and went to sleep.

When she opened her eyes, the gray light of a cloudy morning filled the double–hung windows of the bedroom. She reached out instinctively for Kashi but instead of a tiny, diaper–covered backside, her fingers touched a large, hairy arm.

Gasping, she sat up in alarm, but her racing heart immediately calmed itself. Hunter had crawled into bed on the other side of Kashi and was sleeping peacefully with one arm thrown protectively over the baby.

Shaking her head, she wondered how long he had been there. Then she shook her head again at the youthful audacity that had compelled him to climb into bed with her, albeit with a baby between them. His bare shoulders indicated he was naked at least from the waist up.

She tried to ignore the tingling feeling that spread from her abdomen on down as she looked at him. She'd been trying to ignore the feeling for a week now. She still had not asked him how old he was (or how young he was depending on just how perverse she wanted to be) because she was afraid to know the truth. Trying to push her thoughts away, she closed her eyes and lay down again, pulling the quilt up to her chin, suddenly aware of just how naked she herself was under the covers.

But the movement had been enough to wake Kashi, who was usually up by this time anyway. She sat up, gurgling and cooing, surprised and delighted to be in a big warm bed surrounded by both of her surrogate parents.

"Good morning, baby," Sarah whispered to her. Then they both looked over at Hunter as he groaned and rolled onto his back.

"Hi, ladies," he murmured a second later, his eyes still closed. "Hope you don't mind that I joined your sleepover party."

"I didn't hear you come in." Much as she wanted to know, she was almost afraid to ask him what happened. "What time did you get back?"

"I don't know. I sat outside getting totally wasted because I knew I wouldn't sleep otherwise."

"Was it him?"

Hunter nodded, biting his lip. Sarah could see moisture forming under the eyelashes of his closed lids.

"Oh, God, Hunter, I'm so sorry." She reached for his hand and he squeezed hers gratefully. "How – what happened?"

"They found him floating in some lake near here. He'd been drowned." He sniffed a little and passed the back of his other hand over his eyes before opening them.

"Accidentally?"

"They don't think so, but they're not sure that he didn't try to commit suicide. There was a rope tied around one of his ankles that they think was tied to something else. Shit." He sat up suddenly and covered his face with his hands. "I don't think I'll ever forget how he looked when they made me identify him, no matter how much reefer I smoke."

Pulling her robe off the bed post, Sarah hastily put it on. Then, sweeping up Kashi in one arm, she moved closer to Hunter, putting her other arm around him and leaning comfortingly against his back. She felt sick to her stomach with the unknown possibilities of the future. He answered her next question before she asked it.

"I still didn't tell them about Kashi."

"What about Miles' parents? Do they know about her?"

"I'm almost positive they didn't. He wasn't sure how they'd take it. He wanted to surprise them. He figured it might be easier once they met her." Hunter lifted his head finally and stared unseeingly out the window.

"Do you think we should call them?"

"The police are doing it this morning. His parents live in Ohio. That's where we were headed."

"No, I mean about Kashi. Do you think we should call them about her?"

He twisted around to look at her. Their eyes locked for a brief second before he buried his face between her chest and Kashi's. She tried not to think about how hot his breath felt against her skin.

"I don't know what we should do," was his muffled reply.

Tyler stood in the parking lot at Double Phoenix, trying to decide who might lend him a car. Tracy was out of the question – he might drive him somewhere but he would never lend Tyler his red Ferrari. Victor and Jillian had a Land Rover, nearly as expensive as the Ferrari but far more practical. The only person he'd actually seen driving it was Phoebe when she went out to buy groceries for the farmhouse. There were a couple of other vehicles, a battered and rusty Ford Escort that he thought belonged to Gabriel and a black Volkswagen van that he'd seen Paloma in once.

The only likely prospect seemed to be Gabe, the understudy who no doubt secretly wished Tyler would come down with an incurable illness between now and performance time. Fifteen minutes later, he was rattling down the driveway in car that was missing an exhaust pipe and had a couple of very soft tires. All it had taken was the promise of a full tank of gas on his return. The wipers were in desperate need of new blades; Tyler had to hunch over the steering wheel peering through the narrow arc at the bottom of the windshield as a steady rain beat down on the car and the road.

He realized he would only have about half an hour at the inn if he was going to make it back in time for a quick supper before rehearsal. But he was anxious to pick up Lucy's fax and he did not want to think about the possibility of it going from the mailbox into the wrong hands at the school. Thirty minutes hardly qualified as a conjugal visit with Sarah and the thought left him feeling empty and frustrated.

By the time he left the inn he felt worse than he could have anticipated. He had what he had come for; a copy of the unread fax in the inside pocket of his jacket and all the details of Hunter's experience with the police and identifying Miles' body. But what he really seemed to be carrying away with him were haunting snapshot images of Hunter and Sarah; Hunter putting a forkful of black bean salad in her mouth and asking her what she thought, Sarah absentmindedly plucking a piece of thread out of Hunter's ponytail as she talked to Tyler, the two of them laughing together over some private joke having to do with a couple of elderly customers.

She didn't miss him at all. And the realization made him insanely jealous.

Rehearsal did not seem to be going well for anybody that night, particularly Frieda. She could not seem to relax at all during a scene with Jillian where Christina announced her attraction to Ebba and made sexual advances. Every time Jillian even reached for her, Frieda would physically stiffen or begin to giggle nervously. Finally Victor stood up.

"That's enough for now. After we're finished here tonight, I would like you girls to work on this scene alone, some place private like up at the farmhouse. You need to relax into this part physically, Frieda, if you are going to make the audience believe in you. And you need to conquer this scene before we work on the one between you and Magnus in bed."

Frieda blushed deeply and Tyler had a feeling that, with her mature figure, she had rarely been asked to play the part of a sexually attractive ingénue before.

"We probably ought to get you working in costume as soon as possible too. Your dress needs to be low–cut and sort of laced and trussed up –" Victor demonstrated on his own flat chest– "and you need to learn to feel comfortable like that. Where is Phoebe? Is she here?

As he peered out at the empty rows of seats, several voices chorused, "No." Frieda's flushed color had now spread to the roots of her dark hair and down her neck.

"Well, somebody let her know that she needs to get to work on Frieda's costume right away. Jillian, will you look in our own collection at home? We might have something that can simulate the effect in the meantime."

Tyler was glad when Victor finally called it a night. He was having trouble concentrating – his mind kept wandering back to the disturbing familiarity he had witnessed between Sarah and Hunter. It had been his own idea that Hunter stay at the inn; and now he had to stay on there, working until Tyler was finished with the play, even though Miles had turned up dead.

It would only drive Tyler crazy to dwell on it. He would go back to his room, drink a few beers and read Lucy's fax.

An hour later he leaned back on the pillows and closed his eyes, trying to assimilate all that he had just read.

What had come up again and again in every article was that Jillian Fox was an extremely wealthy heiress to an old family fortune. Not a single reporter had neglected to mention that important fact. An only child, she had been born to middle–aged parents and both had died before she was out of college, making her, at the time, one of the youngest millionaires in England. Tyler hadn't recognized the name of the conglomerate William Rutherford Fox had owned, but from the number of well–known small companies it seemed to have acquired, he imagined it be along the lines of Proctor & Gamble.

The first clip that caught his interest was from one of the gossipy, sensationalist rags that were so popular in London. Dated fifteen years earlier, it claimed that Fox was threatening to cut his daughter out of his will if she went through with her plans to marry a Canadian actor she had met during a summer of touring with an avant–garde theater troupe. Her father was quoted as saying she was not showing the good judgment need to execute an estate the size of the one she would inherit when he died.

The next page was an obituary of William Fox from the Sun Times four months later. He had died of heart failure. His daughter and her new husband, Victor Nesbitt of Ontario, Canada, had been visiting him at his country home at the time. Apparently his wife had passed away a few years earlier. Jillian was the only surviving relative.

The headlines began to get more brazen and bizarre after that. "HEIRESS FIGHTS DADDY'S 'MISS'TRUST'", "JILTED JILLIAN JOUSTS FOR JUSTICE," and "FOX HOCKS STOCKS." Apparently Jillian's father had no confidence in her capacity to manage the family money. He had set up a trust for her so that she would only receive a certain amount per year for the rest of her life. When she died, the trust would be assumed by her heirs and if she produced no heirs, the remaining sum would be donated to charity. One reporter stated that it was obvious that Fox had covered all bases to make sure his new son–in–law would never have a controlling interest in Jillian's estate.

There was an announcement about Jillian's plans to open a theater school with her husband on the outskirts of London. There was a scathing review of a play that reported "the least talented of this untalented troupe seems to be the school's owner, Jillian Fox...it appears she had to fund her own theater and hire her husband to direct because it was the only way she could ever star in a play."

Tyler found that last bit amazing; Jillian had obviously come a long way since then.

Finally he came to the articles on the incident in the Mediterranean. After reading them all, he tried to put the story together chronologically. It seemed that Jillian and Victor had gone sailing on their private yacht in early June of the previous year. They had invited Emma Erikson, one of their "student stars and talented prodigies" to go along with them. Somewhere off the coast of Algeria on a dark and moonless night,

Emma had accidentally fallen overboard. She was never seen again. They laid anchor at the nearest port, a small city called Bejaia, where the accident was duly reported to the international press but not investigated.

As soon as the English papers received the news, they immediately sniffed a scandal and by the time Victor and Jillian moored their yacht in St. Tropez, rumors had grown that the accident was not accidental at all. One story claimed that Emma had been a casualty of a drugged and drunken orgy, another claimed they had done away with her because she was a better actress than Jillian, and the wildest declared she was Victor's daughter from a previous marriage who had been trying to come between the two of them.

All the bad press was apparently too much for Jillian who was no longer the self–confident, outspoken firebrand of earlier, more youthful years. She suffered a nervous breakdown before the yacht ever docked on English shores and was sent to an exclusive retreat to recover from the trauma. During her seclusion there, Victor began to disband the theater school, announcing that he and Jillian were going to retire to the country. After her recuperation, they managed to disappear from London before the press could catch up with their whereabouts.

Tyler shook his head in disbelief and opened another beer. Everything about the story smacked of suspicion and ulterior motives. It was hard to imagine the composed and self–assured Jillian having a nervous breakdown.

He combed the last articles again for information about Emma. She was from Buffalo, New York, a college graduate of Syracuse University, and was working on her master's degree in theater. Described variously as athletic, vibrant, vivacious and spirited, one of her fellow students also added that she was very competitive and had clamored for and won Victor's coveted attention. In the event that she had managed to get to shore and was wandering bedraggled and amnesic through some underdeveloped Mediterranean country, a physical description was included in one piece. Tall, dark–haired, bright–eyed and rosy–cheeked, she sounded like the ultimate American girl.

His stomach grumbled suddenly, reminding him that beer was not exactly a substitute for the supper he had missed because of his trip to West Jordan. Craving something more solid, he headed downstairs to the kitchen. He was surprised to find the hallway door to the living room was closed; he usually walked through the living room to get to the kitchen. He had his hand on the knob when the soft female voices on the other side of the door reminded him of Jillian and Frieda's "private" rehearsal.

"Shit," he muttered. Well, he could go out the front door, walk around the house and come in the back door to the kitchen.

The wet grass felt icy on his bare feet as moved quickly across the side lawn. Despite the nip of the night air, he could not resist stopping at the window and peering through the bottom two inches of glass that the shade was not covering.

His jaw dropped at the tableau he surveyed.

Frieda sat on an upholstered ottoman with her eyes closed; Jillian stood behind her massaging her shoulders and speaking softly into her ear. The action in itself made sense as a remedy for Frieda's stiffness with the scene; what Tyler found surprising was that both women had taken off their shirts.

Frieda was wearing the functional kind of white cotton bra commonly associated with large–breasted women. Jillian, on the other hand, was completely naked from the waist up. Her breasts were so round and well–suspended that they almost didn't look real. Tyler stared at them, wondering if it was just years of exercise that had made them like that or if she'd had silicone implants.

After a moment of wistful lusting, he forced his very cold feet to continue on their way to the back door. As soon as he entered the kitchen, however, he realized that the door between the two rooms was only half closed. Once again he was magnetically drawn to the strip of light that led to the same extraordinary scene. Loathing himself, he moved silently to a position behind the open door.

"No, I mean really touched by another woman," Jillian was saying softly. Were they running lines from the play? Tyler didn't think so.

Frieda's chin rested on her chest as Jillian rubbed along both sides of her neck.

"Well, no, I guess not," Frieda murmured in a very relaxed voice. "I mean, I'm not gay, if that's what you're asking." No, they were definitely not running lines.

"So you've never even wondered what it would be like to explore another woman's body?" Jillian released the barrette that held Frieda's thick, dark hair away from her face. Running her fingers through the heavy tresses a few times, she began to massage Frieda's scalp.

"Well, no, not really, I mean..." Frieda's cheeks flushed scarlet again, the way they had during rehearsal.

"It's really very normal, you can admit to it." As Jillian leaned over, one of her nipples grazed the side of Frieda's face.

Instantly Frieda leaped up, and looked at Jillian with a horrified expression. "Oh, my god, Jillian, where's your shirt? What are you thinking?"

Tyler could see that much as she wanted to avert her eyes, she could not keep from staring at Jillian's perfect breasts.

"Relax, Frieda." Jillian put her hands on Frieda's shoulders and gently tried to force her to sit down again. "I just thought it would make you more comfortable having your shirt off if I took mine off as well."

"But–but you took your bra off too!" Frieda turned her head away as she sat down stiffly on the ottoman.

"No, I didn't. I just never wear one. I find them much too confining." Jillian had resumed speaking in a soft, soothing voice. "I don't know how you can stand it. Don't you ever let them just go free?"

"Well, I don't wear a bra to bed." Frieda giggled and Jillian laughed with her. She still stood in front of Frieda, kneading her shoulders, her lovely chest level with Frieda's face. "But if you had boobs like these you might be a little more self–conscious. They're a pain in the butt."

"Oh, come now, they're beautiful and womanly."

"Do you really think so?" Frieda finally looked up at Jillian.

"I do. They're wonderfully sexy. They should bring you lots of pleasure." Still holding Frieda's gaze, Jillian cautiously ran her fingers over the white seamed cups that Frieda filled to nearly overflowing. Tyler held his breath.

Frieda shivered a little and then seemed suddenly calm.

"Close your eyes," whispered Jillian and Frieda did as she was told. Jillian picked Frieda's hands up from her lap where she held them clenched tightly together. She massaged the fingers until they were relaxed and open. Then slowly she lifted Frieda's hands up until her arms were outstretched and her palms rested beneath the curve of Jillian's breasts. Gently she folded Frieda's fingers up and around so the tips touched her hard nipples.

Frieda gasped and started to pull away, but Jillian held her hands in place. "Relax. Just check them out. See how different they are from your own."

As Jillian reached out to pull Frieda's bra straps down, the door to the living room suddenly burst open. "I found that blouse I was thinking of," Victor announced as he strode in waving something shiny and red.

Frieda screamed and turned her back on Victor, covering her face with her hands. Tyler flattened himself between the kitchen door and the wall.

"Damn it, Victor! We were making good progress here! Why couldn't you knock before you barged in?" He had never heard anyone speak to Victor like that before.

Nor had he ever heard Victor so apologetic. "Oh, sorry, I'm sorry. I didn't realize you'd come so far. Look, why don't you use the study across the hall? You won't have to worry about anybody disturbing you there. I mean, if it hadn't been me it could have been Tyler looking for a midnight snack."

Tyler held his breath again as Victor left the room as abruptly as he had entered. He stayed flat against the wall behind the door for the five minutes that it took Jillian to calm Frieda down and escort her across the hall to the more private "study." He waited another five minutes before he grabbed a box of crackers off the shelf and a block of sharp cheddar from the refrigerator and slipped out the back way he had come in.

He raced across the cold slick grass and then his wet bare feet slid across the front porch. Realizing how bizarre he would look coming in the front door carrying cheese and crackers and wearing no shoes, he was quite cautious about being quiet. The downstairs hallway was deserted but for some reason the door to the coat closet had been left wide open.

Maybe it was the thought of someone walking blindly into the open door after the lights were off and breaking their nose, but some basic instinct made Tyler move forward to close it. His hand froze on the knob as he heard a rustling noise inside the closet. He peered around the edge of the door. The coats had been parted in the middle and pushed aside. Victor stood there, his back to Tyler, working on something built into the back wall.

Tyler crept silently up the stairs and down the hall to his room. He was beginning to have the feeling that there was definitely something very weird going on here.

Leaving his door slightly ajar, he lay on his bed biting off hunks of cheese like a hungry rat, waiting until he heard Victor return to his own room at the end of the hall and firmly close the door behind him. Then, carrying his own jacket as a decoy, Tyler marched loudly downstairs to the hall closet one more time. Grabbing a hanger and pushing the coats to one side, he peered closely at what Victor had been laboring over.

The red light of a small video camera winked at him, indicating that a tape was recording at that very moment. He did not have to peer through the lens to know what Victor was taping. The closet shared its back wall with the private study where Jillian and Frieda were "rehearsing."

CHAPTER SIX

As Sarah pushed the stroller into the parking lot of the West Jordan Inn, she realized that a police car was slowly following her. She stopped walking and frowned, wondering what kind of ticket they could find to give a woman and baby out enjoying a beautiful fall day.

The cruiser came to a halt next to her and the driver rolled down his window. "Sarah Scupper?"

She gave him a curt affirmative nod and he went on. "I'd like to ask you a few questions if you don't mind." She knew it didn't matter if she minded or not. "About Hunter Adams?"

Feeling suddenly flushed and nervous, Sarah hid her face as she bent down to adjust Kashi's blanket. "What about him?"

"Is there some place private we can talk?"

She straightened up, trying to look composed rather than defensive. "Since Hunter is inside the inn, right here is probably as private as anywhere. What would you like to know?"

The cop turned off his engine and got out of the car before speaking to her. He was quite tall and broad–shouldered and cut a much more imposing silhouette towering over her instead of speaking to her through a car window.

"It's a nice day. Why don't we sit on the porch?" Sarah suggested, leading the way. When they sat down on the steps, his name tag was just level with Sarah's eyes; Officer Peter Dussault.

"Hunter's still around then, is he? He hasn't left town?"

Sarah laughed. "No, thank goodness. He's working for me right now, filling in for my cook who was suddenly...called away."

"Were you here when he showed up with his friend Miles Romano?"

"Yes, I was. I met them both at the same time."

Officer Dussault went on for some time, asking her numerous questions about what time they arrived, the car they had been driving, what kind of luggage they had been carrying, and whether they had been drinking.

"After Mr. Romano went out that night, did you see Mr. Adams again?"

Sarah cocked her head, wondering where this was leading. "Yes, later on he came down to the bar for supper."

"About what time was that?"

"I'm not certain but I'd say after nine."

"So you didn't see him for about an hour and a half after Mr. Romano left, is that true?"

Sarah shrugged. "I don't know, I guess so. I was pretty busy."

"Do you think he might have left the inn during that time?"

Sarah's stomach tightened suddenly as she realized what he was intimating. "No, I don't think so."

"And why is that?"

Sarah hesitated a second. "First of all, he had no vehicle and second of all, I know he was sleeping in his room." He had been baby–sitting Kashi, but she couldn't say that.

"How do you know that he was there? Did you see him?"

"Yes," she said clearly. "I saw him there sleeping when I dropped off some bath towels." It was a lie but she didn't care.

"Mrs. Scupper–" Sarah was about to correct him when she understood that he thought Kashi was her baby and that meant she was married. "You know Mr. Adams pretty well now that he works for you, I guess."

"Y–yes. Why?"

"Can you think of anything he and his friend Mr. Romano might have had a falling out about?"

"A falling out? Like a fight?" Sarah looked down at the sweet, chubby face of the baby sleeping in the stroller. It was a possibility she had never even considered. A horrible ugly thought. "No, he's never mentioned anything. They had only known each other a few months but they had become very close friends, the way people do when they travel together."

The more she talked, the more suspicious she herself became. It was ridiculous, she'd seen Hunter's worry and subsequent grief; it had been very real.

But what if the story Miles had told about the baby born in Nigeria wasn't totally the truth. What if there really wasn't any irresponsible Peace Corps worker who ran off after getting a village girl pregnant? What if Hunter really was Kashi's father and –

"Mrs. Scupper?"

"Hmmm? Oh, I'm sorry, I was just thinking, just trying to see if I could remember anything else." She stood up as if to indicate that the meeting was over. "If I think of anything, I'll be in touch."

"Do you remember where Mr. Romano said he was going that night?" Officer Dussault did not take the hint.

"Yes, he was headed over to the Double Phoenix Theater auditions in East Jordan. He wanted to talk to somebody there. That was what he was doing up here in the first place. He was actually on his way home to Ohio." Sarah began maneuvering the stroller up onto the porch.

"So I've heard." He picked up the bottom of the stroller and helped her lift it over the steps. "Cute baby. What's her name?"

Sarah hoped her slight hesitation wasn't too obvious. "Kathy," she said. "Her name is Kathy."

"There you are. We wondered where you were. What are you doing?" Sarah shifted Kashi to the other hip as she looked down at Hunter. He was sitting on the floor of his bedroom next to an open suitcase. He gave a guilty start and made a weak attempt to hide the letter he had been reading.

"Oh, hi. I was just going through Miles's suitcase looking for Kashi's birth certificate. The police told me someone would be coming by to pick up his belongings in the next twenty–four hours."

Sarah put Kashi on the rug and sank down on the floor next to him. "So is that it right there?" she asked, knowing full well that it wasn't.

"No, I couldn't find it. He kept most of his important papers in a small daypack that he must have taken with him that night." Hunter pulled the letter out from behind his back and laid it in plain view on his denim–clad legs. "But I did find a couple of letters from Emma and I thought I ought to check them out. You know, in case she said anything about Kashi in them."

Uncertainty swirled in around the edges of Sarah's thoughts like fog over the river on a cool fall morning. Until fifteen minutes ago it hadn't occurred to her not to trust him.

"But I thought he'd never told her about Kashi."

"Well, I had to be sure." He gave Sarah a sideways glance out of the corner of his eye and then burst out laughing. "Okay, okay, I wanted to read it. I wanted to see if I could tell what she was like from her letters to him."

"And?" Sarah peered curiously at the translucent sheets of onion–skin, air–mail writing paper he was holding.

"It's pretty interesting actually. Sounds like they were drifting farther and farther apart. Kashi may have been a short–sighted attempt at getting them back together again. I mean, listen to this. This is wild." He flipped one of the pages over and began to read aloud.

"*'I'm not going to defend this porno movie thing to you. It's not what you think. Or perhaps I should say, I know how you think and you've always been much more straitlaced about sex than I am. I could make some cracks about Peace Corps missionaries teaching the natives the missionary position but I won't. Believe me, you don't have to worry about anyone you know seeing these movies. They are destined for a private video collection.'* Phew!" Hunter dropped the letter as though it was a burning match. "Hot stuff, huh?"

"Really." Before Hunter could stop her, Sarah grabbed the thin page covered with spidery writing out of his lap. "Well, you can't stop there! What else does she say?"

"Oh, a lot of stupid crap about some part she got in a play. But read this last paragraph." He handed her the next page and pointed to the end.

"*'I've been invited to go on a sailing trip with Victor and Jillian next month. Well, not really invited, actually they're taking me along to cook and clean for them, part of my work/study scholarship. But I can hardly wait to spend some time away from school with them. It should be fabulous – everyone says their yacht is exquisite and that sometimes they throw some very wild parties. I don't know how wild it can be with just the three of us, but I don't care. Victor is such a powerful presence in my life right now, he's done so much for my acting. Swabbing his deck is the least I can do.'*"

Sarah let the letter sink slowly to the floor. "Wow. I wonder if that's the last time he ever heard from her."

"I don't know. This other letter is dated a few months earlier." Hunter unfolded the pages and began to scan it. "Christ, it's all full of how wonderful Victor is. She makes him sound like some Eastern swami."

Sarah was reading over his shoulder. "Actually, it sounds like she's in love with him."

"Oh, here we go, listen to this – *'I've found a way to make money that actually lets me do some acting. I was asked if I wanted a part in a video. When I agreed I didn't know what it was about and then it turned out I actually had to take off my clothes and do a couple of weird things. I was nervous at first but it was really easy. And the money was great compared to what I make cleaning the theater for my work/study job. I'm going to do another one next week. I figure if I do one a week I might actually be able to save up some money for traveling this summer."* Hunter gave a mock shiver and let the page fall to the floor. "Ugh, gives me the creeps."

"Me too. So let's hear some more." Sarah laughed a little embarrassedly. "What else does she say?"

Hunter scanned the last page. "Nothing much. Oh, wait. *'I'm not sure you should expect that our relationship will rekindle itself when you get out of the Peace Corps. I think our paths are drifting farther and farther apart. What's important to you and to me seems to be very different from what it used to be. I don't think we share the same dreams anymore. I'll always love you, of course, but I don't think we'd be happy sharing a life."*

"Whoa, that's kind of heavy. It sounds like she just dumped him. Miles ever mention it?" Sarah pulled a tissue out her pocket and wiped Kashi's nose. Her nose had been running intermittently for days now. "You know, I still can't tell if she has a cold or if this is just part of teething."

"I wouldn't worry about it. I think it bothers us more than her." Hunter put the second letter back in its envelope and then knelt down in front of the open suitcase. "Yeah, he did talk about it a couple of times. I think it really bummed him out how much she changed after going to London. I guess they were pretty tight before that."

Sarah watched him poke through Miles' clothes almost gingerly as though he was afraid to disturb them. "Did you look in that zipper pocket on the top?"

"Yeah, first thing." Obligingly, Hunter slipped his hand into the long flat pocket again. "Oh, wait. What's this?"

Sarah leaned forward anxiously to see what he'd found, but it was only a picture postcard. The scene of camels grazing near a well under date palms had the hand–colored appearance of an antique photograph. "Looks old," she commented. "Where's it from?"

Hunter flipped it over. *"'An oasis on the old road to Tunis',"* he read. "Tunisia, I guess. Oh, it's from her."

"From Emma?" Sarah moved shoulder to shoulder with him again, curious to see what it said.

"'Isn't this a great card? It's hard to believe Tunisia is on the same planet as we are. It's a real time warp here. This yacht trip has been a real eye–opener for me, in more ways than one!'" The ink changed at this point and so did the handwriting, becoming a larger scrawl and indicating another day or time. *"'Don't ever worry about me, Miles. I'm fine. Remember I'll always love you, Em.'"*

Sarah sighed and sank back against the edge of the bed. "That's sad. That must be the last time he ever heard from her." She sat up again suddenly. "But it's also kind of weird. Can I see that postcard for a minute?"

Hunter tossed it to her. But he had barely resumed his search of Miles' suitcase when she exclaimed excitedly.

"Look at this! Did you notice the stamp? It's from Algeria, not Tunisia. Damn, I can't read the postmark."

"So? What's the big deal? She probably mailed it from the next port. Hey, sweetie, don't eat that." He pulled half of a soggy tissue out of Kashi's mouth and held it up. "I guess it's too late to say that now."

"Remember what it said in the fax Tyler got from England? Emma never made it to Algeria. That's where they docked and reported her drowned."

"Hmmm, it did say that, didn't it? Well, they must have mailed it for her when they got there. That's entirely possible, isn't it? Come on, spit it out in my hand, baby." Hunter held his hand open beneath Kashi's chin but she only grinned mischievously at him.

"Oh, come on, don't you think that would be a weird thing to do?"

"It depends how you look at it. Some might think it was a gracious last gesture for a dead friend. But more likely it was in a stack of postcards to be mailed and nobody realized what it was." For someone who liked to smoke himself into oblivion, Hunter had an incredibly down–to–earth way of looking at things.

"You're probably right. But I still think it's weird." Continuing to study the card, she stood up, stiff from the uncomfortable position she'd been kneeling in. "If you let your mind wander, it opens up all kinds of possibilities."

"Like maybe she swam to shore with the postcard in her teeth and mailed it before riding off into the sunset on the back of some Algerian sheik's camel?" The devilish look in Hunter's eyes contrasted with the deadpan expression on his face.

Sarah burst out laughing and impulsively bent down to give him a quick squeeze. Hunter took the opportunity to wrestle her to the floor in a bear hug that made her gasp and giggle at the same time. Finally he released his hold but kept his hands on her shoulders, pinning her down.

"You know, I've been thinking–"

"Oh, really?"

"I mean, we've already slept together. Don't you think we ought to have sex?"

Sarah searched his face as he hovered above her, trying to see if he was just joking again. His cheeks were flushed and his eyes were smiling but it was hard to tell. "Well, I'm sorry but I make it a rule never to have sex with my employees."

"Yeah, right. Seems to me you were sleeping with your last cook pretty regularly."

Sarah felt a warm flush sweep across her face and she struggled to get out of the absurd position he was holding her in. "That was different," she said as he let her slip out of his grasp and sit up.

"So is this."

"THIS is really different." She swallowed hard, realizing how serious he was. "TOO different." She forced herself to ask the question she didn't want to know the answer to. "How old are you, Hunter?"

"Twenty–three." He held up his hand like a stop sign before she could speak. "I know. You're a lot older than me. But so what?"

"So what? I'm thirty–nine! How old is your mother?"

"My mother? What difference does that make? You're not my mother!" He sat up and arranged himself so that he was directly in front of her, forcing her to look at him. "Sarah, I'm seriously attracted to you. And I'd bet everything I own that you feel the same way about me."

She looked away, unable to meet his gaze. He grabbed her hands and squeezed them until her eyes came back to him. "Hunter," she said at last. "Tyler and I have been together for a long time–"

"But I thought that was over now."

"I'm not sure if it is or not. I mean, all his stuff is still here. He hasn't really moved out." Her mind retreated to their last major argument when he had announced his plans to take a part in the play. "I don't know what to think. A month ago I thought he and I were going to make a baby together and live happily ever after. Then he said he never wanted to have a baby in the first place and he couldn't be happy living here forever...Damn, I don't know. I guess it is over. It's hard to accept."

She sat silently for a moment, watching his long, tanned fingers stroke the back of her own hands. She did not want to admit to him the truth she could barely admit to herself.

She and Tyler had always been opposites attracted to each other, complimentary colors, two halves of a whole; although passionate and devoted, they rarely saw eye to eye on anything.

She and Hunter never seemed to argue. She enjoyed how relaxed he was (Tyler would have called it "unmotivated") and his easy–going exuberance for life's simple and basic tasks (which Tyler had always called "boring"). And she especially liked the ease with which he cared for Kashi and the pleasure he seemed to derive from their relationship.

His youthful enthusiasm was infectious; he reminded her of what it was like to be full of dreams and without responsibilities. Despite the difference in age and experience, she felt amazingly comfortable spending time with him – and incredibly uncomfortable with how physically attractive she found him.

"I can't believe you just asked me to sleep with you." She hoped her joking manner would hide what she was really feeling. "We've never even kissed."

Afterwards she realized that was the most leading remark she could have made. In the next second his lips were locked onto hers, his tongue forcing his way into her mouth, exploring and probing, making the rest of her body scream yes while her mind still shouted no.

"Oh, Hunter." She held his face away from hers to keep the next kiss at bay. "I can't do this yet."

"Oh, I think you're doing it pretty well." He grinned and tried to reach her with his mouth again.

"I'm sorry. I'm not ready. It's too soon. Tyler and I weren't married, but we might as well have been. I need some time."

A wet, farting noise next to them brought reality into focus again. "And I think somebody else needs a diaper change."

Hunter looked blankly at Kashi and then slowly let go of Sarah. "Jesus. For a few minutes I forgot she was even in the room! Some guardian you've got, baby girl." He swung Kashi up onto the bed. "Pee–yew. You stink! Let's get you out of that old thing."

Still reeling emotionally, Sarah sat on the floor and watched him as he unsnapped Kashi's overalls and started to remove her diaper. "I mean, think about it, Sarah," he continued as he worked. "I'm the perfect guy for you. I've already given you a baby and you never even had to go through labor. Or have sex for that matter. Like the immaculate conception."

Sarah laughed and stood up. "I'm out of here. Give me that thing and I'll put it in the dumpster outside."

She held out her hand but he stood there holding the taped–up paper diaper just out of her reach as though it were a special prize. "Okay, but I have just one more thing to say." He paused for effect. "I'm not going to pretend that this attraction between us doesn't exist."

"What does that mean?"

"It means I'm going to remind you of it whenever the feeling strikes. I'm not going to ask you to have sex with me, but I'm going to tell you what I feel like doing to you in graphic, descriptive terms–"

"Oh, stop it. Now give me that diaper."

"And I expect you to do the same." He slammed the plastic–coated package into her hand as though it were a snowball. "Now go away. I have work to do."

Sarah was still too stunned to come back with the snappy retort his last comment deserved. As she began moving toward the door, she caught a glimpse of the corner of Emma's postcard sticking out from under the bed. Hunter's back was toward her now; he didn't notice her retrieve the postcard and slip it into the pocket of her sweater.

Even if Hunter didn't think so, she thought it had some significance. And she wanted to share it with Tyler.

It was not until she stepped out the back door that she remembered what she had wanted to tell Hunter in the first place. The police were considering him a possible suspect in Miles's death. And she had lied to protect him.

CHAPTER SEVEN

Tyler had stayed awake most of the night, unable to sleep for all the wild speculations and conjecture going on in his head. The exhaustion etched on his face made him totally believable when he staggered downstairs and told Victor and Jillian that he didn't feel well and thought he would skip the morning classes and try to rest up for the evening rehearsal.

To prove his point even further, he declined a cup of coffee on the grounds of an upset stomach, although coffee was what he wanted more desperately than anything at the moment. Dragging himself dramatically back up the stairs to bed, he lay motionless under the covers, feigning sleep, his ears alert to the morning sounds of the household which had already grown familiar to him.

When he heard the front door slam for the second time, he moved swiftly to peer through the crack in the bedroom window curtains. He watched Jillian walk across the lawn to the barn where she led the morning movement class in the loft area. Victor would be conducting his voice production class on the stage. All the students at Double Phoenix would be participating in one or the other.

In keeping with the sick–in–bed look, he put on a pair of sweatpants and a flannel bathrobe and then headed first for the hall closet. The video camera was gone, of course, and a cardboard box of hats and mittens was pushed in front of the nine– inch–square hole cut in the back wall. Moving the box aside, Tyler had a clear view of the convertible couch in the study. Gingerly poking a finger through the opening, it came in contact with what felt like glass. A one way mirror, no doubt.

Putting the box back where he found it, Tyler decided to check the situation out from the other side, but the door to the study was locked. Disappointed yet not surprised, Tyler moved swiftly up to the second floor, praying that Victor and Jillian had not locked their bedroom as well.

The old wooden door swung inward, revealing a room that was well–lit by large picture windows even on a cloudy morning such as this one. The wide expanses of unbroken glass did not match the multi–paned windows of the rest of the house, but since they were not visible from the front of the building, they did not ruin the classic nineteenth century design.

The windows were in line with the style of the rest of the room, although the piles of clothes, books and papers on the shiny, hardwood floor spoiled the stark, simplicity of the modern furniture. Along one wall was an expensive entertainment center with a state–of–the–art sound system and dual tape decks probably used for creating performance sound tracks. A wide screen TV dominated the wall however, and Tyler searched the surrounding equipment, inspecting all the shiny black plastic machines with buttons and slots until he found what he was looking for.

Pressing the button marked "Eject", he waited while the VCR regurgitated an unmarked video tape. Popping it back in to rewind, he monkeyed around with the controls on the TV, trying not to undo anything that might be preset. Unable to quickly figure out the system, he finally spied a TV remote control on the nightstand. Seconds later he was watching a replay of last night's events in the study as seen through the hole in the hall closet.

He tried to remain an objective observer but it was hard to ignore the mixture of arousal and revulsion he felt as he watched one woman expertly seduce the other.

Jillian obviously knew exactly what she was doing to Frieda who eventually lost her fear and allowed herself to succumb to the pleasures provoked by Jillian's probing and experienced fingers. Fast forwarding through to the end, Tyler was amazed to see Frieda responding gesture for gesture with a look on her face of lustful adoration. She had clearly fallen in love with the way Jillian made her feel.

As he rewound the tape to the beginning, Tyler began a methodical search of the adjoining cabinets for other homemade videos. Finally he opened a door that revealed seventy–five to a hundred tapes, neatly labeled in Victor's handwriting.

Tyler's fingers were trembling a little as they ran across the titles on a very organized shelf. There was a small collection of plays recorded over the last ten years, apparently productions from Victor's theater company in London. The rest of the tapes had cryptic titles that meant nothing to him, a series of initials or a first name. Some of them were merely numbered and dated.

Selecting one at random, he checked his watch before playing it. He still had at least an hour before anybody might return home. It wasn't enough time to do much more than scan a few of the other videos. He was going to have to figure out a way to get some more time alone in the house.

He ran through this tape with the manual fast forward button. This one was full–blown porno and he recognized no one, but they all spoke with English accents, although mostly they didn't speak at all. He watched two men and two women cavorting on a waterbed and then rewound it and quickly selected another.

This one featured one young woman and a succession of six men. Replacing this tape on the shelf where he found it, he noticed that it was the first of a series. He popped the second one in and was astounded to discover the same exact scenario, the same six men but a very different woman. Where as in the first tape the girl had welcomed and encouraged each of the men, this one seemed shocked when the third participant appeared and had to be physically restrained for the last three.

Shuddering, he could not keep himself from reaching for the third tape, knowing full well that it would be another version of the same. He would just take a quick glance at it to be sure and then go on to something else.

Yes, it was the same story again. He was about to rewind it when the camera did a close up of the actress's face as she moaned with pleasure while she sat astride the second man. He paused the tape and backed it up a few feet and then played it at regular speed.

It looked like Jillian wearing a short, dark–haired wig. When she opened her eyes, he was sure of it. Her breasts were much smaller; Tyler felt he had been right about the implants. But as he watched her enthusiastically screwing one man and then another and another, he became sick to his stomach. What kind of man made homemade porno movies of his own wife fucking other men? And what kind of woman let him do it?

It had something to do with the power Victor exerted over everyone, even his wife. Or especially his wife. Actors became almost cult–like in their obsession with him. Whatever Victor said was gospel. If Victor said Miles Romano had never been here, then he had never been here.

The sound of footsteps on the stairs made a cold sweat break out all over his body. Ejecting the tape without rewinding it, he replaced the original one that had been there and began pressing buttons to turn all the machines off.

"What are you doing in there?"

He whipped around guiltily to see Phoebe standing in the open doorway staring at him through her thick glasses.

"Oh! You surprised me! I didn't hear you come in." Flushed and sweaty, Tyler was sure he looked at least as sick as he was supposed to be. "I was just looking for a video to watch downstairs. I thought it might help pass the time. I think I'll take this one." He reached blindly towards the shelf of theater productions. "Taming of the Shrew. I'd like to see how Victor directs Shakespeare."

He closed the cabinet and tried not to worry about the fact that the remote control was still on the floor in front of the TV. It wouldn't seem strange to Phoebe for it to be there, but Victor would certainly notice immediately that it was misplaced.

"Victor sent me over to measure you for your costumes if you felt up to it," Phoebe stated flatly.

Tyler swept past her into the hall, trying to switch her focus of attention. "I guess so, if it doesn't take too long. I feel dizzy when I stand up; I think I have a fever."

He opened the door to his own room and stood back waiting for her to enter. She hesitated, obviously not comfortable with the idea. So much the better, she would leave quickly. "I'm probably not contagious." Tyler didn't move. Looking down at her feet to avoid meeting his gaze, Phoebe finally walked inside.

When he was finally standing with his back to her and she began to take his measurements, she was swift and professional in her movements. Tyler sensed it was the most opportune time to get her to talk. Her access to the farmhouse led him to believe that she had some special status at Double Phoenix.

"So how did you end up here?" he asked, lifting up his arms so she could measure around his waist.

"Jillian and I are old friends. When they came to the U.S. she offered me this job."

Old friends. There was at least a ten year age discrepancy, unless Phoebe was a lot older than she appeared. “Where did you meet?”

“We went to camp together when we were kids.” She jotted his waist measurement on a pad, and moved quickly to his inseam.

“Really? Isn’t she quite a bit older than you?”

“Yes, well, not that much. It was a theater camp so age wasn’t such an issue.”

“So how long ago was this, like twenty years maybe?” He was sure she was fabricating a big one and he wanted to see just how far she would go.

“Twenty years? I don’t know, I don’t think so.” She was on her knees now, stretching the yellow tape from his waist to his ankle. He couldn’t see her face, only the top of her thin curls which were the color of field mice.

“Has she changed much?”

“Jillian?” Phoebe chuckled under her breath. “You might say that.” She was obviously not going to become suddenly talkative.

“So where did you grow up?”

“Upstate New York.” She had the measuring tape around his neck now and Tyler had the briefest sensation that she would love to strangle him.

“Did you ever visit Jillian in London?”

“Oh, sure. A couple of times.”

“Did you meet Emma, the girl who drowned?”

There was a silence and he turned around to see what she was doing. Phoebe was slowing winding her tape measure up around her index finger. She had an angry expression on her face; her lips were pressed into a thin line.

“No,” she said, gathering up her things. “I don’t know anything about Emma.”

He knew she was lying and there was nothing he could do about it. He didn’t know when he would have a chance to talk to her alone again. Sitting down on the bed and trying to look weak and pitiful, he made an attempt at prolonging the conversation. "How long will it take you to make my costume?"

"I'm not sure I'll have to do your robes actually. We're trying to borrow or rent a red choir robe. But I will probably have to make you some kind of cardinal's hat." On safe territory and conversing about her favorite topic, Phoebe became quite garrulous. "And your hair shirt, of course. I'll be making that.

"They did this production before in London, right? Didn't they bring any of the costumes over here with them?" Tyler leaned backed against the pillows and rubbed his forehead.

"A few. But they had rented some and the ones they did bring won't necessarily fit the new actors playing them. There are a couple of costumes that can be altered, but like Frieda – she could never fit into the dress that was worn by Ebba." Phoebe stopped talking as abruptly as she had started. Moving towards the door, she said over her shoulder, "I'll be downstairs picking up in the kitchen if you need anything."

"Thanks. You know what I would like?"

She waited impatiently for him to continue.

"I'd like it if you would go out for a drink with me some night after rehearsal. I mean it," he said, addressing the astonishment in her eyes. "I like you. I'd like to talk to you some more." Shaking her head, she backed out into the hall.

"Thanks, but I don't think so."

"Well, think about it!" he called after her, showing surprising lung strength for such a sickly person.

Phoebe knew plenty. If she was Jillian's good friend, she probably knew about everything. She had obviously been warned not to speak about Emma. If he could just get her away from here and loosen her up, he could probably get lots of answers. He would do it somehow, even if he had to trick her into it.

As soon as he heard the sound of water running and the clanking of dishes in the kitchen, he picked up "The

Taming of the Shrew," slipped silently out of bed and returned to Victor's room. He knew how important it was to leave everything exactly as he had found it. Especially with someone as strange and obsessive as Victor.

To his surprise, he actually fell asleep. When he awoke he could hear voices downstairs in the kitchen. Jillian and Victor must have come back for lunch. He wondered if he should act as though he felt better or try for another period of home alone time. He really wanted a second chance to go through Victor's video collection. He had a feeling there was probably some really pertinent information caught on those tapes. On the theater videos there was probably some footage of Emma.

He sat up, feeling rather dizzy and realized he hadn't eaten anything since his fateful excursion for a snack last night.

"Tyler? Are you awake?"

Jillian stood in the doorway. She held a tray with a small metal pot of tea and a bowl of chicken soup surrounded by crackers. The smell of it was intoxicating and Tyler could not pretend to ignore his hunger any longer.

"I thought you might like something to eat. Phoebe said you seemed feverish earlier."

Tyler hoped that was all Phoebe had said. "Thanks, I am kind of hungry." He let Jillian set the tray up over the blankets covering his legs. As she turned to go, he spoke up quickly. "Would you stay and keep me company while I eat? I'm kind of bored."

Jillian glanced at her watch and appeared to mull the question over in her mind for a few seconds. "Okay. For a little while." Unlike Phoebe, who had been intimidated by being in the bedroom with Tyler, Jillian perched herself on the foot of the bed and leaned her back against the bedpost of the wooden footboard.

Overcome by her physical closeness, he involuntarily shut his eyes as video images of Jillian in sexually gratifying positions closed in on him. For a split second he was one of those lucky six, Jillian sitting astride him, riding both of them to a powerful climax.

"Tyler? Are you all right?" His eyes flew open. She was five feet away, looking concerned not orgasmic, fully clothed in tight blue jeans and a pale pink leotard that picked up the soft color of her cheeks and set off her straw blonde hair. It was hard to imagine someone so innocent being so... "naughty" was the word that came to mind. Of course, that made the fantasy even more exciting. As did her upper class British accent.

"No, I'm fine." He forced himself to meet her worried gaze. "Just a little nausea from that first spoonful of soup. I'll be fine now," he assured her as he ate some more.

"You're sure? You shouldn't eat if you think it's not going to stay down." Apparently the thought of being puked on did not appeal to her.

"It tastes great. So talk to me. Tell me about why you and Victor decided to move to the sticks of northern Vermont from a cultural metropolis like London. I mean, why not New York or L.A.?"

Jillian picked at a loose thread on the quilt. "Victor thought it would be a better place to raise a child."

Tyler choked on the dry cracker he was eating. His eyes travelled immediately to Jillian's flat stomach and shapely waist. "You mean you're pregnant?"

She shook her head. "Not yet. But we're trying."

Tyler fought back the images of Jillian's tongue on Frieda's skin, of Jillian's mouth on some stranger's penis, of the probable scenarios on the videos he hadn't viewed yet. He could not picture that Jillian as a mother.

"Excuse me for asking, but is this something you want to do? Or something you feel you have to do?"

She tilted her head and looked at him without answering. Fearful of losing her before they'd even begun, Tyler kept talking.

"The reason I ask is that my girlfriend feels like she has to have a baby in the next couple of years before she's too old. But I finally had to tell her that I'm really not into it. I'm not ready for kids. I may never be ready for kids. And our relationship may be over because of it."

Still staring at him, she got up, shut the door and sat back down on the bed. "It's Victor idea, really," she admitted. "I don't think he realizes how much I'll be giving up. He says we'll just hire a nanny and I'll be back in the theater in no time. But what's the point of having children if you're not going to care for them?"

Tyler found it hard to imagine that Victor wanted a family at all. "Does Victor know how you feel?"

She nodded, a grim expression playing on the lines of her face. "He's older, you know. He says he doesn't want to be having children at the age most men are having grandchildren. And– and I'm not that young either."

"But you look it. And you're in great shape. Pregnancy should be a breeze for you."

The compliments rolled off her like rain on a marble statue. She shook her head. "It will change everything. Everything."

Regarding the curves of her splendid breasts beneath the snug leotard, Tyler was inclined to agree with her.

"Sounds like you better get yourself some birth control pills, lady."

Her cheeks suddenly became a brighter pink and Tyler suspected that he had guessed something he wasn't supposed to. "Hey. Sorry. Our secret, okay?" As he touched her knee reassuringly, he realized that he finally had the leverage he'd been needing. "Let's talk about something else. Tell me about the production of

'The Abdication' you did in London. How was it different from this one?"

Jillian laughed. "There's no comparison. The actors were superb. We had so little to choose from this time. This is exactly what it looks like; small town theater."

"You must miss it."

"I do."

"You must curse the way that unfortunate yachting accident changed your whole world."

Her eyes narrowed suspiciously. "You always come back to that, don't you? You can't just leave it alone."

"I can't," he agreed.

"You know that Victor will toss you out on your ear if he hears you bring it up and yet you keep insisting." She frowned at him defiantly.

He crossed his arms and leaned back confidently. "And what would Victor says if he knew why his little sperm weren't finding any little eggs to fertilize?"

Her mouth opened and closed and her round blue eyes widened. "Okay," she snapped angrily. "I'll tell you what happened that day if you'll promise to get off my back about it."

"Absolutely."

Glancing hesitantly at the door, she began to speak very softly. "We were on summer holiday. We'd been having a lovely time. It was just three of us, Victor, myself and Emma. Victor doesn't like me to do any housework, he insists that if we can afford to pay someone there is always someone who needs the work. I always wished that we could go on a trip alone, just the two of us, but he insisted on bringing at least one person along, sometimes two or three. He didn't have the wealthy upbringing that I did. After all these years, he still adores the idea of servants waiting on him hand and foot."

Tyler wished he'd had the forethought to set up his tape recorder, but he had never expected this windfall conversation. He would have to rely on his memory this time for details.

"Emma was one of our more promising students. In fact Victor was quite taken with her." Jillian stopped suddenly as thought she'd said too much. "Anyway, it was an extraordinarily windy day when it happened. It all happened so quickly really. It's hard to believe one's whole life could change in the space of a minute."

"I know what you mean." A few incidents of a similar nature in his own past flashed through his mind.

There was a hard silence as Jillian sat there, contemplating the accident that had altered the course of her future. "They were fixing the sail," she said at last.

"Victor and Emma."

She nodded. "There was a gust of wind, the end of the sail blew out of her grasp and the boat heeled over on a forty–five degree angle. She lost her footing and fell overboard."

"Surely someone threw her a life preserver."

"We tried but she couldn't grasp it. The sea was very choppy that day. The mainsail was flapping wildly and I couldn't steer the boat properly."

"So you were watching the whole thing from the tiller."

"Yes. It was horrifying. I still have nightmares about it. It's one of those things you never think will happen." A tear slid off one of her cheeks. "She should have been wearing a life jacket. But she wasn't."

"What was she wearing?"

"Not much. Only the bottom half of her bathing suit. It was the Mediterranean," she added swiftly as though Emma needed defending. "That's how women sun bathe there."

Tyler didn't remind her that Emma hadn't been working on her tan at that moment. It wasn't hard for him to embroider the details of what the relationship of the ménage–a–trois on board must have been.

"Did you radio for help?"

"We tried, but the radio wasn't working. We never used it much, we're not social sailors – we go out on the water to be alone. We headed for shore as quickly as we could but it took us the better part of an hour to get the sail out again and then the wind was blowing from the south so we had to tack our way in. It was night before we made port."

Tyler shut his eyes, trying to imagine how Emma must have felt being abandoned at sea, treading water in the choppy waves as twilight descended into the navy blue Mediterranean. "Could she swim?"

"Emma?" Her shrill giggle made his eyes fly open. It was the sound of someone who was on the verge of losing it. He had almost forgotten about the breakdown she'd had as a result of the accident. "Of course. Can't everybody?" In an odd gesture, Jillian rubbed the knuckles of one hand vigorously as she spoke.

Trying to avert a possible flashback, Tyler reached for her hand. It felt like ice. She did not respond to his touch. "I just wondered if she was a strong swimmer," he said gently. "Whether there was a possibility that she could swim to shore."

Jillian shook her head. "It was thirty miles. I don't think so." Her icy fingers suddenly folded around his own in a grip of distress. "Even though I went through months of therapy, it still haunts me. Wasn't there some way we could have saved Emma? Is it possible that an Algerian fishing boat picked her up and she's still alive somewhere?"

"Surely your therapists taught you some way to deal with those fears," Tyler said gently.

"Yes, they did." She released his hand and sat up straight, staring at the wallpaper across the room. "Emma is dead. There's nothing I can do to bring her back. I know that."

"Miles couldn't accept it either," Tyler mused aloud, half to himself.

"What?" Despite her stoic demeanor, her eyes looked wild and unstable as she turned to him.

"Miles, the fellow I told you about who came here looking for Emma. She had been his girlfriend in college. It might have helped him if he'd had a chance to talk to you that night. He might have come to terms with her death and maybe he'd still be alive today."

"What? What are you saying?" The way she was acting should have been a warning signal for him to stop. Reliving the boating accident had obviously put her in a precarious state. But he could not leave her hanging now.

"They found his body in Walker Lake. It's creepy, you know; they both drowned. They think he committed suicide."

Jillian just sat there, staring beyond his shoulder, seeing something she wasn't sharing with him. Tyler went on talking a bit nervously.

"But I don't know. What guy kills himself over an ex–girlfriend he hasn't seen in two years? It turns the whole story into melodrama, into a gruesome romance. But I guess that's the kind of story the general public likes to believe. Me, I think it was accidental. I think he might have been stressed out, missed a turn and landed in the lake. Of course, that's just a theory, they haven't found his car yet. I don't really know the details–"

"Can we talk about something else, please." It was a command, not a question. With a deep exhalation of breath, Jillian had pulled herself back together, suppressing the issues that made her feel weak and vulnerable. She was a Valkyrie once more, large, impressive and aware of her own cool beauty. "I've answered your questions. Now you can answer some of mine. What's this thing?"

With her toe, she poked at the carrying case of his laptop computer that lay on the floor next to the bed.

"My laptop computer. I'm still a journalist at heart. I never go anywhere without it." He hoped she wasn't going to ask him to turn it on.

"They're expensive little numbers, aren't they?"

Tyler thought it was an odd remark for a "million–heiress" like Jillian. "They're not as expensive as they used to be. The demand for them has given birth to no–name clones and lots of competition." He couldn't believe he was talking computer marketing with her. "I guess you theater people don't use computers as much as the rest of the world."

"Oh, I used one a lot in college. I'm not computer illiterate." She stood up suddenly. "Time for me to go now. And you need your rest. Do you think you'll feel well enough for rehearsal tonight or should we work around you?" She picked up the tray of dirty dishes and waited by the door for his answer.

He was tempted by the opportunity to be alone in the house for another few hours. "I don't know. Why don't you check in with me again around suppertime?" He slid down between the sheets, pulled the quilt up to his chin and closed his eyes, trying to look as though all the conversation had worn him out.

Jillian left without answering, closing the door behind her. As soon he heard her footsteps on the stairs, he reached for his notepad. He quickly jotted down the key points of their conversation, shaking his head as he did. There were a few things that did not sit right. Until he had started weaving his "romantic" version of Miles death, he hadn't really made the connection that both Miles and Emma had died by drowning. Now he wasn't sure how coincidental it was.

He needed to know more about Jillian. And Victor. And a lot more about Emma.

His eyes drifted sightlessly to the ceiling. If only he could make some calls. It was ridiculous that he did not have a private place to talk on the phone here. It seemed like an insurmountable first step in doing any further investigating.

What he really needed right now was a cell phone. There was a place in Jordan Center where he could get one. He'd seen the advertisements in the paper; they gave you the phone free along with ten hours of calls. Then you paid through the nose for the rest. He just had to figure out how to get there. A speedy recovery by suppertime was definitely the diagnosis for his illness now.

Kicking off the bed covers, he began making a list of the people and places he wanted to call.

CHAPTER EIGHT

"Hey, Red, what's happening?" Sarah automatically put a frosted mug of draft beer in front of the bearded old man. Red was one of the regular patrons of the West Jordan Inn and had lived on the outskirts of the village all his life. A dairy farmer who had been getting up before dawn for more than thirty years, Red usually came in after the evening milking was done but always left before nine.

Tonight his clear blue eyes had a distracted look about them. "You okay?" Sarah asked in concern.

"Yeah, I'm all right. But I thought I saw a ghost this afternoon and I've been straining my memory ever since."

"Saw a ghost?" Sarah laughed uncertainly, as did a couple of the customers who were sitting within earshot at the bar. It was now high foliage season, and both the dining room and bar were as busy as they might ever be. But Sarah put everything else on hold for a few minutes to pursue Red's remark.

"Yeah, I saw someone who died twenty–five years ago. He was in the liquor store today over in Jordan Center." Red sipped the foam off the top of his beer. "It was the damnedest thing. It wasn't like he looked the same as he did back then. He looked the age he'd be if he'd lived."

"Oh, come on, Red, it must've just been someone who looked like this guy." Sarah cleared a few empty glasses off the bar and tossed a couple of dollars into the tip jar.

"I know you think I'm crazy, but I'd swear to it on a stack of Bibles. Hey, Jack!" He hailed another old–timer who was seated on a stool at the other end of the bar. "You remember Claudie Ledoux, don't you?"

"Claudie Ledoux? You mean the Ledoux family used to live out to Walker's Lake?"

"Yeah, those Ledoux. You remember Claudie, he was a few years behind us in high school, always in trouble?" Red picked up his beer and moved down to stand beside Jack, a chubby bald man with a ring of white hair around his head that matched his handlebar mustache.

"Claudie...didn't he die in some car crash up in Quebec?" Jack was assuming the same distant look that Red had been wearing since he had entered the lounge.

"Well, that's what I remember. And then his old man drank himself to death a few years later and that was the end of the Ledoux. But I could swear I saw Claudie himself walking out of the liquor store this afternoon. Carrying a case of French wine."

Sarah could hear Jack snorting with laughter as she turned to wait on someone else. "That couldn't be Claudie. Those Ledoux were the Vermont equivalent of Southern white trash. Did you ever see the shack they lived in? It's still standing – I see it sometimes when I'm out fishing. Besides, Claudie's dead. Must've been a cousin or something."

Red was still protesting that he had to be right when Hunter backed through the kitchen door carrying a tray of food. "It's getting cold, Sarah," he said warningly as he transferred it to her arms. Then he leaned over and whispered something in her ear that made two bright red spots appear on her cheeks. Before he had finished, she was pushing her way past him headed for the dining room, grinning and shaking her head.

"What'd you say to her?" Jack asked Hunter. "I've never seen her blush like that before."

Hunter winked and disappeared back into the kitchen.

"What do you think, Red? You think he's doing her?"

"Sarah?" Red's tone expressed his opinion of the idea. "Are you kidding? All these years Tyler's come and gone, she's never been with another guy. Besides, he's just a kid."

"Red, you are a poor judge of character. Always have been, always will be." Jack knocked back his bourbon and water as Red began protesting again.

The lounge was still full a few hours later when Tyler showed up with a pale, skeletal man whose most distinctive feature was a frizzed–out Afro in an improbable shade of red. Tyler caught Sarah by surprise as she came out from behind the bar lugging a bag of garbage, and gave her a big hug and a kiss. Her response was perfunctory; she did not even put down the full garbage bag.

Tyler stepped back uncomfortably and filled his embarrassment by introducing Tracy. "He's the entire set design and construction department of Double Phoenix. We're bar–hopping tonight. I'm showing him the hot spots of the Northeast Kingdom."

"But we seem to be having a bit of trouble finding the action," Tracy added looking around at the relaxed atmosphere of the homey country inn. "I'm waiting for Tyler to take me to some tacky disco with mirror balls and flashing lights."

Sarah could not keep herself from smiling at how Tracy made the most of his displaced person's status.

"Let me help you with the bag," Tyler said, heaving it over his own shoulder. As Sarah held the outside door open for him, he whispered, "I'm trying to get him loaded so he'll talk. He's drinking rum and coke."

"Yeah, but who's driving home?" she hissed back.

"I will. You should see the Ferrari he's got."

Sarah shook her head; she would never understand the high men got from fast, expensive cars. "What are you drinking, Tracy?" she asked as though Tyler hadn't said anything.

"Rum and coke. Make it Myer's. I love that sweet dark stuff. Hot in here, isn't it?" He slipped off his black suit jacket and hung it carefully on the back of a chair. Sarah could see the sweat circles beginning to form underneath the arms of the white silk shirt he was wearing. Before he had turned back to face the bar, she had poured a double shot of rum over a glass of ice and shot some coke into it.

"Would you be a love and add a slice of lime? Thank you."

Two carpenters in plaid flannel shirts exchanged meaningful looks as Tracy took an empty stool next to them.

Sensing the tension that was brewing, Sarah tried to make small talk with Tracy until Tyler returned.

"So how did you end up over in East Jordan?" she asked. "My guess is you're not from around here."

"You got that right, honey. I spent the last ten years in London designing sets for Victor Nesbitt's productions." He dropped Victor's name as though it had as much clout as Spielberg or Lucas. "When the school closed down, he asked me to accompany them on their next venture. Little did I know we would end up here!"

His implication was so clearly derogatory that Sarah tried to gloss over it before he ruffled anyone's feathers. "Where are you from before London?"

"Pittsburgh, Pennsylvania. The armpit of the nation. Couldn't get away from there fast enough." Tracy was drinking quickly, obviously ill at ease.

Sarah wondered what was taking Tyler so long to get back from the dumpster. "So if you were in London all that time, you must've known the woman that our friend Miles came here looking for information about." She wondered why she'd called Miles her friend; she'd only known him a few hours.

"What woman would that be?"

"Emma was her name. She was a student at that theater school you worked for."

Tracy scrutinized her a moment. His small gray eyes were wide spaced and heavily hooded –or maybe he was just getting drunk. "Yes, I knew her. What's the big deal?"

"Well, that's what we've been wondering. I mean what kind of person was she that this guy Miles would come all the way up here on his way home from Nigeria just to find out more about how she died? She must have been pretty special."

"Maybe he thought so. Most people didn't. I mean, I certainly didn't think she was worth it."

"Worth what?" Sarah was already mixing him another drink.

"Worth what?" Poking at the remaining ice cubes in his glass with a red plastic stirrer, he repeated her question. "That's a good one. What was Emma worth? Certainly more now that she's dead than when she was alive."

It was a callous remark and Sarah was not sure what he meant or how to respond. "You mean all the trouble her drowning caused?" she asked pushing the fresh drink towards him.

"You know an awful lot about it for a bartender from north of nowhere." Tracy was eyeing her suspiciously now and she was relieved that Tyler finally returned, entering through the kitchen door.

"I met your chef out by the dumpster," he remarked to Sarah. "He was letting go of today's garbage, so to speak." The slightly smoky smell that clung to Tyler's clothes filled in the unspoken spaces between his words.

"Ah, yes. He gets rid of his garbage every evening about this time. Did you talk?"

"Yes, he told me about the letters he found." Tyler helped himself to a beer. "Interesting stuff."

"That reminds me, I have a postcard for you too. Tracy and I were just talking about Miles' ex–girlfriend, Emma."

"You mean the one I'm not allowed to mention for fear of excommunication from Double Phoenix?" Tyler was amazed that Sarah had managed to accomplish in five minutes what he had been working up to all night. He looked sideways at Tracy, whose body posture was beginning to suggest inebriation.

"Yeah, well, I wasn't talking to you about her, I was talking to your girlfriend here. Victor didn't saying anything about her." Tracy's voice was little louder than necessary. Tyler wondered if he realized what he had just admitted about Victor.

"Well, in that case," Tyler stood up and nodded at Sarah, "Carry on." He picked up his beer and headed for the kitchen. "Besides, I've got a few things I'd like to talk to my replacement about."

The way he said the word "replacement" made Sarah wish she could ask him what exactly Hunter had said to him outside. She didn't think they were going to be discussing how to make beef stroganoff and the thought of Hunter spilling his honest guts to Tyler made her extremely nervous.

"Hey, where's he going?" Tracy complained. "I thought we were only stopping here for one drink."

"He'll be back in a minute." Sarah waved goodbye to a group of local schoolteachers who had been sitting by the fireplace. There were only a few customers left now and the lounge began to take on the more intimate atmosphere that it was known for. "So it sounds like you didn't like this Emma much."

Tracy shrugged. "Oh, for God's sake, she was just another little whore vying for Victor's attention." It was pretty clear that this was how he felt about women in general. "You make a good drink. I'll have another." Pulling out his wallet, he rifled through a thick wad of cash. "Smallest I've got," he said, laying a hundred dollar bill on the shiny wooden surface of the bar.

"So you must make pretty good money doing this job." Sarah tried to conceal her astonishment at how much cash he was carrying. "I always thought small town theater groups were dirt poor."

"Honey, we may be in East Bumfuck, but we are not small town. I do all right." Tracy tried to assume a superior stance but couldn't quite pull it off.

"I don't know much about theater companies." Sarah began clearing dirty glasses off the tables by the fireplace. "I mean, who gets paid? I thought the students at Double Phoenix paid to be there."

"I'm the only one really. And Phoebe, she does the costumes, she gets a small stipend. They're not making any money here really. It's all in the bank back in England."

"So tell me." Sarah stopped close to Tracy's stool, holding the tray of dirty glasses off to one side and affecting a confidential air. "Are they millionaires?"

"Well, so to speak. If they liquidated their assets they would be, but they live off the dividends. Almost blew it all when Jillian had that cancer scare a few years ago."

"They did?" Sarah began loading the dishwasher beneath the counter, and tried to sound only half interested.

"Yeah, turned out Jillian didn't have proper health insurance. Operations and chemotherapy ate into their dividend checks and they had trouble accessing the other money because of some stupid trust that Jillian's dad set up when she was young and flighty. Almost put them under."

Sarah remembered reading about the trust fund in the faxes that came from London. She was surprised that there hadn't been anything about Jillian's cancer in the tabloid articles that Lucy had sent.

"So how is she now? Is the cancer gone or in remission?"

Tracy laughed for the first time, an unpleasant wheezing sound. "Oh, it's in remission all right. Where's Tyler anyway? I'm ready to get out of here." He pushed the hundred dollar bill towards her, indicating that he wanted to pay his tab.

Sarah gave him his change and then peeked through the kitchen door. It was clean and quiet except for a small but steady drip from the kitchen faucet.

"He must have gone upstairs. I'll tell him you're ready to go." Quickly scanning the bar to make sure everybody was taken care of, she hurried to the second floor.

Tyler was reading instructions from a book and Hunter was examining something on the coffee table in the apartment. "It's my new cell phone," Tyler explained. "That's really why I convinced Tracy to take me on this outing. I'll call you with my number tomorrow. What'd you learn, Sherlock?"

On the way back downstairs, Sarah told him briefly about the huge amount of cash that Tracy was carrying and about what he had said regarding Jillian's battle with cancer. "You ever hear anything about that?"

Tyler shook his head, clearly puzzled. "I wonder what kind of cancer she had? And how'd they ever keep it a secret? The rest of their lives have been so public."

"I think you'd be surprised how much people can keep to themselves. Especially if they have money."

Tyler stopped by the front desk. "I'm going to send Lucy a quick fax about it. See what she can come up with. Can you keep him busy for another a minute?"

"Tyler–" Sarah hesitated thoughtfully. "Do you really think it's important? Or fair?"

"What?"

"What difference does it make if Jillian had cancer? Can't you respect her right to privacy? It doesn't have anything to do with Miles's death. Or Emma's." She opened the top drawer of the desk and handed him the postcard from Tunisia. "Here. I thought you might find this interesting."

Without waiting for his response to her questions, she moved quickly back into the lounge.

"You're wrong, Sarah," he said after she had left. "I know you are." Finishing his hastily scribbled fax, he put it in the machine and dialed Lucy's number in London.

"Guess it's time for your friend to go home," Sarah commented to him when he came back into the bar.

Tracy was slumped over the bar sound asleep. His cheek rested on a paper napkin, his jaw hung open in an unflattering way.

"We can't have him sleeping at the bar," she went on. "You'll have to put him out in the car if you want to stay any longer."

"I should probably get going anyway. It's late. I'll go see if I can get Hunter to help me wrestle him into the Ferrari."

"Tyler–" Something in her tone stopped him as he turned to go. "The police came to ask me some questions this morning about Hunter."

"What do you mean?"

"Like maybe they suspected that he had something to do with Miles's death." Tyler let out a low whistle. "I haven't said anything to him about it."

"Why not? Do you think the cops might be right?"

"No! You were here, how could they be? I didn't tell him because – I didn't want to upset him anymore than he already is about this whole thing." Now she was lying to Tyler as well.

"I'm surprised they haven't been back to talk to Victor. I don't know how I could have missed it if they'd been by." Tyler stopped by the chair that Tracy had hung his coat on and deftly plucked the car keys out of the right pocket. Holding the keys in the air, he said reverently, "This alone will make spending the evening with him worth it."

"I thought you had rehearsal every night."

"I lucked out. Tonight they were working on some flashback scenes that I'm not in. But tomorrow night it's back to the grind for the heavy climactic scene between Christina and the cardinal. Well, I better go get Hunter."

"Please don't say anything," Sarah warned.

Tyler bit back the remark he really wanted to make and said instead, "I won't. But it certainly is a new way of looking at everything."

"Don't wake the baby!" she called after him.

There was something about how he left the room and the familiar way he walked that made her palms begin to feel sweaty and her stomach turn. Tyler's presence made her realize what an emotional upheaval her life was in right now. With no end in sight.

"'I do not want to lose myself again, Christina!'" Tyler pretended to remove the hair shirt which he had just revealed to Jillian. As Jillian reach out to touch him, Victor interrupted.

"What is this little phony action here?" he called out from the front row. "Take your T–shirt off, Tyler. Show us what wearing the hair shirt has done to you, show us what loving Christina is doing to you. Show us your bleeding flesh!"

Tyler stepped back to where he had been kneeling a moment before, repeated the line and pulled his shirt over his head. Jillian gasped and ran her fingers along the imaginary scars on his chest. Tyler tried not to shiver at the sensation of her touch.

"'God have mercy!'" she whispered. "'How long have you been wearing this? Since that time long ago?'"

Tyler closed his eyes for a second, feeling very much like the cardinal he was playing as he tried to shut off the way Jillian's fingers made him feel. "'No. Since you.'" He stood up. "'I knew, even before you knew, how much there could be between us.'"

Suddenly his confession began to seem very real to him. He had been suppressing his attraction to Jillian from the moment he had learned who she was. It was easy to channel his true feelings into the words he was saying, words he didn't even have to think about, words that came to him as though they were his own.

When he finally turned away from her, after confessing that his greatest faults were feeling love and desire, he felt as though he had turned himself inside out. There was no one in the theater but Victor and surely he had seen that Tyler wasn't acting.

"'Do you desire – me?'" Jillian spoke her line very softly, intimately.

Tyler paused as he had been directed to before replying. "'Yes. I do.'" When he looked up at Jillian he could see she was astonished by what she saw in his eyes.

Being a good actress, she used that surprise to feed her next line. "'Dear merciful God!'"

"Okay, we skip over the flashback scene with Ebba and Magnus and pick up with your next line, Christina. By the way, the energy between the two of you is fabulous. Don't lose it now."

Tyler barely heard himself saying his lines, he was so captivated by the electricity between himself and Jillian. He knew this scene was headed for their one and only kiss and he wanted to be psyched up for it. In previous rehearsals, he had held himself back, feeling uncommonly shy about giving it his all in front of everyone.

"Don't forget you're on stage, you two! Don't let it get too personal. Share what's going on with the audience!"

Victor's admonitions seemed to come from a faraway place but Tyler followed his directions mechanically. He let his hand fall from Jillian's cheek and moved away from her, saying, "'Christina, we would be damned–'"

"'If I don't have you I will have no one.'" As Jillian spoke, Tyler's head filled again with visions of her videos. As he tried to shut out those images, there was a silence and he knew it was his line. Unable to remember what he should say, he turned around and took her in his arms.

"'Christina–'" He fumbled for his words, his face inches from her own, and finally gave up. Pulling her body against his, he kissed her. It was long, thorough and satisfying and left him feeling totally aroused.

"That was beautiful," Victor announced loudly. "But you skipped about five very important lines. Let's take it again from Azzolino's 'we would be damned.'"

While Victor was talking, Tyler had been searching deep in Jillian's eyes trying to see if what was happening was real or if she was just a good actress. Reluctantly he released her and moved to his position, wondering if Victor could see the bulge in the front of his jeans and whether it bothered him to watch someone else kissing his wife.

He dismissed that thought immediately. This was Victor the voyeur who made movies of his wife having sex with other men. It was probably turning him on to watch Tyler kissing Jillian.

As he made them repeat the kiss over and over, Tyler began to find that idea increasingly disturbing. Victor was forcing them into a state of unrequited passion, making them experience the sexual frustration of the two characters in the play, encouraging them to be as physically demonstrative as possible in their one moment of carnal contact. By the time they moved on to the last few pages of the play, he felt ready to explode with unfulfilled desire.

Everything about Jillian excited him, her shiny blonde hair falling seductively across her face, the moist, bruised look of her lips after having kissed him, the way her impossibly large eyes actually filled with tears as she cried out her last anguished lines. She had an amazing presence; he could not understand how anyone could have ever found her performing ability second rate.

"Okay, why don't we take a break here, say half an hour?" Victor's voice cut through Tyler's haze of infatuation. He looked up and saw someone standing next to Victor, apparently the bearer of an important message. When he finally focused on the person as Phoebe, she blushed and looked away, apparently embarrassed by the sight of Tyler naked from the waist up and glistening with sweat like a field worker on a hot day.

"I have to go back to the house to make an overseas call," Victor explained, speaking more to Jillian than Tyler. "Take a break and let's see if you can recreate this same scene when I get back."

As Phoebe followed him up the aisle, she could not keep herself from stealing a furtive backward glance at Tyler as he wiped the sweat off his face and chest with his T–shirt.

"Wow. I need some air," Tyler said as the slamming of the door echoed hollowly in the empty theater. Jillian was still kneeling center stage in her final position, watching him with an expression that was both thoughtful and amused. "What?"

She shook her head, her moving hair creating a lustrous cascade even in the harsh work lights. "Nothing. Let's go outside." She got to her feet with a fluid motion that carried her across the stage, stopping for what looked like a choreographed moment to pick up her sweater and his denim jacket. "Here." She tossed it to him. "Don't catch cold."

He walked behind her down the steps and up the aisle, watching the rounded curves of her buttocks moving up and down inside her tight jeans, wishing he never knew that she made private porno movies, wishing he had never seen her go down on Frieda, wishing he could put her back on the Scandinavian goddess pedestal from which she had fallen off.

Maybe she just needed some help getting back on track.

The evening air had the arctic chill that can accompany a crystal clear, autumn night in the mountains. A shaft of light from the windows of the theater doors illuminated the walkway for a few feet.

Instinctively Tyler stepped into the concealing darkness and as Jillian followed him, he turned and gathered her into his arms. Without a word, her own arms went around his neck and she pressed her lips and her body against his.

Tyler slid his hands inside the back of her pants and pulled her hips tightly towards his own so she could feel the heat and hardness in his groin.

"Let's go back to the house," she whispered, slipping her own hands under the back waistband of his jeans.

Tyler froze for an instant, seeing in his mind Victor's TV paused on a frame of himself and Jillian in bed together. Was this really all part of some perverted plan the two of them had cooked up? What if he was being set up, just like poor, unsuspecting Frieda?

"No," he said, still holding her tightly while his mind raced. "I have a better idea."

He led her across the lawn to the parking lot, where the cars were just dark shapes, hulking shadows under the moonless sky. He moved to the largest one, running his hand along the cold metal until he found a door handle. He pulled it open, illuminating the inside of Paloma's VW van. A silky black sleeping bag was unzipped to cover the platform in the back.

"She'd kill us," Jillian laughed breathlessly. "She hates me."

"She'll never know." Tyler pulled her inside after him and shut the door, pitching them into blackness again. "Climb over the seat and be careful."

The inside of the van smelled like incense and patchouli oil. They tumbled over the back seat like a couple of high school kids, struggling to get their clothes off as fast as possible. "Ouch. I was hoping there was a mattress under this," Tyler said as he rolled on his back. "It's just a piece of plywood."

"This is crazy, Tyler, I can barely sit up straight back here without my head bumping the ceiling. Wait." He could sense Jillian feeling around for something and then suddenly they were illuminated by a tiny circle of light from a slender metal flashlight the size of a pen. "I always keep it in the pocket of my sweater, for finding my way around this place at night."

Tyler was starting to shiver a little as he wiggled out of his pants and he guessed the temperature was near freezing, inside the van and out. He held the flashlight on Jillian as she peeled off her leotard, her unconfined breasts springing to life, the nipples were already standing at attention. Again he wondered about how much bigger they were then the breasts of the Jillian in the old video but this was no time to ask delicate questions. He hadn't felt such a burning lust since he'd moved in with Sarah. Sarah. This was no time to think about her either. Not now. Not when Jillian was climbing on top of him and he was about to erupt like Mauna Kea.

"I guess we'd better go back. Victor is probably wondering where we are." Tyler ran his fingers lightly down Jillian's back, tracing the line of her spine. She kissed the middle of his chest and attempted to sit up. "Do you think he'll know?"

The afterglow of instant gratification was already fading, making way in his mind for the hard, cold facts. He'd just had unprotected sex with a married woman who'd done some pretty indiscriminate screwing in her lifetime. It was one of the most irresponsible things he had done in years.

"Do you care if he knows?"

She was on her knees with her back to him and he wished he could see her face. "What do you mean? You're not planning to tell him, are you?" He could feel his chest constricting at the thought of a confrontation with Victor.

Jillian's shoulders moved up and down in a casual shrug. "He wouldn't care. He's really not possessive of me that way. Victor still has one foot back in the early seventies in the days of alternative theater and experimental sex."

"So do you two still have a good sexual relationship after all these years?" Tyler's curiosity forced him to ask the question.

There was a trace of bitterness in her reply. "Good?" she laughed softly. "Let's just say it's unusual. But Victor is a very unique person. Everything with him is going to be different. I will say that he keeps me satisfied." She laughed for real this time giving Tyler a chill that had nothing to do with the air temperature.

He had a feeling that what she meant went layers deeper than what she said. "He has a lot of power over you, doesn't he?"

She was instantly still, her fingers freezing for a second on the zipper of her pants. "More than you'll ever know, Tyler." She grabbed her shoes and climbed over the back seat to put them on. "This was fun. We'll have to do it again sometime. In a real bed."

Her casualness slapped him in the face as effectively as the back of a hand. This was nothing to her, just another round of drinks in the bar of life. She didn't realize that he didn't do this all the time, that he had really felt something for her, or so he thought.

But it was a way to be alone with her and very pleasurable to boot. Time was running out, he only had a few weeks left here to learn what he could about what really happened to Emma.

When they got back to the theater, Victor was pacing the aisle restlessly. Before they could even apologize for being late, he came forward and swept Jillian away. "The rest of the rehearsal is cancelled tonight. I'll work with the two of you again tomorrow afternoon before we do the run–through tomorrow night."

Tyler sat down heavily on one of the benches in the theater, feeling very much alone in the silence after they left. What had caused Victor to act like that? The phone call he had received? Or knowing that Tyler had just fucked his wife?

He was losing all perspective here. Sometimes he felt as though he was living on the edge of reality in this world of memorized lines and forced emotions. He needed to concentrate more on finding out the answers to the questions that had brought him to Double Phoenix in the first place.

Doing a quick check around to make sure he was really alone, he pulled his cell phone out of his jacket pocket and punched in a number in London.

CHAPTER NINE

"Rochelle, what are you doing here this time of the morning?" Tyler felt suddenly self–conscious. He was standing at the kitchen counter, ravenously eating piece after piece of toast straight from the toaster, buttered on the counter, and shoved into his mouth. He was surprised to see Frieda's pale, petite roommate hovering uncertainly by the door to the hall. Students rarely ventured uninvited into Victor's house.

"I need to talk to Victor. Or maybe I just need to talk to Phoebe." Rochelle's words tumbled over themselves; she seemed unusually nervous.

"Victor hasn't come down yet and Phoebe doesn't usually come over until they leave for class." Taking another bite of toast, he held out the coffee pot in an offering gesture. Rochelle shook her head and bit her thin lower lip. "Why don't you talk to me?" He straddled the back of a wooden chair. "What's on your mind?"

"Well, it's nothing you can really help me with," she said, but she sat down at the table opposite him as though she wanted to talk. "I was just hoping it would be okay if I moved in with Phoebe. She still has that empty bed in her cabin since Courtney left."

"What's the matter? You and Frieda aren't getting along?" He could almost guess where this was leading already.

Rochelle's eyes filled with tears as she shook her head again. "Ever since she started working on this role of Ebba, she's got this idea that maybe she's a lesbian."

"Really?" Tyler acted surprised. "But Ebba's the most heterosexual woman's role in the play. Next to yours." Rochelle played the feminine side of the young Christina.

"Not really. If you think about it, she responds to Christina's advances until she gets together with Magnus. Anyway, Freida says she's been exploring that side of herself and now she thinks she likes women. I think she's crazy. I don't know how a person can change, just like that." She snapped her fingers.

Tyler wondered how Rochelle could have missed the way Frieda had been mooning over Jillian the last several days. Maybe her strange behavior had no meaning to someone who didn't know what had happened between them.

"So what you're saying is, it bothers you that she's come out about her sexuality? I thought you guys were best friends."

Rochelle blushed and began carefully inspecting the wood grain of the butcher block table. "Well, it seems like she wants to be more than just friends now."

"Oh. Wow. You mean she came on to you?" Tyler's overactive imagination easily pictured the scene.

Rochelle nodded and chewed on her already–mutilated lower lip. "I don't really want to talk about it." Her voice was little more than a whisper now. "I just want to move out. I don't care if she wants to be a lesbian, I just don't want her to involve me."

"Have you tried telling her how you feel?" Tyler asked. Inside he was thinking about how, once again, Victor had managed to exert his Svengali–like powers, although this time he had done it indirectly, using Jillian as his conduit.

"It wouldn't matter. Frieda has her mind set on this thing. She's even been hanging around with Paloma and Cassandra and you remember how she always used to talk about them." Rochelle smiled a little and wiped her eyes with the back of her hand.

Tyler smiled with her, trying not to show how foolish he felt. How could an investigative journalist like himself not have realized that Paloma and Cassandra were gay? He was usually pretty good at picking up sexual vibes, but in this community of actors nothing was ever exactly what it appeared to be.

The sound of footsteps in the upstairs hallway announced the imminent arrival of Victor and Jillian. "Well, it sounds like they're coming," Tyler said, pushing back his chair and standing up. "I'm sure there won't be any problem with you moving. Don't worry."

He lingered at the top of the stairs for a while, listening to how their conversation was going. He hid silently around the corner as Victor and Rochelle came down the hall, still talking.

"Let me just give you the other key to that cottage and then you can be on your way." He heard Victor unlocking the door to the study. What he wouldn't give to get into that room. He wondered if Phoebe ever cleaned in there and if she had a key. There had to be a way.

Two hours later, he slipped quietly out of the darkened theater during acting class. Gabe and Frieda were holding everyone's attention with their interpretation of a scene from "A Streetcar Named Desire."

Tyler startled Phoebe while she was scrubbing the sink in the downstairs bathroom. He explained to her that he thought he had lost his notebook in the study the previous evening while he and Jillian were rehearsing their final scene for "The Abdication." Phoebe's face reddened as she nodded without questioning his story and he realized that she must be aware of some of the unorthodox activities that went on in that room in the name of theater.

He followed her into the kitchen and pretended to read an open magazine on the counter, watching her out of his peripheral vision as she rummaged around in the back of a drawer for the key to the study. When she let him into the room, he walked right to the couch as though he had been there before and began shoving his hand down between the cushions. When he got down on his knees to look under the couch he was able, with a little sleight of hand, to extricate his notebook from his pocket and pull it out as though he had just found it.

Impatient but apparently satisfied, Phoebe locked the room and headed for the kitchen to return the key. Tyler was still in the hallway, standing next to the telephone when it rang. "I'll get it!" he called to her.

"Mr. Nesbitt? Northeast Kingdom Travel calling."

"Uh, I'm– yes?" The blood rushed to his head as his heart began to beat faster.

"I've got some information about those travel times you requested earlier?"

"Oh, yes. Good."

"If you don't want to go through Montreal, it looks like the best we can do is fly you out of Burlington to L.A. with one change in Chicago, and then you can catch the 7 PM Air New Zealand flight to Auckland."

Tyler tried to sound calm. "To Auckland. Right. And which day are we talking about again?"

"You asked for Sunday October 20th. That's still what you want, isn't it?"

"I'm sorry, I'm a little distracted here, I'm in the middle of a class. Could you call back in an hour or so?" Tyler hung up the phone and pulled his hand away as though he had burned himself.

"Who was it?" Phoebe asked.

"It was for Victor. I told them to call back in an hour." Tyler left the house quickly, sprinting back across the field to the barn. Something was up and it was time to go into high gear.

He slid back into his seat, hoping his absence had been attributed to a bathroom visit. Marcus and Paloma were on stage now taking their own turn at Stanley Kowalski and Blanche Dubois. Victor sat in the middle of the theater, his attention totally focused on the scene taking place on stage.

New Zealand. October 20th was a week after the last scheduled performance of "The Abdication." As far as Tyler knew the school was supposed to be in session until Christmas time, with another production to be performed before the end of the season. Some sort of emergency must have come up. He thought about Victor's behavior after he received the phone call during rehearsal the night before. He had canceled the rest of the rehearsal and then he and Jillian had spent the remainder of the evening in their room with the door closed. He had heard raised voices a couple of times and had egocentrically assumed they were arguing about how Jillian had behaved with him. No, something else was going on, he was sure of it.

He'd tried calling Lucy a few times last night but had only gotten her answering machine. It was five hours earlier in London, she had probably been sleeping. He had left a message for her to fax the inn if she had found out anything more about Jillian's bout with cancer.

Jillian did not fit the profile of someone who'd had a bout with death in recent years. Or maybe she did. Or maybe she was just a very good actress.

He needed more time alone in the farmhouse. Probably all the answers he needed were there.

October 20th. It was only a few weeks away. He just needed more time.

Later that afternoon he decided to boldly take his chances. Victor was upstairs in his bedroom with the door closed. Jillian and Phoebe were in the front hall; Jillian was giving Phoebe some money and instructing her on just exactly which kind of mushrooms to buy for the Oriental stir fry she wanted to make for dinner.

Tyler walked past them into the kitchen and went directly to the drawer where the key to the study was kept. After pocketing it, he stayed in the kitchen for a few minutes, making small talk with Jillian as she began chopping vegetables. He put some music on for her to listen to while she worked and then he excused himself. With a quick glance up the stairs, he quietly let himself into the study, locking the door behind him.

He headed first for the file cabinet next to the desk. There was a file on each student, which included their applications, references, emergency phone numbers and billing records. Some of them had copies of Victor's evaluations of their work and performances. He scanned through them quickly until he found what he was looking for.

Courtney Miller, from South Portland, Maine. He quickly scrawled her home phone number in his notebook. He flipped to Victor's evaluations. They were glowing reports of a gifted young actress who was still a bit too headstrong and opinionated for ensemble work. The last page was one sentence dated September 9th. "Dismissal due to extreme lack of respect for authority and inability to cooperate."

That was the girl he needed to talk to, all right. He quickly flipped through the other files, looking for one on Phoebe, but there was nothing with her name on it.

He closed that drawer and slid the top desk drawer open. A large black checkbook filled most of the space. Without removing it from the drawer, he began to flip through the entries.

It was the Double Phoenix account and there were no unusual entries. The deposits were neatly recorded as tuition or box office or donations. The debits were all carefully itemized; printing expenses, costume accessories, lumber, paint, electricity. There were no checks made out to Tracy or Phoebe, however.

As he closed the back cover in disappointment, another check register of the same size was revealed beneath it. Opening this one, he immediately realized this was Victor's personal account. The beginning balance was staggering but so was the number of checks written against it. Deposits were only made into this account quarterly, refreshing the enormous sum but never bringing it back up to where it had begun.

Within the first month's entries he found the name he was looking for. Tracy Lane...he ran his finger across the line to the check amount and his jaw dropped. Victor had written Tracy a check for $10,000 the first month the school was open. His eyes quickly scanned down, looking for Tracy's name again. $8,000 this time, a month later. And $8,000 each month up to the present. What services could Tracy possibly provide that required such a fee? It sure as hell wasn't building sets and teaching stagecraft to twenty students. Besides, he was being paid out of Victor's personal account.

The sound of the front door slamming made him remember his time was limited. Phoebe was back with the mushrooms. He hurriedly looked for her name in the checkbook but, as far as he could tell, it never appeared. She was probably paid in cash.

He began jotting down the names, dates and amounts of checks that interested him. The biggest by far was an entry marked as a donation to the Raeburn Clinic for $50,000. There were large payments to credit card companies each month. There was a regular check for $1,000 a month each to Robert Thompson, Elaine McFee, and Cyril Somerset. Each of these were sub–noted as a donation. He wrote a check for $500 each month to someone named Sybil Erikson.

Tyler's pulse quickened. Erikson. That had been Emma's last name.

His hands were shaking as he replaced the checkbooks the way he had found them and slid the drawer shut. Opening the door a crack, he could hear Jillian and Phoebe talking in the kitchen. He silently slipped into the hallway, locking up behind him.

"I'm going for a walk," he announced, hoping his voice did not sound as odd as he felt.

"Dinner's in fifteen minutes, luv," Jillian called after him.

He walked down the driveway until he was not in sight of the house and then pulled out his cell phone. Lucy's message machine was still taking all her calls. Damn, he hated leaving information like this on a tape but he had no choice. After reciting his name, date and the time, and his usual plea for urgency, he read off the names in his notebook. "Raeburn Clinic, Robert Thompson, Elaine McFee, Cyril Somerset, Sybil Erikson. Oh, and Tracy Lane. Anything you can tell me."

His call to South Portland was more successful. He waited anxiously, pacing back and forth in the dead leaves on the driveway, while Courtney's mother called her to the phone. It took only seconds for him to remind Courtney of who he was.

"Yes, I know who you are. If it hadn't been for you, I'd still be at Double Phoenix." Her tone conveyed all the bitterness she felt.

"Look, I'm really sorry, but just between me and you, I don't think this place is going to last the season. They're in serious financial trouble." Half–truth, half–lie, but the right effect. "I just need to know that you really did talk to Miles that night."

There was a silence at the other end of the line. "Look, I know he was there and I respect you for standing up to Victor. Nobody else here dares to tell him what they really think."

"Isn't that the truth," she agreed darkly.

"I've read your file. I know that's the reason Victor expelled you from the school." Another half–truth. "You must have some very strong feelings towards him now."

"That's putting it mildly."

At least she was talking to him. "I want to tell you something. The man you saw that night is dead now. You were the last person we know of who saw him alive."

"Dead?" she repeated in a horrified whisper.

"I'd like to give the police your address and phone number so they can talk to you about this." He had no intention of doing any such thing but he wanted to hear her reaction.

"No. Please don't. Please. I can't talk to the police."

She was still whispering.

"Why not? It's the right thing to do."

"Because I promised Victor I wouldn't."

That power again. "But does it matter now what you promised Victor? What can he do to you now?"

"Because... he said something awful would happen to me or someone in my family if I ever told anyone that I saw that man." She sounded terrified. "I believe him. It's just not worth it. It was such a stupid thing." She was crying now. "I should never have said anything to Victor. He had promised me such a good part in the play and I ruined all my opportunities to ever work with him again."

"Courtney. Calm down. I promise I won't go to the police." Shit, what had he started here. "And listen, just for the record, I read your file. Victor thought you were a great actress with plenty of potential.

"He wrote that?" she sniffed.

"He did. And I'm sure it's true. Good luck to you. And pretend I never called." He closed the phone and put it back in his pocket.

Feeling increasingly uneasy, he walked slowly back to the house for dinner.

He waited on the line for ten minutes while a recorded male voice with a strong Australian accent told him about the great package deals Air New Zealand offered to Auckland or Sydney with a free stopover in Fiji. Finally an operator broke in.

"Air New Zealand. How can I help you?"

"I'd like to confirm some reservations I have."

"Certainly. And you are flying when?"

A few minutes later, he stretched out on his bed and stared at the ceiling. He had confirmed what he had already expected. Leaving October 20th, with an open return date in the next six months. He was sure Victor had no intention of ever using the return part of the tickets. He wondered what explanation he would give to his students or would he just disappear.

In the morning, he continued his new tactics of bold aggression. He waited in his room until he heard both Victor and Jillian leave for their morning classes. Then he moved swiftly into their bedroom and began removing video tapes from their covers, replacing the covers back where he had found them, flipping them over so that it was not obvious that they were empty. He took a couple of the theatrical productions and a random selection from the private porno collection. Stashing the tapes in his daypack, he made sure he left the closet looking the same as before. He slung the pack over his shoulder and quickly exited the house, heading across the field for his morning movement class.

The next trick would be to borrow a vehicle for the afternoon so he could go over to the inn and view his contraband. He was sure Gabriel would lend out his rusty station wagon again for a full tank of gas and ten bucks.

It was hard to keep his mind from wandering as he stretched and pranced with the other students under Jillian's direction. He was just not interested right now in turning his body into a finely tuned instrument that would respond and convey at his command.

By twelve o'clock he was behind the wheel of Gabe's old station wagon, headed for West Jordan.

He was surprised to find no one home at the inn. It was an exceptionally glorious day, the mountains were a tapestry of luminous autumn colors. In local vernacular, "the foliage was peaking." Sarah and Hunter were probably out for a walk. With the baby. Sarah always hated to "waste" a beautiful day.

He made himself a sandwich, noting a few changes Hunter had made in the kitchen and that things were not quite as clean as he usually kept them. He wondered what would happen in a few weeks when the play was over, whether he could really ever come back to the inn and cook again. He could not think that far in advance. There was too much to do between now and then.

Popping a tape into the VCR, he stretched out on the couch in the front room and punched the buttons of the remote.

He fast forwarded through the first tape; it was typical porno featuring a well–built young man and woman with oversized breasts and genitals. The woman was not Jillian.

The second tape was more interesting. It showed the whole film session from the moment the actors walked through the door in their street clothes. He could hear Victor's voice off camera telling them what to do, there was no background music and apparently no script. There was a lot of nervous giggling, these were obviously amateurs, and a lot of realistic close–ups of unstaged and unattractive poses.

He did learn one interesting thing from that film. At the end, after the actors had put their clothes back on and left, Victor was heard saying, "Okay, Tracy, you can break it down now."

The camera stayed on as Tracy appeared with a crowbar and a hammer and began removing the flats that had formed the back wall of the set. He grinned self–consciously as he turned to the camera to ask Victor a question. "Do you want me to stash these or are you going to use them again tomorrow?"

So Tracy knew all about Victor's private passion for film–making. Tyler thought that might explain a few things.

The next one he watched was "The Taming of the Shrew," the same tape he had taken the day he had been caught by Phoebe in Victor's room. He was curious to see if Jillian had acted in it.

He was not disappointed. He recognized her in the lead role of Kate, the rebellious and passionate daughter. She was wearing a long haired wig of fiery red hair. The woman who played her sister looked unusually like her, adding to the interesting stage illusion. She had Jillian's straw colored hair, but she was a paler, more washed out version of Jillian's brightness. He wondered with increasing interest if that was Emma.

He skipped through, watching only the scenes these two women were in, wishing there was a way to know the names of the actors. Unfortunately, it was not a real movie and no credits rolled across the screen at the end.

The next tape was bits and pieces, not a whole story like the others. About half way through there was about fifteen minutes of Jillian which he stopped to watch. Her hair was short and black again, she must have gone through a few years of wearing it that way, and she seemed a bit awkward as though perhaps this was her first time at performing nude in front of a camera.

"What shall we call it – Orgasm, American Style?" she asked using a broad American accent and then giggled self–consciously.

Then the camera stopped and when it started up again, this time she was waving two small American flags as she announced the title. She looked around trying to figure out what to do with them and then finally wove their little wooden ends into her pubic hairs, laughing hysterically at the effect it created.

When she calmed down, she began to stimulate herself while trying to keep close eye contact with the camera. As she became more aroused, her self–consciousness slipped away and she had to make a supreme effort to keep her eyes open.

Tyler felt uncomfortably excited watching her. If this had been a screen test for professional porno movies, she would have been hired on the spot.

The sound of footsteps on the porch made him jump. Feeling oddly guilty, he quickly paused the tape at the same time that Sarah came flying through the front door in the next room with Hunter in close pursuit. She was shrieking with girlish laughter in a way Tyler had never heard before.

"Right on the kitchen floor!" Hunter shouted.

"No way!" was Sarah's taunting reply. "You won't catch me anyway!"

"Oh, no?"

The sudden silence made Tyler sick to his stomach. What was happening to his life? Maybe he could gather up the tapes and sneak out and they would never know he'd been here.

There was a gasp and a sigh and then Sarah's voice. "We left the baby on the porch."

"She's asleep. She's fine." As Hunter spoke, a whimper from outside indicated otherwise. "Never mind. I'll get her."

Although Tyler remained motionless on the couch, Hunter glimpsed him out of the corner of his eye on his way back to the porch. "Oh, hi, Tyler. Didn't know you were here."

"Tyler's here?" Sarah appeared instantly in the door to the living room. Her flushed face gave away all the feelings she was trying to hide.

"Hi, Sarah." He felt about as comfortable as she did.

"What are you doing? Watching movies in the middle of a sunny afternoon?" Her opinion couldn't have been more apparent.

"They're some tapes I took from Victor's private collection. I thought I might learn something from them. About Victor and Jillian, I mean," he added as Sarah turned to view the picture paused on the screen.

"What is this? One of his porno flicks?" She stared at the frozen image of Jillian masturbating.

"Yes."

"And what do you think you're going to find out from watching this?" Her tone indicated her doubt and disgust.

"I've already learned plenty."

"I bet you have." She reached over and took the remote from him and defiantly pushed the play button. The sound of Jillian bringing herself to orgasm filled the room in an embarrassing and overwhelming way. Sarah watched in contemptuous fascination.

Now that she was closer, the smell of smoke drifted towards his nostrils from her clothes. Her strange, youthful entrance suddenly made sense.

"Sarah, are you high?" Tyler asked in astonishment.

She refocused her look of contempt on his face. "Oh, give me a break, Tyler. Just because you're sitting here doing something abnormally freakish and deviant this afternoon doesn't mean that I am."

But he didn't believe her.

The canyon between them was widening to an unbreachable point. He was beginning to realize there would be no return.

He stood up abruptly and turned off the television. "I've got to be going," he said, gathering up the tapes. His head felt as though he were being sucked into a downward vacuum of depression. "Is there any mail here for me?"

Before Sarah could reply, they heard the front door opening and the sound of a stroller being pushed across the old wooden floorboards. "I got her back to sleep," Hunter whispered.

"Good." Sarah touched his arm in a familiar way as she moved past him into the other room. I'm getting Tyler's mail for him."

Tyler followed her out to the desk. "Any faxes from Lucy?"

“Yes.” She handed him a sheet of paper that had been folded in half.

Tyler opened it, not knowing what to expect. In the center of the page was a line drawing of an open soup can with dozens of earthworms crawling out of it. Beneath was printed “but I’m working on it.” And beneath that, “Please be careful.”

“Damn,” he said aloud. He looked up. Sarah was watching him with an unreadable expression on her face.

“So. Are you going to be able to catch the play?” he asked her as he took the handful of letters she held out to him.

“I – I don’t know if I’ll be able to get someone to cover for me.” She looked away.

“It would be nice if you could see what I’ve been doing for the last month. So you can judge for yourself whether it was worth it.”

“I’ll try. What nights is it?”

“Wednesday through Saturday, next week and the following week.”

“That’s our busiest time.”

“I know. But I’d really like it if you would come.”

She still would not look at him. He packed his mail up and turned to go. Hunter had been leaning against the doorjamb, listening and watching. He slapped Tyler on the shoulder.

“Hey, don’t worry, we’ll be there, man. I’ll make her shut the place down for a night if it’s the only way.”

“Thanks. I’ll see you guys.” He stepped out into the sunshine. He wasn’t sure if the door he heard slamming behind him was in his head or in his heart.

CHAPTER TEN

Tyler was in a gray funk by the time he pulled into the Double Phoenix parking lot. On the drive back he had finally admitted to himself that he had not really thought about the possibility of his situation at the inn changing so drastically. In the back of his mind he had expected Sarah to go on with business as usual and, when he was done sowing his wild oats (so to speak), she would be ready to begrudgingly welcome him back as always.

On the front porch of the farmhouse he had to step aside to let Tracy pass by. Tracy was carrying a wooden box full of tools.

"Doing a little household repair?" Tyler asked, attempting to be friendly.

Tracy's only response was a self–satisfied smirk. Tyler shook his head as he went inside. He was beginning to hate everything about this place.

He stood on a chair backstage in the theater while Phoebe pinned up the hem on his cardinal's robe.

"See if you think you can manage it tonight with the pins in it," she said as she moved around him. "Victor wants you to start working in it and there's not enough time to hem it before rehearsal."

"Phoebe, I hope they pay you well enough for all you do here. You work harder than anybody."

She blushed and filled her mouth with pins so she wouldn't have to answer. Tyler thought the pinkness of her face was the perfect complement to the squirrely–ness of her hair.

"What are your long range plans? After Double Phoenix."

She shook her head and mumbled carefully, "Don't have any."

"Oh, come on. Don't you want to do costumes for a big Broadway production? I thought everybody had aspirations of that sort."

"No, I like it here. Northern Vermont suits me just fine." He had to agree with her there. She didn't have an aggressive enough personality for the New York scene.

Frieda was waiting impatiently nearby, holding out a couple of extra inches of fabric at the waist of her costume. "I've lost weight since you first measured me," she complained to Phoebe. "And now my dress doesn't have that snug appearance it's supposed to."

Over the last few weeks Frieda's plump curves had begun to slip away. She now had the beginnings of an hourglass figure that was accentuated by the full skirt and tight, low-cut bodice of her 17th century costume. It was obvious to everyone that Frieda felt good about her body for the first time in her life. At least that was one point in favor of Victor's perverse rehearsal methods.

It was also evident that Tony, the young actor who had the role of Ebba's husband, Magnus, in the play was very much aware of Frieda's burgeoning sexuality. He had begun hanging around her a lot of the time, trying to transfer her fascination with Paloma and Cassandra onto himself.

It was all an interesting melodrama from which Tyler felt totally removed. His isolated position as a guest in Victor's house had kept him from forming serious personal relationships with any of the students. All part of Victor's plan, he was sure of that.

He looked out at the aisle where Jillian was getting into character, strutting up and down, wearing her 17th century doublet and pantaloons. When she saw him watching her, she stopped and gave him a seductive smile. He was not sure if it was Christina smiling at him or Jillian. Or both.

He knew by now the best way to forget his own troubles was to throw himself completely into his role. At least for a few hours he would be someone else in a different time and different space with different problems.

After rehearsal he stretched out on the floor of his room and drank brandy until it made him feel like vomiting. He was trying to suppress the erotic memory of Jillian's tongue inside his mouth at the end of the play. He was trying to stop recalling the little sounds of pleasure he had heard come out of Sarah's throat at the inn that afternoon. He was trying not to feel anything.

It must have worked for a while because suddenly he was opening his eyes and there was Jillian hovering over him. She was wearing a white cotton lace robe and a concerned look in her eyes.

"Are you all right?"

"Sure. I just passed out drunk on the floor which is exactly what I wanted to do." The back of his head ached and he was afraid if he stood up that he might get the spins.

"Tyler." Her tone was disapproving, but a grin played on her lips.

"What are you doing here?" he asked curiously. His mouth felt very dry.

"I saw your light was still on and when I knocked and you didn't answer, I thought you'd fallen asleep with it on. So I came in to turn it off and found you lying here."

He doubted that was the real reason she had appeared in his room in the middle of the night, but he was too out of it to care if she was lying. She reached down to grab his hands and he let her pull him to his feet.

"Come on, let's get you into bed." She moved him backwards until he sat down abruptly on the edge of the mattress. He was not at all helpless, but he liked the fantasy that was he playing out in his mind, the fantasy of Jillian undressing him and putting him to bed.

Instead, as she leaned over him, he reached up and tugged on the sash of her robe. It fell open to reveal a matching lace bra and tiny bikini underpants. Her skin seemed to glow in the lamplight and he felt dazzled by the sight of so much of it.

"Is that what you sleep in?" he laughed, marveling at how the half cups of the bra seemed suspended on her perfectly sculpted breasts.

"What do you think?" she countered teasingly, letting the robe slide from her shoulders.

"I think that you didn't come in here to turn my light off." He was more awake now and beginning to wonder about the folly of her motive. "But more important, what is Victor going to think about where you are?"

"He's not thinking, he's dreaming." She began to unbutton Tyler's shirt and he closed his eyes, enjoying the sensation of being caught up in his own dangerous fantasy. A moment later his eyes fluttered open; he did not want to shut out the sight of her amazing body as she hovered over him, unbuckling and unzipping now.

"I thought you never wore a bra," he said and then reached up to tweak the lace down three–quarters of an inch so that her brown nipples and the bottom half of her amazing breasts could be fully appreciated. The boning of the bra still held them up at an extraordinary angle, pushing them against each other to create an unnatural but incredibly erotic cleavage.

"Only for fun," she replied. "Are we having that yet?"

He grabbed her wrist as she began to slip her hand into his pants. "Wait," he whispered. "Let me enjoy you first."

"My pleasure, luv." She straddled him and his eyes moved down to the little vee of white lace that barely covered her open crotch. Jillian put her hands behind her head and flexed the muscles of her flat, well–toned stomach. She remained in this flagrant and uninhibited pose as she said, "It unfastens on the sides. Go for it."

As the scrap of lace drifted to the bed, Tyler gave a little sigh of contented anticipation at the thought of what the next hour would bring. Then he leaned forward and ran his tongue up the inside of her smooth thigh.

Several hours later, he awoke alone. His head rested against the footboard, the bed sheets in a twisted tangle next to him. He could still taste Jillian in his mouth, still smell her on his fingers. His head pounded and his back ached, but he regretted nothing. In fact, if he had his way, he would spend the whole day in bed drinking and fucking the real world away.

He held his watch up to his face. Nine fifteen. Victor and Jillian were already gone off to teach their classes. And he wouldn't have to make any excuses for why he hadn't been there. He could tell the truth; he'd just overslept. He didn't have to say why.

He could not remember the last time he'd had such wild and intense sex with anyone. Jillian threw herself into the act with the same intensity that she brought to the theater. Her total absorption combined with her amazing strength and flexibility created an unparalleled experience. It was sex purely for the sake of sex, absolute animal lust, an energetic endeavor that was only gentle when necessary as a means to its explosive end. It was not the compassionate, caring lovemaking that he had carried on with Sarah for the last several years.

It had been unbelievably exciting and he would do it again in a heartbeat.

He staggered to the bathroom, hoping that a hot shower would clear his head. As he let the water pound on his stiff neck and shoulders, his mind was full of images of Jillian. He had carefully inspected nearly every inch of her body. The only scars he had found were the one hidden under her bangs and the ones underneath her breasts where the enlargements must have been done. It made his stomach turn to wonder why someone so close to physical perfection would need to go that far. But there was no evidence of any operations which made him wonder what kind of cancer she might have had. Sure, many kinds of cancer were treated with chemotherapy and radiation which of course, probably explained the black wig in the videos. Cancer patients generally lost their hair from that kind of treatment. But he bet they didn't usually make porno movies at the same time.

There were two things he had to do right away, besides drink about a gallon of coffee. He had to call Lucy and he had to get the videos back into Victor's cabinet.

He sat on the edge of the unmade bed listening to the sounds of the international call going through, still wearing just a towel wrapped around his waist. He was enjoying his mood of rebellious debauchery; he did not feel like getting dressed yet.

Amazingly, Lucy answered on the first ring. "Oh. Hi." She sounded unusually nervous. "Look, can I ring you back in ten minutes?"

"Sure. Do you have my cell phone number? It's–"

"Yes, I've got it here. I'll talk to you soon." She hung up without saying goodbye.

Tyler frowned. Something was up. He decided to return Victor's movies while he waited for her call.

Even in the warmth of the morning sunlight, everything about Victor's bedroom seemed cold and calculated. Just like Victor himself, Tyler reflected. The polished wood floor, the black frame of the bed, the spotless white down comforter, the orderliness of the video cabinet. He began quickly slipping the tapes back into the empty boxes which he had left to hold their spots. He froze suddenly as he realized there was one missing.

The box for the "The American Orgasm" tape was not where he had left it. The other tapes had been pushed together to fill in the space where it had been yesterday.

Goosebumps covered his bare chest and shoulders. It meant Victor had to know someone had been in here. He stood with the pilfered tape in his hand, not knowing what to do. His eyes roved the other shelves, frantically looking for another place to put it.

Maybe the best thing to do was just keep it for a while longer. He would have to hide it somewhere that Victor would never find it which meant that no place in the house was really safe. He stared out the window for a moment, an idea forming in his mind.

Back in his own room, he dressed quickly. Returning the tape to his daypack, he put on his denim jacket and headed downstairs. His cell phone rang just as he reached the kitchen.

"Tyler? It's Lucy." She was breathing heavily as though she had been running. In the background he could hear traffic and street noises.

"Lucy? What's going on? Where are you calling from?"

"The booth on the corner. I think my line may be tapped. I'm not sure whether to thank you or curse you, Tyler."

"Why? You're not in any danger, are you?"

"Let's just say I've received some serious threats from some major bad dudes. Which leads me to believe this is a big time story we're cracking here."

Cradling the phone on one shoulder, Tyler poured himself a cup of coffee. "No kidding? So tell me what you've found out."

"The easy part was that list of names you gave me. Thompson, McFee and Somerset are all editors at different London papers. Sounds like he must be paying them some kind of a bribe or hush money. But the clinic is the part that's a ball breaker. It's a privately owned place down in Cornwall that won't give out any information about what they do unless you've been specifically referred by a particular list of doctors. I pretended I was an insurance agency doing some research on the medical histories of Victor Nesbitt and Jillian Fox. I left a fake name and my phone number with them. The next thing I know a couple of ugly thugs are pushing their way into my flat wanting to know who I really am and warning me about trying to get information from the Raeburn Clinic under false pretenses."

"Holy shit, Lucy!" Tyler was beginning to worry that he'd led her into some kind of danger. "They didn't hurt you, did they?"

"No, they just scared the daylights out of me! I can't decide whether to go on with this or not. Truth is, I'm really curious now what kind of place this clinic is."

"It could just be a retreat for celebrities who want to improve their appearances without the world knowing. I think Jillian has had her breasts enlarged in the last couple of years."

Lucy laughed. "Enlarged? You've got to be joking. Her knockers were already big enough to put your eye out."

Tyler let that one slide. He knew he never made points arguing about the size of one woman's breasts with another woman. "Do you think the place might have anything to do with the cancer she had?"

"Now what about this cancer thing? I can't find any mention of it in any article in any magazine or paper in the last ten years. Where did you get that idea? Hang on – a big lorry is passing, I can't hear a thing."

Tyler waited until the truck had rumbled by before he replied. "A guy who came with them from London mentioned it the other night when he was drunk. Tracy Lane. Did you find anything out about him, by the way?"

"Nothing except that it's the name of a street near Kensington Gardens. Probably an assumed name, wouldn't you think?"

For some reason that thought hadn't occurred to Tyler before. "You're probably right. Lucy, I wish I could be over there with you right now to find out more about this clinic." He lowered his voice and moved out to the back porch. He felt better talking about Victor when he wasn't inside the house. "Time is running out here. I found out that Victor and Jillian are flying to New Zealand when this play is over and they haven't told anyone yet. It seems like they're on the run from something but I can't pinpoint what."

"New Zealand? What could possibly be there for them? Look, Tyler, I'm going to head down to Cornwall tomorrow, see if I can find out anything from the locals in the nearest village about what goes on at this clinic. I'll call you in a day or two. But whatever you do, don't leave any more messages on my machine."

"Sorry, Luce. I'll be more discreet from now on."

He pocketed the phone and downed the rest of the coffee. Leaving the empty cup on the back steps, he headed across the field in the opposite direction from the theater. Towards the cottages. He wondered if Tracy had gone off to work yet.

Even the front porch of Tracy's cottage gave the appearance of being a lot more lived in than the others. Tools and equipment were piled on one side of the door; the other half of the tiny porch was filled with an expensive looking hammock on a wooden stand. After a cursory knock, Tyler reached for the door handle only to find himself locked out.

"Damn," he muttered. He peered through the window behind the hammock, trying to get a glimpse of Tracy's living quarters. In the opening between the pair of dark curtains, he was able to see a tiny kitchen area built into one wall and some contemporary speakers that were nearly as tall and thin as Tracy himself.

He had hoped to unload the video here. It had seemed like the perfect place. Stepping off the side of the porch, he walked around the back of the building.

He found the open window he was looking for on the opposite side of the cottage. He tried to jimmy it up but it seemed to be locked into place leaving an opening of about six inches. Peering inside, he saw that Tracy's bed was pushed up against the wall next to the window. Without a second thought, Tyler pulled the tape out of his pack and then stretched his arm through the opening, letting the tape fall into the crack between the bed and the wall.

Satisfied that he'd disposed of the incriminating evidence, he made his way back across the open lawn to the theater. Acting class was nearly over. It was a good thing he wasn't really a student here or he'd be failing.

He was not surprised when Jillian followed him up to his room after lunch and locked the door behind her. No words were exchanged until half an hour later, when they collapsed in a sweaty embrace on the still unmade bed. "That was the best afternoon nap I've had in a long time," Tyler whispered in her ear. He was curled up behind her, his chest against her back. Lifting the hair off her neck, he blew softly on the dampness there.

Before Jillian could respond, there was a creaking noise above the ceiling of his room. Tyler stared up in puzzlement.

"What do you suppose that is up there? Is there a third floor to this house?"

Jillian laughed. "Just an attic. Victor must be poking around up there for something. Ever the investigator, aren't you?"

Tyler had never considered the possibility of an attic in this house. People always hid things in attics that they didn't want anyone finding. "What does he keep up there?" he asked, his lips grazing her shoulder.

"Costumes, props, you know. We brought all sorts of whatnot with us." Jillian rolled over to face him. She covered his lips with her own, successfully preventing him from saying any more.

Tyler knew that there was a huge loft in the barn used to hold costumes and props but he had no intention of pointing this out. As their tongues intertwined he wondered where the trap door to the attic was and why he had never noticed it.

"Where does Victor think you are?" he asked when he was finally able.

"Rehearsing lines with you. Missed most of class again this morning, didn't you?"

"Got a phone call from my mother. My Aunt Etta just came down with cancer. First person in our family to have that happen. I don't know much about it, what they are going to do to her or if she'll recover." He was fishing, hope she'd rise to take the bait off his line.

"I'm sorry to hear about your Aunt. Were you close?"

The only thing she was rising to was her knees as her mouth made its way down his body towards his groin again.

"Not really. Anyone in your family ever die of cancer?"

"Both my grandfathers. Gruesome subject to discuss at a time like this."

He was not going to let the moment escape him. "How'd you get this?" He asked lifting the bangs off her forehead and running his fingers across the faint scar there.

She jerked her head away from him so that the hair fell down in a concealing curtain again. "Swimming accident in college. Hit my head on the concrete edge of the pool. How'd you get this scar?" She touched a C–shaped mark on the side of his thigh.

He grinned. "Rusty nail sticking out of a windowsill of an old building I was jumping out of. Your turn. Any other scars on your body you'd like to tell me about?"

She shook her head as she bent back down to continue the task she had in mind. He stopped her again with a light touch beneath the breasts.

"How about these? What happened here?"

She clucked her tongue and wagged a finger at him. "You should know better than to ask a question like that, luv. Show some respect for a girl's integrity."

Integrity, my ass, he wanted to say but instead he blushed deeply as she scolded him. "Sorry," he mumbled. "Just curious, that's all."

When she left him twenty minutes later, he was resting in a satisfied stupor. He was getting nowhere at learning more about Jillian and in his present state of being he felt rather inclined to just leave the stones unturned and enjoy the ride.

Maybe he should try a different tactic for a while. Let Lucy look under the English rocks, he'd stick to the American ones. With a lazy stretch, he reached over the edge of the bed for his pack. He shuffled through the ever–increasing contents until he found the copies of newspaper articles Lucy had faxed him.

Emma Erikson was from New York; she grew up in Buffalo and went to the university in Syracuse. That was where she had met Miles. There must be plenty of people at the university who still remembered them, or at least her. Theater students were usually easy to recall, especially by the professors and directors.

Syracuse was probably a six hour drive. Or a very short plane hop from Burlington. Finding the time to get there was another issue. Meanwhile a few phone calls might help get things rolling.

Suddenly the urge to sleep had mysteriously disappeared. He piled up the pillows and settled down with his notebook and telephone. "Syracuse," he said into the phone. "The number for the university."

He punched in the number. "Can you tell me who the head of your Theater Department is? Can you connect me with him please? Yes, I'll take his voice mail."

Tyler left an urgent message for Stan Silverman to call him back regarding an ex–student of his. He made a note of the name and extension number. He was not sure where he was going with this but at least he was going somewhere now. Then, as suddenly as it had come, his burst of energy left him. Exhaustion covered him like a warm blanket and he slipped into a dreamless sleep.

CHAPTER ELEVEN

"Paloma is passing out the schedule for the next two weeks," Victor announced. "To run over it briefly, tomorrow night we are having spot rehearsals on a few troublesome areas. Then we have dress rehearsal Wednesday and Thursday night, Friday is opening night and we have performances Saturday and Sunday. Then Monday and Tuesday you have off to rest, Wednesday we perform at Goddard College, Thursday at UVM and then Friday through Sunday final performances here.

"It is a very strenuous schedule," he admitted, "but you will see how keeping our momentum up builds the energy of the show night after night. You will need to get lots of sleep, no late night parties–" he gave Tony and Marcus a warning look– "and try to keep your body tuned and toned."

Tyler was no longer hearing Victor's advice; he had noted his window of opportunity on the schedule in his hand. He had two and a half days off next week, easily enough time to get to Syracuse and back. Now he just had to find a way to get there.

The last few days had gone by in a haze of activity and exhaustion. Jillian was subtly running his life, making sure he went to classes, requesting his help with set production, volunteering him to help hang the stage lights, and filling any leftover hours with exciting and inventive sex. He was playing along with it for several reasons. He was, of course, hoping to learn more about her secrets. But he also found that she kept his mind off Sarah and the heavy loss he was beginning to feel.

There was the nagging feeling in the back of his mind that he was being used for some alternative purpose. Time and again he asked her where Victor was or what he would think if he knew about their fiery affair. Since she always had a ready answer, he made a game of asking her more and more personal questions, trying to trip her up.

"Is your sex with Victor as exciting as your sex with me? Who is the better lover? Would you leave him for me?"

She had pouted in response to the last question, a mournful look in her round blue eyes. "You know I can't," she had answered. "He's my life. My destiny."

"Doesn't it bother him that you're spending so much time with me?" He asked her this at least once a day.

"It's not changing my relationship with him. If I'm happy and satisfied, then he is."

Right, in a perfect world, Tyler would grumble to himself. Then he would let her dissolve his suspicions in intense physical pleasure.

Three days had passed without any word from Lucy. Stan Silverman from Syracuse had returned his call in the middle of rehearsal. Tyler had had to stop everyone in the middle of a scene to answer his cell phone. Incredibly embarrassed, he now made sure to turn the ringer off during class or rehearsal times. He had told Stan he would get back in touch with him. He had not been able to reach him since.

He suddenly realized that Victor was done talking and everyone was standing up to leave. He looked up to see Frieda hovering by his shoulder.

"A few of us are having a little get together tonight in my cabin," she said to him quietly. "If you want to come by, feel free."

"Uh, sure. That would be nice." He tried not to display how surprised he was that she had invited him. Since Jillian had commandeered his presence, the other actors had been steering an even wider circle around him.

"See you later then." She turned towards Tony, who was quickly approaching at the sight of Frieda talking to another man. Not missing a step, he hooked his arm through hers and started walking her up the aisle. Tyler strained his ears to hear their conversation.

"See, I told you he would come," he heard Frieda say. "He's not really like her at all."

Tyler knew he was referring to Jillian. He wondered how much the other actors knew about their relationship. Maybe he would find out tonight. He left the theater without a backward glance.

It was an unusually warm night for early October. He had heard that a hurricane was heading north up the east coast. This warm weather was probably caused by the tropical depression that was being pushed along in front of it. Hopefully the bad weather would peter out by the time it hit the mountains. In the meantime, the warmth of the evening seemed to lift the spirits of everyone.

At the inn, the surprisingly mild temperatures created little rivulets of sweat on Sarah's cheeks and forehead. In the kitchen, Hunter stood at the stove wearing only a pair of shorts and sandals.

"You can't come out like that," Sarah warned him. "The health inspector would have my head. You're breaking the law."

"Well, that's nothing new," Hunter laughed. "You ready for these two orders of beef tournados?"

A few hours later they sat outside on the porch swing, massaging each other's feet and relaxing after another heavy night of foliage seekers.

"Thank God it's not like this all year," Sarah remarked. "But this is what will get us through the next few months."

"So when do we close the inn and go on vacation together? I'm ready for our honeymoon."

"You just got back from a year and a half of vacationing!" Sarah laughed.

"That wasn't vacationing, that was traveling. There's a big difference. All right, forget the vacation, it's the honeymoon part I'm really ready for."

Sarah did not know why she continued to hold out on him when it came to physical intimacy. After her last unfortunate conversation with Tyler, she had realized it was foolish to think that they could ever repair the damage now done to their relationship. When he had accused her of being high, she realized he didn't recognize the way she acted when she was euphorically happy and having fun. It had been years since she had felt that way around him. Sometimes she thought she spent more time worrying about Tyler than being in love with him.

"Tell me about your last girlfriend," she said, sidestepping the issue again.

"My last girlfriend? Or do you mean the last woman I was lovers with?" It was too dark on the porch for her see the expression on his face.

"You decide." She was not sure what the difference in terminology meant to him.

"Well, the last meaningful sexual relationship I had was with – actually change 'meaningful' to 'meaningless' – was in Kenya. She was the wife of a coffee plantation owner, a stunning woman, much older than me, bored to death with her own existence. Her husband spent most of his time away, traveling on business. She offered me a place to stay in her enormous bungalow. Fed me incredible meals that were actually served by servants, took me on safari, gave me clothes. All I had to do was fuck her every night."

He stopped and reached for Sarah's hand. "At the time I called it making love. In retrospect I know it was just fucking. Anyway, one afternoon I found her in bed with the groundskeeper. All right, so he was a big handsome black guy with a huge member. I had nothing to lose, so I decided to forgive her that one. But then her husband came home one weekend and I was ignored like a stray dog. Oh, I shouldn't say that, she did send the cook's teenage daughter to my room as a consolation prize. That was when everything lost its meaning. I left the next morning."

"The cook's teenage daughter."

"No, I didn't sleep with her." The sour tone in his voice changed to humorous. "I may be a hedonist, but I'm not a cradle robber. Like you."

"You turkey." She tried to punch him but he held her down and tickled her until she gave up. "Okay. Go on. Who was before her?"

"You want a rundown on all my sexual activities for the past year and a half? Oh, I'm sorry, 'girlfriends'. So that means I can leave out the one night stands, right?"

She wasn't sure if he was teasing her or not. "Right. Unless you didn't practice safe sex. Then I absolutely have to know."

"Relax, lady. I am a modern boy. I may have had a few women in the last year but I'm not crazy." There was a flash of light as he lit the remainder of the joint he had been smoking all night, off and on. Sarah took another hit off the beer she was nursing.

"I don't know." Hunter exhaled the smoke he had been holding in his lungs. There were a couple of chicks from New Mexico I met in Thailand who I traveled with for a while. I got pretty tight with one of them. But then the other one got jealous, I think she had kind of a crush on me, and they had a fight. When they made up they decided their friendship was more important to them than I was. They left me in Kuala Lumpur. Traveling can be weird that way sometimes. I may catch up with Natasha again someday. I've got her address in Santa Fe."

Sarah was beginning to feel sorry she had asked him to talk about this. She had thought it would make her feel closer to him to know more about him, but instead she could feel age and experience widening the distance between them.

"How about in Nigeria? No girlfriends there?"

"Nobody but Kashi." He gave a brief laugh. "No, I got there after that Peace Corps jerk who got Kashi's mother pregnant left town. Mostly all I felt was animosity from the women in the village. A few of the young girls were still flirtatious in an idealistic way."

"Idealistic?"

"You know, maybe they could marry the California man and he would take them back to live in Hollywood with Clint Eastwood and Sylvester Stallone. They show movies sometimes, outdoors," he explained. "With an old–fashioned projector, using a sheet hanging on the side of a building for a screen. It's a big night out for the village."

They were silent for a few moments after that, Hunter remembering and Sarah trying to imagine the scene he was describing.

"Speaking of big nights out, I talked to Jennifer and she can baby–sit on Sunday night, so I think we are all set for going to see Tyler's play." Hunter's tone was purposely casual, knowing this was still a volatile subject.

"As long Clyde can do the bar. He still hasn't called back about it. Listen." Sarah sat up suddenly. "Is that the phone?"

Hunter cocked his head towards the screen door. "Fax machine. Maybe it's from Tyler's friend in London."

"I don't know why Tyler thinks any of this stuff she's dredging up for him over there has any bearing on Miles's murder." Against the pureness of the night air, Sarah's comment sounded petty and whiny. "I guess it's the journalist in him. He'll look for the mystery in anything."

Tyler breathed a sigh of relief as, after a final good–bye, he shut the door to Freida's cottage behind him. It had been fun drinking a couple of beers with the group gathered there, but as the night progressed, instead of feeling closer to them, he had felt more and more removed. He could not relate to their music, their opinions, or their incessant chatter about all things theatrical.

At one point, Tracy had knocked on the door and for a few seconds all gossiping stopped. Tracy swept dramatically into the room and, after a quick inventory of faces, had asked Tony where he had left the electric drill. Tyler knew it was a trumped up excuse for the visit. Tracy had been sent by Victor to keep tabs on Tyler's own whereabouts.

"I hate that faggot," Marcus remarked distastefully after Tracy had departed. "There's got to be someone better for his job than him."

"Don't be so homophobic," Freida admonished.

"Ooooh, big word, Freida." Tony laughed.

"Well, you shouldn't hate him just because his sexual preference isn't the same as yours," Freida retorted, reminding them all of her own preferences of the last month.

"I don't hate him because he's gay. I hate him because he's so full of himself. Thinks he's so special just because he worked in London for five years banging nails in English wood instead of American."

Tyler listened carefully while they trashed Tracy for the next five minutes but learned nothing he didn't already know. When they moved on to the topic of what play they thought Victor would be choosing to do next after "The Abdication" was over, Tyler made his excuses and left.

The night was still exceptionally warm as he walked back across the field towards the lights of the farmhouse. Out of habit, he headed around the side of the house. That way he could come in the back door and grab something to eat in the kitchen before heading up to his room.

As he reached for the door knob, the sound of arguing voices came from somewhere above him. Startled, he stepped back and looked up.

A dim light illuminated the large picture window in Victor and Jillian's room. The casement windows on either side were open to let in the unusually mild air. Flattening himself against the wall, he stood perfectly still and listened to their conversation.

"...A full night's sleep," he heard Jillian say. "It's beginning to wear me down."

"You can manage. It's just another week and a half. And don't tell me you're not enjoying it." The lower pitch of Victor's voice made it a little harder to catch all his words.

"Of course I'm enjoying it." Jillian laughed. "You know I am. I would just love to get a full night's sleep sometime soon, that's all."

Tyler leaned against the wall, letting the white clapboard siding take his weight as the strength seemed to leave his limbs. He knew what they were discussing and he knew he had to keep listening even though it left him feeling weak and empty.

"I know you would, dear." Victor's voice was soothing, almost hypnotic. "And he could probably use more than a few hours of sleep as well. But that's the whole point. He's too smart. He knows too much already. We must keep him on the edge. And you must be there for him. Make him reach for you, make him trust you."

"He doesn't trust me. You hear how he's always trying to trip me up, make me give something, anything, away."

"You mustn't worry. You hold a lot of power over him right now. And the continuity of that is so important. I love to see it happening."

There was a silence and then the sound of a drawer being slammed shut. "Why don't you sleep a little right now? I'll listen for him."

Tyler lowered himself slowly and silently to the damp grass until he rested on his hands and knees, his forehead touching the ground. He wanted to throw up, he wanted to disappear, he wanted to be somebody else.

They were using him, pulling his strings like a marionette, and Victor was the master puppeteer. Jillian was returning to his room night and day, not out of passionate desire but because her husband was jerking her strings as well. Why were they doing this to him, what did they want from him?

More important, what were they afraid of him finding out?

He sat up on his haunches, feeling like a rabbit or a fox who has found temporary sanctuary from the baying hounds on his trail. He could not bring himself to go inside the house knowing that sooner or later Jillian would come to his bed and that Victor would be behind it all. How could he have sex with her again? Victor had probably told her which position to use and when. He'd probably coached her in how to act passionate the same way he did for his porno flicks.

Tyler covered his face with his hands. He couldn't let them know he knew. He would have to go on pretending everything was the same, even if he what he felt now was disgust and humiliation. He realized it was not Jillian he felt that way about, it was himself he loathed.

How could he have allowed himself to believe even for a second that she actually cared about him in any way? He had always though she was an incredible actress on stage. It hadn't occurred to him that she was one in real life as well.

He stumbled to his feet and headed blindly away from the house. He couldn't face her tonight; he would never be able to pull it off. He had to sleep somewhere else.

More than anything right now he wished he could go home. Instead he crawled into the back of Paloma's Volkswagen van and wrapped himself up in the shiny black sleeping bag. Let them worry. He wanted to be alone and he wanted to sleep.

A persistent beeping sound drew him out of the swirling blackness of his slumber. He had no idea what it was or where he was. When he opened his eyes, the utter darkness surrounding him provided no clues. Not until he flung out an arm and hit cold metal did he realize where he was. He was in Paloma's van and, somewhere in the recesses of the sleeping bag, his cell phone was ringing.

"Tyler, I'm sorry, I woke you, didn't I? I am at a call box in the underground on my way to work and it seemed like a safe place to ring you from."

"Lucy, hi. No, it's fine. I'm just a little disoriented." He shut his eyes, trying to picture Lucy waiting for a subway with hundreds of London commuters. "What's up? You back from Cornwall?"

Yes, and I've got some very interesting news for you. I was getting nowhere until I parked myself in a pub that the clinic nurses frequent on their way home from work. Bought a few rounds and got chummy with the most gossipy of the bunch. She stayed on after the others left and for an order of fish and chips and a few more ales, she told me more than I'd bargained for."

"So tell me! What'd she say?"

"Well, it seems your friend Jillian has been to the clinic on a couple of occasions. The first time was about three years ago for uterine cancer."

"Uterine cancer? But they must have cured her, right?"

"After a complete hysterectomy, they did. But plenty of women go through that, I didn't know why they made such a big secret about it. But Alice, that's the woman, she made me promise I wouldn't breath a word about it – right, she had no idea I was a journalist. Alice said the only reason she knew was because she worked the night shift and one of Jillian's private nurses took ill in the middle of the night and she had to cover for her for a couple of hours. Read the chart, she did."

"But – that means she can never get pregnant."

Lucy was too caught up in her tale to comment on the shock in Tyler's voice. "Bingo, bonzo! I kept thinking about it all the way back to London. For some reason Jillian Fox doesn't want the world to know she can't have kids. I started looking through all the old news articles I collected for you and finally found a possible reason."

"And what would that be?" Tyler was feeling more like a fool every minute.

"It's that trust she inherited. If she doesn't have any children to pass it on to, it all goes to charity when she dies."

"That's pretty farfetched, don't you think?" Tyler could feel a pounding headache coming on. "Why should she care what happens to her money after she dies? It's more likely that she might want to adopt a child and pass it off as her own. I mean, she certainly fed me a line of bullshit about Victor wanting to raise a family in Vermont."

"Why do you sound so annoyed? It's just an idea." In the background, he could hear a loud speaker booming out some garbled words. "They're announcing my train. I'm going to have to ring off."

"What about the second visit to the clinic? What was that for?" Tyler asked quickly.

"Cosmetic surgery and boob job. You were right on that one. She did have them made bigger last summer."

"Last summer?"

"Right. When all the papers said she was recuperating from her nervous breakdown after the traumatic accident on the Mediterranean. Got to go. I'll call you again soon."

Tyler stared sightlessly at the back window of the van which was steamed over by his breath. He could not remember the last time he had felt more disturbed by how poorly he had assessed someone's character.

Jillian was not just a superb actress. She was a cold–hearted, lying, two–faced bitch.

CHAPTER TWELVE

Opening night was more terrifying than Tyler could have imagined. It was a different sort of panic than being trapped in a burning building (he had experienced that terror a year before). Despite the fact that he knew his lines backwards and forwards and felt totally confident in his ability to portray the anguish of a man caught between faith and desire, there was still the anxiety of having his performance judged by an audience. Could he make them believe he was Azzolino?

He did not feel comfortable confiding his apprehension to any of the other actors. They all assumed that he had complete confidence in himself; he was older, more mature and kept company with troupe's prima donna. He didn't want them to know that he had not been able to eat any dinner or that his hands shook when he buttoned up his cardinal's robe. And he especially did not want them to know how his relationship with Jillian had changed.

Jillian had acted concerned, like a rejected sweetheart, when she had questioned where he had slept on Monday night. Tyler had tried to be casually caustic in his reply.

"Why should that matter to you? Or do you only have an open relationship with your husband and not your lovers?"

Jillian appeared momentarily stung by his cruel answer but instantly regained her composure. "I was worried about you, that's all. I care a lot about you, Tyler. I thought you realized that."

He had coached himself repeatedly in the fact that he could not blow off their relationship. He had to pretend that nothing had changed, that he was no more suspicious or curious than before. But the reality of pretending he still desired her when he actually despised her was more than he could manage.

"I miss Sarah," he said simply. That was the truth. "Being with you reminds me of how much I miss her." That was a lie.

"You shouldn't look at it like that." They were sitting alone at the kitchen table. Lunch was over and Victor had discreetly disappeared. "This is just a pleasurable interlude. It has meaning, but it's not permanent. Pleasure rarely is."

Her large turquoise eyes peered at him innocently from beneath the fringe of blonde hair covering her forehead. She was such an exquisite liar. Actress. Liar. Was there a difference? Where did one draw the line?

"I like being with you," he said carefully. "I just don't feel comfortable having sex with you right now. For a few days, anyway. Let's see if we can just be friends until opening night."

"Platonic, then?" Her British inflection seemed to put poetry into the simplest phrases. He would have to keep his revulsion forefront in his mind if he was going to be able to resist the carnality she still stirred in him.

"Platonic then. What do you think, luv?" he said, imitating her accent and expression. "Do you think we could get through a midnight visit just chatting? Or do you only want me for my body?"

He could not decipher what emotion she was feeling as her cheeks seemed to relax and the lines around her mouth softened. "A midnight chat? Sure, why not?" She reached across the table and squeezed his hand. "I'll be looking forward to it. And as to my willpower – I'm stronger than you think."

No, you're not, Tyler said to himself as he watched her pick up their dishes and turn to the sink. But I am a lot stronger than you or your sicko husband could ever imagine.

So Jillian had kept him company for the next two days, acting more like a friend than a watchdog although he knew that's what she really was. One afternoon he asked Phoebe for a ride into town when she went on a grocery run. When he went out to get in the car, he was surprised to find Jillian sitting in the front seat of the Land Rover next to Phoebe. In the weeks he had been in residence at Double Phoenix, he had never seen Jillian leave the yard.

"I thought I'd come along. I haven't been to town in at least a month," she explained. "There are a few personal things I need to pick up."

That was probably true, but Tyler didn't think that was the reason she had chosen to accompany Phoebe today. He had hoped for a chance to talk to Phoebe alone and Jillian knew it.

He rode in the back seat, listening to the two women make small talk about totally innocuous topics; what spices to put in lentil soup, whether Jillian should use a rhinestone pin or a large blue glass jewel to hold the feather onto the hat she wore in the first act, finding someone to repair the dishwasher which had ceased working the night before.

"Tyler's from around here. Maybe he knows a repair man," Jillian remarked, casting a glance over her shoulder to see if Tyler had been listening.

"Repair man for what?" he asked, pretending that he hadn't been following their conversation.

"For the bloody broken dishwasher, of course."

"I might," he replied, wondering how he could use the situation to his own advantage. "Let me think about it."

Because the conversation was so guarded, throughout the afternoon he found himself watching the two women more than listening to them. He noticed that after an hour or so they began to seem more similar. He felt this was probably a result of Jillian's chameleon–like ability to mimic people. Phoebe's gestures became her own and when they laughed it had the same rolling pitch. Even their facial expressions were the same at times.

Tyler tried to imagine what Phoebe would look like if she had shiny blonde hair, no glasses and lost about forty pounds. He couldn't make his imagination go there. He tried to picture Jillian with Phoebe's colorless curls and coke–bottle lenses. He couldn't do it.

Perhaps the truth was that Jillian had no personality of her own, that she just took on the characteristics of whoever she was with. Maybe that was why he felt such a connection to her, because she was just reflecting his own qualities back at him.

Lost in the profoundness of this contemplation, he almost missed the most significant event of the afternoon. They were in line at the drugstore after waiting for Jillian to have a prescription filled. Tyler paid for his purchases – shampoo, some film, and a bottle of aspirin – and then stepped aside to wait for Jillian. She put a whole basket of items on the counter. Vitamins, allergy medicine, shoelaces, batteries, a six pack of blank video tapes, bobby pins, deodorant, she had something from nearly every aisle. But it was the big box of Tampax that made Tyler's jaw lock and his lips form a grim line.

He didn't know a lot about hysterectomies. But he did know that if you didn't have a uterus, you didn't get your period.

Lucy must have got her information wrong. It must have been somebody else who had uterine cancer or something else that Jillian had. Otherwise it didn't make any sense at all.

She came to his room that night wearing a slinky little ivory chemise of shimmering rib–knit silk with string straps that would not stay up on her shoulders. The fabric clung sensuously to her body revealing the dark hardness of her nipples and the muscular separateness of each of her buttocks. She might as well have been naked, but she obviously was aware that the luxurious stretchy silk made the invitation much more erotic.

She struck a pose at the end of the bed and shivered; the drafty farmhouse was still pretty much unheated at this time of year.

"Get under the covers, you idiot," Tyler said throwing back the blankets. "You'll freeze to death standing around in that outfit."

"Silk is a thermal fiber," she replied, sliding beneath the sheets and wrapping her icy limbs around Tyler. "It reflects your body heat."

"Of which you seem to have none at the moment." He wound his arms around her and pressed his face into her sweet–smelling hair, trying to remember why he didn't want to have sex with her.

What was it he had heard Victor say to her that night? "Make him want you, make him trust you."

He would never trust her. But he certainly wanted her right now. She was rich, beautiful and talented. Who wouldn't want her? He knew her beauty and her talent inside out. What he didn't know a lot about was her money.

"What should we talk about?" Jillian asked, slipping her glacial hand up under his T–shirt, resting it against his heart.

"Money. Let's talk about money. I don't have any but you have lots. What's it like? Do you ever wonder if that's why people befriend you?"

Jillian laughed. "I don't have to wonder about that. When you have money you don't have to prove yourself. You can publish your own book, star in your own play, buy whatever clothes you want wherever you want. The tricky part is getting people to believe you really have talent and character, to really see you for who you are."

Tyler nodded as though he agreed with her. "So if you were to die tomorrow, who would get your money?" he asked casually.

"Morbid bugger, aren't you?" She pinched him playfully. "Why – you thinking of bumping me off?"

"Just curious. As your husband, Victor would inherit it all, I suppose."

"Actually not. It would all go to charity. Victor doesn't get any of it. My father saw to that."

"So it would be in his best interest to hire a full time bodyguard for you then, wouldn't it?"

"Why?" she teased. "Are you applying for the job?"

"That's a thought. I can't think of a body I'd rather guard." His fingers stroked the gossamer fabric of her nightgown. "So what if you ever have kids? Surely grandpa didn't cut them out of the will too."

"No, all the money would go to them. But if they didn't have children, then the money would go to charity. And so on."

"So what if you had kids and then you died before they were old enough to manage the trust themselves? Does it go to some estate lawyer or does Victor do it?"

"Would you like a copy of my father's will?" was her sarcastic comeback. "I'll ring up my solicitor and have him send one round to you. I had no idea you were so detail oriented." She pulled away from him and sat up with a troubled look on her face.

"I'm a pushy journalist, what did you expect?"

Instead of replying, she rested her chin on one knee and stared at him, deep in thought. One shoulder strap fell down again in a provocative manner. He watched her for a moment, wondering what was going on in her head. According to Lucy, Jillian couldn't have any children so his question had been pointless. Or maybe it was just thoughtless.

"Do you still get nervous on opening night?" he asked gently, changing the subject.

She smiled and relaxed, obviously glad to talk about something else. "Do you have the jitters, luv? You know you're brilliant in your role. You've nothing to worry about." She slid back under the covers again and snuggled up to him. "I know something that would help you forget your anxiousness for a while. And help you get a good night's sleep."

"Some killer weed?" he joked and then wished he hadn't because the reference to pot–smoking reminded him of Hunter and Sarah and put his nerves even more on edge.

She gave him a crooked smile before saying, "Killer something else," and then dived head–first between the sheets.

"No – Jillian – we agreed – stop – no – don't –" he gave up protesting and sank back on the pillow, once again a helpless slave to the pleasurable sensations created by the wet warmth of her mouth and tongue. He couldn't think of why he was arguing with her sound reasoning. He couldn't think at all.

Afterwards he asked her to leave, something he had never done before. He felt ashamed and disgusted with himself, and he wanted to get some sleep. If she was surprised or hurt by his rejection, she didn't show it. She just kissed him goodnight and left.

He managed to avoid her most of the next day, putting his energy into helping Paloma run off the programs for the play using the theater company's very slow, secondhand copy machine. Afterwards, in an attempt to clear his head, he took a long walk on a trail through the woods that lead to a high, look–off point with a view. He tried to think of the future, what he would do when the play was over. In the end, he gave up. Jillian and Victor had won – he could think of nothing but them and their damn production.

The opening night audience was small but receptive. Halfway through the first act, Tyler began to feel as comfortable with his role as he had during rehearsals. He was exhausted but elated by the curtain calls; he had done well, the rise in applause when he took his bow assured him of that. The whole cast was ecstatic about how well the show had gone.

After removing their costumes and make–up, most of the students congregated in the dining pavilion to congratulate each other and discuss in detail the ups and downs of every angle of the performance. Once again Tyler was astounded by the obsessive enthusiasm they all showed for their craft. He was certainly proud and excited by what he had done but he would never be totally preoccupied by the experience the way they were. He reserved that kind of passionate fixation for investigative journalism.

Saturday night the house was full and by Sunday night, when Sarah and Hunter showed up, it was packed. Obviously word was going around about what a great production "The Abdication" was. Several people stood in the back or sat in the aisles, breaking all fire regulations but no one seemed to care. Tyler was glad that the theater was so crowded the night that Sarah was in attendance. In some small way it justified his reason for dropping out of their life at the inn and leaving her holding the bucket.

Despite the fact that he was happy that she had come, he found he was distracted by her presence as well. He realized that, in comparison to how he worried about Sarah's opinion, he cared very little what other people in the audience thought. He was glad he had not invited his parents up from New York. He saw how intense that experience was for the other actors.

After the show, Hunter and Sarah were waiting outside for him. "Hey, excellent performance, man," Hunter greeted him, clapping him on the back. "You were superb. I really believed you were that priest."

"Thanks, Hunter. How'd you like it, Sarah?" He could see her eyes were red–rimmed as though she had been crying, apparently moved to tears as half the audience usually was during the final scene between Christina and Azzolino.

"I loved it. It was a really wonderful play. That woman who played Christina was incredibly convincing. And you were good too." Her tone was so sincere that he knew she meant it, but still he was hurt by the fact that she mentioned Jillian's name before his.

"Well, let me just get my things and then we'll get out of here." It had been prearranged that he would drive them back to West Jordan and then leave with the car for Syracuse. With luck he should be at the university by the time it opened in the morning.

He had not told Jillian and Victor he was leaving Double Phoenix for his two days off. He knew they would protest and find some reason he had to stay just so that they could keep an eye on him. But he had told Freida and Tony and a few others, that if anyone asked, he had gone home to the inn on Sunday night and would return Wednesday morning to go to the Goddard College performance with them.

"We'll meet you at the car," Hunter called after him. As they walked away he threw an arm around Sarah's shoulders in a familiar way that spoke volumes. Volumes Tyler wished he didn't have to read.

Returning to the dressing room of the theater, he shouldered his day pack, trying not give away how heavy it was. Before leaving his room, he had filled it with what he would need for the next few days, including his laptop. That way he would not run the risk of encountering Victor or Jillian on his way out of the house at this time of night.

Sarah was already behind the wheel with the engine running. Hunter was in the passenger seat beside her. Tyler opened the back door, wishing that the ride to the inn was over already and that he was on his way to Syracuse.

"Watch out for the baby seat," Hunter warned him. "Oh, Sarah, don't forget we need to stop and get apple juice before we get home."

They made easy conversation about the play for a while until Sarah abruptly changed the subject. "I still don't see what you think this trip is going to prove, Tyler. It could be an awful lot of driving for nothing."

"It might be." Tyler did not feel like arguing with her tonight. "I just haven't come up with any other way to find information about Emma. I've never even seen a picture of her – I'm not even sure which person she is in the theater videos I watched. I can't get anyone at Double Phoenix to talk about her. It's a long shot, I know. I'm just hoping to pick up some stray clue to her personality that might tip me off why Victor and Jillian get so weird when her name comes up. Or Miles's name for that matter."

"I've got those copies we made of Emma's letters if you want to take them with you," Hunter reminded him. They had turned over all of Miles's possessions to the police, including the letters, but Sarah had had the foresight to Xerox them before turning them in. "I've also got his parents' phone number if you want it."

"Thanks." Tyler knew that Hunter was still struggling with the fact that he had concealed the truth about Kashi from Miles's parents. To the eyes of the world, Kashi was Hunter's offspring now, and anyone who thought they had heard otherwise had been persuaded that they must have been mistaken. Two travelers had shown up at the inn one night, one was the father of a Nigerian baby, the other one disappeared and turned up floating in Walker Lake. The rental car had still not been found.

"Victor writes a check to someone named Sybil Erickson every month," Tyler told them. "Erickson is Emma's last name. I don't think it's a coincidence. He also sends money on a regular basis to several editors of London newspapers. He's paying people off for some reason, probably to keep quiet about something. They're leaving the country in two weeks and they haven't told anybody yet. These people are incredibly powerful and incredibly sleazy. I think they've done something really wrong and I want to get them."

They rode in silence for a few minutes, each one of them deep in their own thoughts. "Do you think Emma's really still alive somewhere?" Sarah asked finally. "And they know it?"

"You mean, like they're hiding her somewhere?" Hunter's voice expressed his incredulousness. "Why would they bother to do that?"

"Victor and Jillian are very secretive about their past," Tyler answered darkly, thinking about the Raeburn Clinic. "And I think they might go to some strange and extreme lengths to protect themselves."

Sarah shuddered. "Tyler, be careful. If you know so much, you might be their next target."

"Don't worry," he said grimly. "They need to keep me alive at least until next Saturday."

But Sarah was right. He might have to plan his next disappearing act – before Jillian and Victor pulled one on him.

CHAPTER THIRTEEN

By eight o'clock the following morning he was leaning against a wall in the hallway outside of Stan Silverman's Modern Dramatic Lit class, drinking another cup of coffee. He hoped he didn't look as bad as he felt. His eyes ached from squinting at the road through the last hundred miles of torrential rain, his head pounded rhythmically like a set of windshield wipers, his throat felt like highway exit gravel.

But as he watched the students filing into the classroom, he realized he didn't look any worse than most of them did as they dragged themselves to an early morning lecture after a late night in the dorm. A few of the young women even gave him the once over which boosted his depleted self–assurance.

Stan Silverman was easy to pick out but not so easy to catch. Short, balding and overweight, he came streaking down the corridor like a bowling ball headed for a strike. A heavy beat–up leather briefcase swung menacingly from one arm, the other held a pile of textbooks like a medieval shield in front of his chest. Tyler quickly stepped out in front of the classroom door to insure that Stan would have to stop on his hell–bent route.

"Mr. Silverman? Tyler Mackenzie. We spoke briefly on the phone last week. About Emma Erickson," he added in response to Stan's blank stare.

"Oh, right. Well, look, this is a hell of a time to accost me. I certainly can't talk to you now." The professor was more than mildly annoyed.

"I understand that. I just wanted to catch you first thing to find out when you might have some free time today. I'm only here until tomorrow." Tyler spoke quickly.

"Monday mornings are always jammed..."

"How about I buy you lunch?"

He could see Stan assessing his desperation. "Insistent, aren't you? Like a damn reporter or something. All right, I'll meet you at twelve thirty in front of the theater."

Tyler didn't dare ask where the theater was. He had all morning to find it.

"I'll get it!" Sarah shouted up the stairs as she reached for the phone. "Kashi, you stay put for a minute, okay?"

The baby sat on the floor and gazed up at her innocently, but as soon as Sarah spoke into the phone, she was down on all fours and crawling across the room. Moving as fast as her tiny hands and knees could take her, she cooed in delight at the newest skill she had acquired.

"West Jordan Inn. Damn. Kashi, get back here! Sorry, how can I help you?" Sarah's distraction was evident.

"Is Tyler there?" a low–pitched, resonant voice asked.

"Tyler? Who's calling?"

"Victor Nesbitt, his director."

"Oh, Victor. Hello. I've heard a lot about you. And I really enjoyed your production last night." Sarah tried to sound casual and chatty.

"Thank you. Can I speak to Tyler please?"

"Actually he's out right now. But I'll tell him you called."

"I'd like to speak to him as soon as possible. When do you think he'll be back?"

"Oh, probably not until this evening. He had a lot of things he wanted to get done today. Can I give him a message?" Out of the corner of her eye she saw Kashi pulling herself up on a low windowsill.

"Just tell him it's urgent that I talk to him. Have him call me as soon as gets in." Victor's tone conveyed the arrogant attitude of someone who had spent his life bossing people around.

Across the room, Kashi was methodically ripping off the leaves of a philodendron plant. "OOPS, gotta go. I'll tell him to call you."

So it's already begun, she mused as she pried the poisonous green leaf out of the baby's sticky fingers. By tomorrow morning, when they still couldn't reach him, they would begin to suspect that either Tyler was avoiding them or he wasn't there. It was time to let the answering machine pick up the calls for the next few days.

Tyler had located the theater building easily enough and wandered inside. At that time of the morning there wasn't any activity on the stage. But as he turned to leave, he heard a lone hammer banging some place backstage. The sound was muted by the heavy stage curtains. Wandering through the darkened wings, he followed the noise to the lights of a workshop where he found a heavyset woman in coveralls building scenery alone.

"Can I help you?" she asked loudly, her tone of voice indicating her feeling towards uninvited visitors.

"I'm Tyler Mackenzie." He held out his hand and flashed her his dimples with a charming grin. She shook his hand with her own strong, fleshy one, but her unwelcoming expression did not change. "And you are..."

"Cindy Petrovsky. Technical assistant. That means I'm expected to build the whole set single–handedly. So if you don't mind–" She picked up an electric drill with a mildly threatening gesture.

"You do nice work," Tyler complimented her as he looked around at the flats and platforms cluelessly. "Have you worked here long?"

"Long enough to be more than a damned assistant. It was four years last month."

Tyler's pulse quickened. "Four years. So you must remember Emma Erickson then."

"Emma? Sure I remember her. Why? Is she famous yet? I thought she moved to England or something." Cindy looked at him curiously. "You another one of her ex–boyfriends?"

"Another one? She have a lot those?"

Cindy cackled and handed him a box of screws. "Here, hold these, make yourself useful. Did Emma have a lot of ex–boyfriends? You might say that. She could be pretty wild at times. But you know that, right?"

Tyler waited until the electric drill stopped whirring to reply. "Actually, I don't know much about Emma at all. That's why I'm here. I'm a private investigator hired to look into her background."

"Is that a fact now?" Cindy put down her drill, showing a small spark of interest. "Well, I can't really help you much, I wasn't a friend of hers, I just knew her because of working on the plays. We didn't have much to say to each other but I saw a lot of her, if you know what I mean." She laughed again. "Well, everyone saw a lot of her, she ran around during most rehearsals bare–legged, wearing nothing but a sleeveless leotard, like a bathing suit."

It didn't take much guessing to figure out that Cindy wouldn't feel comfortable doing that herself.

"Besides, Silverman cast her in the lead role of every show. Most of the women hated her because of that."

"Jealous."

"Yes and no. They just never got a shot at any good parts when she was around. Most of them were glad to see her go."

"I wonder how they'd feel if they knew she drowned last year."

Cindy reacted with predictable astonishment. After a few minutes of repeated no kiddings and holy this's and that's, she finally stopped staring at Tyler and sat down heavily on a set of steps painted to look as though they were carpeted with an Oriental runner.

"It's more than a damn shame," she said shaking her head. "It's – what do you call it – ironic, I guess."

"Ironic?" Tyler squinted in puzzlement at her.

"Yeah. She was like the captain of the swim team or something while she was here. She swam all the time, that was how she stayed in such great shape. I can't believe she would drown."

"Well, there must have been extenuating circumstances." Tyler's wheels were spinning. Like maybe a cement block was tied to her foot, or maybe she'd been drunk or drugged. Which would mean her death wasn't accidental. Or maybe she had actually made it to shore and disappeared into some teeming North African port city.

"Whatever. Boy, it makes me kind of sad. I don't feel much like working anymore."

When he left her a few minutes later, she was staring forlornly at the flat she had been screwing together, the drill hanging idly in her hand. He hoped his visit wouldn't have the same effect on Stan Silverman.

He spent the next few hours in the library, looking through old yearbooks, trying to find a graduation picture of Emma. He found Miles without a problem, but there was no sign of Emma in the years before or after.

When that proved fruitless, he tried to find her in a picture of the swim team. A tiny little face under a bathing cap in a row of clones showed him less than nothing.

"Did you find what you were looking for?" the sweet–faced library assistant asked him as he passed the front desk on his way out.

He shook his head. "Her picture wasn't in any of the yearbooks."

"I guess she didn't graduate." The girl giggled. "Lots of people don't."

He slapped his forehead in a self–deprecating gesture as he hurried on to the theater, giddy with exhaustion. That made perfect sense. Why hadn't he thought of it himself?

In the few minutes he had to wait for Stan Silverman, he sat on a low stone wall and watched the dynamics of the students as they socialized between classes. Many of them seemed so incredibly young. It was hard to believe Miles had only been a few years older. His experiences had made him seem so much more mature.

Stan burst out of the theater doors and glanced around for Tyler, giving the impression that if he didn't see him immediately he wasn't going to spend any time waiting. When Tyler approached him, his face fell a little as though he had been hoping to be able to give him the slip.

"Can I take you out somewhere for lunch?" Tyler offered quickly. "My treat. My car's just over there in the visitor's parking lot."

Stan shrugged and fell in step with him. "You know, if this was about anybody but Emma Erickson I wouldn't give you thirty seconds of my time. But Emma was one of the most promising students I ever had, an incredibly gifted actress. I'd do anything to help her succeed. So what are you doing, some kind of background check on her for an employer or something?"

Tyler swallowed. "Not exactly. Do you know about what she did when she left here?"

"Of course, I do. I suggested the Phoenix Theater company in London to her. Victor Nesbitt has a reputation for doing fabulous things with talented students. I wrote her recommendation myself."

"So you know Victor." Tyler spoke more slowly than usual, wondering whether he was getting deeper in trouble.

"Not personally. I just know of him. I did see a couple of his productions in London several years ago. Very impressive. They say that wife of his was an incredibly mediocre actress until he got a hold of her."

They had reached the Subaru by now. Tyler was unlocking the door on the passenger side for Stan.

"I've had only a very few students who I thought would thrive under Victor Nesbitt," Stan continued when they were settled inside the car. "Of the ones who applied to his school, only Emma got in. So what is she going for now?"

Tyler looked at him blankly.

"I mean, who do you represent? Another theater company? A university?"

Tyler pretended to focus on his driving for a moment, while he organized his thoughts. "You obviously haven't kept up with Emma since she left here," he said carefully.

"A postcard once, I think. Why? Hey, is she in some kind of trouble with the law or something? That's it, isn't it?" Stan Silverman put a large heavy hand on Tyler's arm. "Tell me what she's gotten into now."

Tyler sighed. He hated breaking the bad news over and over again. "About year and a half ago, she fell overboard on Nesbitt's yacht in the Mediterranean. She's presumed drowned; her body was never recovered."

"No. Tell me that's not true." Stan began involuntarily squeezing Tyler's arm.

"We have only Victor and his wife's word on it, but that's the story." Stan's grip was beginning to hurt.

"It can't be true. Emma was an excellent swimmer. I can't believe it." Something in Stan's voice led Tyler to suspect there was a little more going on here than the usual beginning of the grieving process.

"Well, I can't believe it either. And that's why I'm here." He was about to ask Stan ease up on the arm when his fingers suddenly released their hold. "I was hoping you could help me."

"Emma....My God, life isn't fair." Stan slammed his fist into the dashboard. "What are you doing the rest of the afternoon, Mackenzie?"

"Uh – why?"

"Because I'm canceling my appointments. I don't want to counsel any half–assed students about their failing grades. Pull into that convenience store up there. I'm going to buy a couple of six packs of Bass Ale. Then we'll go to my house and talk about Emma."

Sarah gently put Kashi down in her crib and covered her with a flannel blanket. She looked at her watch. It was one–thirty; hopefully Kashi would nap for a good solid two hours.

When she turned around, she was startled to see that Hunter was stretched out on his own bed, hands behind his head, regarding her thoughtfully.

"I didn't see you there when I came in," she whispered. She sat down next to him on the edge of the bed. "What are you thinking about?"

"I'm wondering what's going to happen next week when Tyler returns from Double Phoenix. Do you think he's going to want his job back? I mean, should I start planning my trip home to California?"

Sarah looked down at her feet, pretending to study the painted pine floorboards. He was right, it was time to face the music. She had begun to feel so very distant from Tyler in the last few weeks, she didn't think their relationship could ever be re–tuned to the fine instrument it once had been.

"Tyler is sick of working here," she said slowly. "The only reason he took the job was for me, so we could be together."

When Hunter didn't respond she raised her eyes to meet his. My God, how she had grown to adore him, how close they had become. She couldn't bear to think of the empty space that would be left in her life if he and Kashi were gone.

He was waiting for her to go on, to say what he really wanted to hear.

"I don't want you to leave," she heard herself saying. Overcome by a wave of emotion, she leaned over to kiss him on the mouth. When their lips met, he pulled her down on top of him. She could feel the heat running the length of their bodies as they pressed against each other, hungry for ultimate closeness.

"But I guess if you're going to stay," she murmured in his ear, "we better find out right away if we're compatible in bed."

"How could we not be?" he teased. "I'm so hot for you, you could fry an egg between my legs."

While she laughed uncontrollably, he began unbuttoning the tiny buttons that ran down the front of her sweater. "Don't bother, this way is quicker," she said, gasping for breath as she sat up and pulled the sweater over her head.

Hunter sighed with pleasurable anticipation as she straddled him in her jeans and bra and began to undo the buttons of his flannel shirt. Across the room, Kashi made a small sound and stirred in her sleep.

"Wait," Hunter whispered, grabbing her hands and sitting up. "Let's go down the hall to your room. I've waited so long for this moment, I want to be able to shout my joy when the time comes."

"Good idea." Instead of moving, she locked her arms around his neck and buried her tongue inside his mouth, wondering not only how she had held out for so long, but why. While they kissed, his fingers found the hooks of her bra and slid the straps from her shoulders. When they pulled apart and stood up, the bra floated to the floor.

"You look incredibly sexy like that," he said softly. "Come on, cowgirl, hop on." He turned his back to her and slapped his backside. "I'll give you a pony ride over the threshold."

Sarah rode him piggyback down the hall, naked from the waist up, her long braid slapping against the bare skin of her back, her breasts bouncing free. She could not remember the last time she had been so aroused. By the time they fell onto her big bed, she was a wild jungle animal embarking on an exhilarating adventure into a rain forest of released desire.

"As I recall, she came from a rather dysfunctional family." Stan opened another bottle of beer and put his feet up on a worn leather ottoman. "There was no father figure to speak of, her mother died while she was in high school and her older sister finished raising her. I met the sister once. There was only a few years difference between her and Emma but they were like night and day. She was as plump and plain and shy as Emma was stacked and stunning and personable."

"Sybil was her name, right?" Tyler stood up and moved closer to the blazing fireplace. So far he'd had one beer to Stan's three and it seemed like the right ratio to keep Stan reminiscing.

"Maybe. I don't remember. For me, Emma was like this brilliant fiery star that obscured everything and everyone else around her."

It was clear to Tyler now that Stan had been hopelessly in love with his student. When they had entered his one story bungalow, Stan had apologized for the disorder, saying that he hadn't done much cleaning since his wife had left him over a year ago. It wasn't polite to ask why his wife had left him, but Tyler wasn't wondering too hard now.

"So you must have known Emma's boyfriend, Miles." He chose his wording purposely.

Stan snorted. "Miles was hardly what you'd call her boyfriend. More like a father figure."

"Really?"

"I guess they got together the first week they were both here. Miles had transferred from somewhere else and must have appeared worldly and self–assured to Emma. I see this happen all the time here – where new students bond together when they first arrive and then retain a very strong loyalty to each other even after they've moved into other social spheres. After about six months she'd already outgrown their relationship but she never really let him know. She liked how he took care of her."

"You seem to remember it pretty clearly." Tyler took the open beer Stan held out to him and placed it on the mantel behind his head.

"I remember everything in terms of theater productions. What I'm recalling is the cast party I had here for Twelfth Night. Miles didn't relate to the theater crowd very well and he left early. After he was gone, Emma got totally wasted on banana daiquiris. At one point I found in her my bed with Paul Sorvano, an empty–headed stud who looked good on stage. Charlie Keller and Jimmy Belinski offered to give her a ride home and an hour later I could see their car still in the yard with the windows steamed up. When Miles came over to look for her the next morning, I didn't know where to tell him to go."

"Wow. She sounds pretty wild." Tyler wondered how Stan himself fit into the scheme.

"Only when it came to sex. She was one of the most disciplined actresses I've ever worked with. Although Miles probably had a lot to do with keeping her feet on the ground when it came to school work. Do you know Miles?" Stan asked curiously, peering up at Tyler through his thick glasses.

“I’ve met him,” Tyler replied carefully. He was not sure whether to tell Stan about Miles’s death or not.

“Then you know what a righteous, ethical bastard the guy can be. The Peace Corps was the perfect place for that Dudley DooRight.” Stan’s tone was clearly bitter. “Emma was way too much fun for him.”

“How about for you?”

To Tyler’s surprise, Stan blushed deeply. “Yeah, I guess she was too much fun for me too. But, Jesus, I loved working with her,” he said quickly regaining his composure. “She was incredible with accents; she was another Meryl Streep. I did Pygmalion when she was here just because of her. She played a fabulous Eliza Doolittle.”

“Do you have any pictures of her?” Tyler asked suddenly. “The only one I could find was a tiny one of her with the swim team.”

“You mean you don’t even know what she looks like? Oh, My God, she was gorgeous. Old–fashioned, Greta Garbo, sultry movie star gorgeous.” Stan was on his feet now, moving unsteadily across the room to a bookshelf. “Let me find my photo albums. She almost did herself in with that diving accident, did I tell you about that?”

Tyler was following him closely, ready to catch him if he lurched the wrong way. “No, what diving accident?”

“Oh, she smashed her head on the side of the pool. People thought she was dead, lying there unconscious on the concrete with all that blood running down her face. Luckily all she was left with was an inconspicuous scar near her hairline.”

Something familiar tickled the back of Tyler’s brain but he couldn’t place it.

“Shit, this is going to make me cry, I know it.” Stan had leafed through one of his albums to an eight–and–a–half by eleven, glossy black and white photo. “Here, look at her. Wasn’t she something else?”

Tyler took the heavy book from him and carried it over to the window so he could see better. Stan hadn't turned any lights on and the living room had taken on the gloom and darkness of the rainy afternoon.

He stared at the photograph in speechless awe.

"So what'd I tell you. Was she beautiful or what?"

And Tyler echoed softly, "Or what."

CHAPTER FOURTEEN

It was another extraordinarily busy night at the West Jordan Inn. The dining room was full, the bar was crowded and even the two guest bedrooms were rented.

Sarah and Hunter both seemed oblivious to the stress created by so much extra work. Sarah had called in Jason, the high school student who washed dishes on the weekends, and Clyde, the auxiliary bartender. But the additional help had nothing to do with why Hunter couldn't stop grinning or why Sarah felt as though she was sailing smoothly around the inn a few inches off the floor.

"All I can think about is how soon all these customers will go home so that we can be alone," she murmured into the warm flesh of Hunter's neck as she passed him in the kitchen.

Reaching out with one long arm, he grabbed her around the waist and pulled her pelvis against his own. "If Jason wasn't here, I'd take you right now on this counter," he said softly, running his hand provocatively across the gathered silk skirt that covered her buttocks. "Later," she laughed pulling away from him. "I'll look forward to it."

Flushed and smiling, she returned to the lounge to find that two young women had taken seats at the bar and were waiting to be served. One had long, straight flame–red hair and a gold hoop in her nostril; the other had short spiky locks in a striking shade of blue and wore a studded dog collar. Their pale, serious faces looked vaguely familiar to her but she could not imagine why.

On the next barstool, Red, obviously intimidated, was trying not to laugh and stare.

"What can I get you ladies?" Sarah asked. She would not have been surprised by anything they ordered. When they both asked for Black Russians, she wondered if the drink had been chosen purposely to match the cocoa brown nail polish that both of them wore on their extremely long nails.

She was surprised some time later, however, when she returned to the bar to find them engaged in animated conversation with Red.

"These girls have seen that play Tyler's in," Red explained to Sarah. "They say he was real good in it. They didn't know he lived here."

She was about to say he didn't really live here anymore, but she could not bring herself to admit the truth to one of her oldest and most loyal customers. "He's not here tonight," she said apologetically. "Or I'm sure he'd love to talk to you about it."

"He still staying over at that place?" Red asked.

Sarah nodded, taking a sip from a glass of ice water beneath the bar. "The play goes on for another week. You ought to go see it, Red. You'd be amazed by him."

Not wanting to talk about Tyler, she moved to the other end of the bar where a couple of local auto mechanics were signaling her with their empty bottles. "Your new tires came in, Sarah," one said to her as she placed fresh beers in front of them. "If you want, I've got time to put them on tomorrow morning."

"Damn, Tyler's got the car and I don't know when he'll be back with it."

"Where'd he go on those nearly bald babies? Not too far I hope."

Sarah grinned sheepishly. "Upstate New York. I forgot how bad the tires were getting."

"Well, I hope he doesn't have to ride all the way back on that skinny little spare that's in the engine." The two mechanics laughed.

"Where in upstate New York?" asked the tourist sitting next to them. "My grandmother lives in Rochester.

"Syracuse," Sarah replied shortly, trying to end another conversation centering around Tyler.

If she wanted to maintain her euphoric mood, she would have to get out of the bar. Motioning to Clyde who was coming out of the dining room with a tray of dishes, she said, "Clyde, if you want to do the bar for a while, I'll reset the rest of the tables in the dining room."

With romance forefront in her mind, she began to realize how tired she was of working. Maybe after Columbus Day, when foliage season was over, she would close the inn for a week. And get a new perspective on relating to Hunter, one that didn't include the role of employer and employee.

It was nearly eleven o'clock on Tuesday night when Tyler finally called. "Do you mind if I bring the car over in the morning?" His voice was raspy with exhaustion. "I got a flat tire around five this afternoon, and then the damn spare was flat also and I had to hitchhike with it to the nearest gas station to pump it up."

"Sure, not a problem. We're not going anywhere tonight. And the only place the car is going tomorrow is to get new tires on it. Sorry, I forgot to tell you how bald they were." Sarah changed the subject quickly. "So was the trip worth it?"

"Totally worth it. I just have to figure out how to use what I learned to crucify these guys. I can't really talk about it now. I'll tell you when I see you."

Sarah wondered what he could have discovered that was so earth–shattering. "Victor's been calling for you since yesterday morning. He's left half a dozen messages about how urgent it is that you contact him as soon as you can."

"Yeah, he gave me some bullshit story about needing to change the blocking on a particular scene. I told him I thought two days off were supposed to be two days off. I told him I went to visit my dying aunt in upstate New York."

"I'm sure he believed that one." Sarah propped the phone against her shoulder as she poured two more glasses of red wine for an elderly couple from Arizona.

"Look, I've got to go inside before they come looking for me. I'll talk to you tomorrow when I see you. I'll call you in the morning to let you know when I'm coming."

Sarah hung the phone up with the uneasy feeling that once again Tyler was in way over his head.

When the telephone rang again at dawn, her legs were locked around Hunter's waist, her damp chest resting again his and she could still feel him warm and large inside her.

"Who would be calling at this time of the morning?" she groaned.

Hunter pulled her arm back as she reached for the receiver. "Let the machine get it."

"It might be important."

Hunter extended one lanky arm and turned up the volume so they could listen.

"Sarah, it's Tyler. Victor says we've got to leave here by eight for Goddard College so I'm not going to be able to bring the car over until later. I can't even tell you when. I hope this doesn't leave you stuck. Sorry and I'll call you later."

"Now aren't you glad you didn't break this cozy embrace to answer that? It would have ruined our mood entirely."

He moved his hips against hers and she could feel him stirring and growing hard again deep within her warm, sensitive recesses. She was still astonished by his youthful ability for a repeat performance within minutes of an explosive, all–encompassing orgasm. In the last two days, the brilliance of their sexual relationship had nearly blinded her, making her unable to see or think of little else. She moved about in an exhausted daze, performing her daily tasks by rote, completely satisfied yet aching with anticipation at the same time.

As she gasped with pleasure for the second time in half an hour, the sound of gurgling laughter came over the baby monitor on the nightstand. Within a few seconds, Hunter climaxed again and collapsed against the pillow beside her. Although he was breathing hard, she knew he was keeping one ear carefully tuned to the babbling baby talk being broadcast from down the hall. As soon as Kashi's happy noises began to sound desperate, he was out of bed, moving with long swift strides down the hall to retrieve her.

Sarah lay alone in the disheveled bed, savoring the moment. It was almost perfect. Almost.

By nine pm, Sarah was harboring a new set of vicious feelings about Tyler. He had not called again all day to let her know when he was coming with the car. He knew full well that it meant that somebody was going to have to spend an hour and a half driving him back to East Jordan and that she did not have that kind of time on the Wednesday night before the Columbus Day weekend. At this point he better know enough not to show up until the morning.

A few hours later, just as the midweek bar crowd was beginning to thin out, a familiar–looking older man appeared suddenly at the end of the bar. The sharpness of his features was accentuated not only by silver hair pulled back severely into a short ponytail, but by the high turtleneck of a black sweater under a black wool blazer. His cold eyes did not match the genial smile he flashed her.

"Sarah?" he inquired softly as she approached, trying desperately to place him among the hundreds of customers she saw every year.

"Yes. Hi. What can I get you?" His steely gaze unnerved her and she became business–like in defense.

"I'm Victor Nesbitt. From Double Phoenix. Tyler couldn't make it tonight so I brought your car back." His voice resonated with all the pleasantness that his face could not convey.

"You did?" Sarah stared at him open–mouthed for a few seconds, unable to process exactly what was happening. "Is Tyler all right?"

"He's fine. Just slightly indisposed at the moment. He said you would be able to give me a ride back..." Victor's voice rose questioningly, but there was obviously nothing to discuss.

"Oh, he did, did he?" Sarah's own tone smacked of sarcasm and impatience. "Well, as you can see I'm rather indisposed myself at the moment." She waved a hand to indicate the handful of customers remaining in the bar. "I'll probably be another forty–five minutes, if you want to have a drink or something."

If Victor was taken aback by her attitude, he didn't show it. He ordered a dark ale and then settled himself on the couch in front of the fireplace, apparently content to wait comfortably until she was ready to leave.

Sarah slipped quickly into the kitchen where Hunter was just hanging up his apron. She moved close to him and spoke softly. "Victor is here. He brought the car."

"Victor? Isn't that weird. Is Tyler sick or something? Victor?" He repeated himself in disbelief. "Tyler said he never goes anywhere."

"Spooky, isn't it. He said Tyler was 'indisposed,' whatever the hell that means. Not only that, but I've got to drive him back to East Jordan when the bar closes."

"Well, I can close up if you want to go in a few minutes. Just let me go out back and smoke this after–work doobie," he patted his breast pocket, "and I'll be all set."

She was about to tell him she didn't want him working behind the bar if he was high and then she thought better of it. He was doing her a favor, which was more than Tyler was at the moment. The prospect of spending forty–five minutes in the car with Victor gave her a serious case of the creeps.

It would be best to get the ride over with as soon as possible.

A few minutes later she had pulled a wool sweater over her head and was accompanying Victor across the parking lot to her car. "Why don't I drive?" he suggested. "You're probably tired from working all night and that way you can close your eyes if you want to."

"Thank you," she answered gratefully. She could at least pretend to be asleep so she would not have to carry on a conversation with him. "I haven't had much sleep the last few nights."

As she tilted the passenger seat back into a reclining position, she began to realize just how exhausted she was. Maybe a forty–five minute cat nap was exactly what she needed.

"Well, I know how that can be." Victor's voice was warm and sympathetic and in the concealing darkness, without having to endure his iron gaze, Sarah did not find him quite as intimidating. "Why don't you just relax now? Make yourself comfortable. I'll put the heat on."

His power of suggestion was very strong. Vaguely she remembered Tyler's description of Victor's hypnotic effect on people.

The hum of the engine and the rhythmic sound of the spinning tires were soothing and familiar. Within moments her eyelids grew heavy and she fell into the heavy sleep known only to the extremely overtired.

She had no idea how long she had been sleeping when a sudden jolt awoke her, banging her right temple into the passenger door of the car. Other than the glow of the dashboard lights, from her reclining vantage point all she could see was total darkness on either side of the car. As she struggled to a sitting position, the car went over another bump big enough for her to hit her head against the carpeted ceiling of the vehicle.

The headlights illuminated a narrow dirt track through overhanging trees. The unmaintained surface was punctuated with enough roots, rocks and ruts that only a four-wheel-drive vehicle could manage to traverse it. It was definitely not the driveway to Double Phoenix and nothing about it looked even remotely familiar to Sarah.

"Where are we?" she asked, trying to keep the panic rising in her throat from reaching her voice.

She could not keep from gasping, however, as a large pine tree blocking the road loomed into view. "You can't drive my car over that!" she exclaimed grabbing Victor's arm.

"Of course not," Victor replied matter–of–factly as he put the car into neutral and put the parking brake on. "We walk from here."

"What are you talking about? Where are we?" Now Sarah sounded as alarmed as she felt.

Before she realized what was happening, Victor had closed the bracelet of a handcuff around her left wrist with an ominous click. When she instinctively jerked her arm away, his right arm came with her. He had handcuffed her to himself.

With a swift motion, he turned off the engine and opened his door. "Come along," he commanded, climbing out of the vehicle and dragging her along behind him. "It's just a few minutes walk."

Tumbling to the ground outside the car, Sarah staggered to her feet and angrily tried to maintain her dignity. "What the hell is this all about, Victor? Where the fuck are we and who do you think you are?"

Victor slammed the car door, pitching them both into the disorientation of utter darkness. "Sarah." Apparently unmoved by her fury, his voice had taken on that soothing hypnotic tone again. "You will find that this will all go much smoother if I have your complete cooperation from the beginning. If you do exactly as I say, no one will get hurt."

Fear washed over her like a tidal wave, numbing her extremities. Her blood felt as though it had frozen in her veins. As Victor jerked her forward into the woods, her legs buckled unsteadily beneath her.

Handcuffed together as they were, she knew there was little point in trying to escape him at the moment. She wished desperately that she had not fallen asleep; then she might at least have an inkling of where they might be.

Victor was illuminating their path with a tiny mag light which gave off just enough of a glow to keep him from tripping. Finally he raised the small circular beam to shine on the sagging door of a ramshackle building. Holding the flashlight between his teeth, he inserted a key in the shiny padlock that was clearly much newer than the rusty hinged hasp it held shut.

Several smart, sarcastic remarks spun through Sarah's head, but instead she croaked in a tiny voice, "Where are we?"

Victor's relaxed laughter only heightened her alarm. He pocketed the padlock and removed the flashlight from his mouth. "I can't very well tell you that now, can I?"

He pulled the groaning door open. The dank smell of musty mildew rushed out to meet the clean air of the forest. "After you, madam," he said in mocking politeness as he grabbed Sarah by the shoulders and pushed her inside before him.

The small shaft of light swept around what appeared to be a crude hunter's cabin and came to rest on a kerosene lamp that sat on a dirty table.

"Hold this for me, will you?" Victor held the flashlight out to Sarah. Knowing there was no point in refusing, she obeyed, taking it in her left hand. Her handcuffed right hand was jerked awkwardly along as he struck a match, lit the wick of the lamp, and then replaced the dusty glass shade.

"The whole place could use a good cleaning," he remarked as they both surveyed the interior in the dim glow of the lamp flame.

They were in what at one time had been a kitchen, indicated by the rusty metal sink and wood cookstove against one wall, as well as an ancient refrigerator, the door of which gaped open. A couple of metal kitchen chairs with ripped plastic upholstery matched the scratched and scarred Formica of the table. A filthy curtain hung on a rope across a doorway, partially concealing the dinginess of another room. There was a liberal covering of mouse droppings on nearly every surface.

Despite her growing panic, Sarah found her voice. "I would have pegged you for something a little fancier than this in the way of a summer cottage, Victor."

"There's a lot you'll never know about me," he replied in a matter–of–fact manner. "I think you'll be more comfortable in the other room."

He shone the flashlight into the darkness behind the curtain as he pulled her along behind him. An old–fashioned black iron double bed took up most of the small space. The sagging mattress was covered by a dull blanket of an indiscriminate dark color. There was a large wooden wardrobe against one wall and a battered nightstand.

New fears ran through Sarah's mind as she remembered some of the perverse stories Tyler had told her about Victor. "Suppose you tell me why we're here." Amazingly her voice sounded loud and confident.

"Momentarily. Would you hold this for me?" He handed her the flashlight again as he rested their handcuffed wrists on the iron bars at the head of the bed. He fished in his pocket and came out with a key in his hand. Before she realized what was happening, he had swiftly unlocked his own cuff and clamped it around the metal piping of the bed.

"You son of a bitch!" Sarah swung out at his face with the small flashlight but he neatly sidestepped away. "Don't think you're going to get away with this! Kidnapping is a federal offense in this country!" She continued to rant at him, tears of anger streaming down her face, as he moved into the next room to retrieve the kerosene lamp.

"Why don't you sit down?" Victor spoke in that infuriatingly calm way of his. "You might as well relax, you're going to be here for a while." He pulled the nightstand out of her reach and set the smoking lamp on it.

"Why? What does anything about me have to do with you?" She remained standing and shivering in the dampness.

"Truthfully, you're nothing to me. But your boyfriend – there's another story. I need him to behave for the next few days. I need him to keep his mouth shut and perform like someone's life is at stake." Victor dragged the least pitiful of the kitchen chairs into the room and sat down. "And someone's life IS at stake now. Yours."

As the inevitable deductions became clear to Sarah she sank slowly down onto the decrepit mattress. The groaning of the bed springs could have been the mournful sound of her own heart.

"We're going to call him right now," Victor announced. From his inside coat pocket, he removed a cell phone that looked suspiciously like Tyler's. "It's all in his hands now. If he steps out of line between now and Sunday, I leave you here to die. If he acts the way he should, in real life and on stage, I'll see to it that you are properly fed and cared for until then. And if you should try to escape, well, then the shoe is on the other foot so to speak. A convenient accident can be easily arranged to take care of him. So let's call him, shall we?"

As he began to punch numbers into the phone, Sarah's nervous laughter stopped him. "You're out of your mind," she said, shaking her head in disbelief. "Don't you realize I run an inn? I even have overnight guests right now. If I'm not there in the morning to give them breakfast, somebody's going to get suspicious. If I'm not there tomorrow when my employees come in, don't you think people are going to wonder? Someone will undoubtedly call the police and the first place they'll look for me is with Tyler."

"Don't be ridiculous." The warm mockery in Victor's voice was suddenly replaced with calculated coldness. "Of course I know you run an inn. And you're going to take care of that yourself. You must have someone who fills in for you when you can't make it. You're going to call that person and tell them you've been called away on an unexpected family emergency. That you'll be back on Monday."

Sarah stared at him in astonishment.

"If you don't play along with this, Sarah, I can assure you that neither you or Tyler will live to see each other again. Now don't make this an ordeal. If you cooperate with me, everything will work out fine."

Sarah eyed him grimly and did not respond.

"Look, it's obviously hard for someone like you to let go of having control of your own life. But I think you're smart enough to realize that in your current situation, you are going to have to let me run the show for the next few days. If you cooperate, I will try to make you as comfortable as possible in these mean surroundings. It's all up to you. So what do you say?"

Sarah realized she had no choice but to act as if she was playing along. But already her mind was running through the options she would have in the few minutes she would be allowed to make a phone call to the inn. Clearly she could not just scream for help and shout out that she had been kidnapped. She didn't even know where the hell she was. She was going to have to outsmart Victor without Victor knowing what she was up to.

Beads of cold sweat broke out on her brow as she made eye contact with him. He held the phone up once again. “Shall we call Tyler now? Let him know our little plan?”

Unable to speak, she nodded her assent.

CHAPTER FIFTEEN

Sarah sat in dazed silence as Victor explained the situation, as well as his terms and conditions, to Tyler over the phone. After a few moments he held the phone up to her ear and said, "Tell him you're fine."

She swallowed hard and tried to speak without crying. "Tyler, it's me. Don't worry, I'm okay."

"Oh, God, Sarah, I'm so sorry–"

"Tell him not to try anything stupid," Victor commanded her.

"Tyler, you've got to play by Victor's rules right now. I don't know what's going on, all I know is he wants you to behave."

"I will, I will. But I don't trust him –"

"For now you have to." Before she could say any more, Victor took the phone away from her and spoke into it again.

"That's it, Tyler. If you have anything else to say, you can tell me when I get home. Until then, you do whatever Jillian tells you. And if you try anything funny, then Sarah doesn't get fed tomorrow."

Sarah clamped her arms to her sides to try to control the trembling that threatened to take control of her whole body. "I need to call someone about the inn now." She sounded much braver than she felt.

"You wouldn't rather wait until morning? It's after midnight."

"No. It will be easier to reach this person now and I need someone to be there to give my guests breakfast when they wake up. And also to check them out." Sarah's plan was beginning to take shape in her mind.

"It would look rather odd if no one was there to take their money, don't you think?"

The overnight guest angle was apparently one Victor hadn't counted on. After a few seconds he handed her the phone. "Don't try anything funny," he warned. "Don't forget that your level of comfort or misery is all up to you. Now here's your cover story – you were called away on a family emergency; a friend drove you in your own car to the airport and will be leaving the car back at the inn before daybreak. You will be gone through the weekend and will check in on a daily basis to answer questions."

"A family emergency." Here was her first lucky break. Victor obviously didn't know that she had no family, both her parents were dead and she had no siblings. Her only living relative was an aunt who was a missionary in Southeast Asia.

"Do you need more details to make it real?" Victor paced back and forth a few times on the uneven floor boards of the cabin. "Let's say that your older brother had a massive heart attack and may not make it through the night. You had to fly to Seattle immediately. Is that enough?"

Sarah nodded. Her palms were sweaty as she held the phone with her cuffed right hand and awkwardly punched the number in with her left. Hunter answered on the second ring.

"Hello, Hunter? It's Sarah Scupper calling." That should clue him in right away that something was off.

"Sarah? What the hell – is something wrong?"

"Sorry to bother you so late, but a family emergency has come up. I'm calling you from the airport. I'm on my way to Seattle. My brother just had a massive heart attack and he might not make it."

"Your brother? What airport? Sarah, is this some kind of bizarre joke?" Hunter was not catching on yet.

"Thanks. Anyway, this couldn't have happened at a worse time of the year and I was wondering if you could help me out with some shift coverage at the inn. I can give you some names of people to call, but right now I really need you to be there first thing in the morning to make breakfast for some guests staying in the front room."

"Sarah, you're in some kind of trouble, aren't you? Are you with Victor?" Hunter's voice was low and breathless now.

"Yes, that's right. That would be fabulous. And keep track of your extra hours." She tried to keep the emotion out of her voice but then realized it didn't matter. She could work with it.

"Are you all right? Tell me that he hasn't hurt you or done anything weird to you, Sarah." Hunter sounded desperate now.

"I'm fine. Just a little stressed. I don't want him to die." She let herself cry a little just to relieve some of the tension she was feeling. "Listen, a friend drove me to the airport and he's going to leave my car back at the inn. I told him to stash the keys over the sun visor." She looked up at Victor for confirmation. "Will you get them in the morning and put them in the front desk for me?"

"Victor's bringing the car back here tonight? God, I wish you could tell me where you are. Are you at Double Phoenix?"

"No, I don't think so. I don't know."

Victor was moving in closer now like he was ready for her to end the conversation. "Listen, I have to go, my plane is about to leave. There are some phone numbers on a list to the left of the answering machine. You'll see it there when you come in tomorrow morning." She was directing him to the pad they wrote phone messages on. "You want to find the first person on that list."

"You talking about here where it says Victor called?"

"Yes, him. He knows the most about what's going on. If you can get a hold of him, just follow him around for a day or a night. He'll show you what to do."

"I think I'm with you here. What about Tyler? Should I call him?"

"You can try. I don't think you'll get through though. There's also a list of numbers on the wall for part time bartenders and waitresses who might be able to help out. And if all else fails, call Woody."

"Woody?"

"He's the owner of the inn. He'd be there in a minute if he thought I – I couldn't handle this problem myself. But I don't want to bother him if we don't have to." She began crying again as she thought about her old friend and how much he cared for her and how worried he would be if he knew where she was right now.

Victor made a cutting sign across his throat to signal her to end the conversation. "Okay, I have to go. I'll try and call you tomorrow night to see if everything is going smoothly. But you know what to do, right?"

"Shit, Sarah, I guess so. Oh, God, I'm worried about you. Don't let him hurt you, I love you, I'm with you–" Hunter was rambling on, trying to prolong the conversation so he wouldn't have to face the reality of what was happening.

"Me too. Gotta go. Bye." She put the phone in Victor's outstretched hand and then rubbed her sleeve across the stream of hot tears that would not stop flowing down her face. She had to try to get a hold of herself here.

"All right then. It looks like we're all set for tonight." Slipping the phone back into his jacket pocket, he stood silent for a few seconds, observing Sarah's condition. "I'm afraid you're not going to be too comfortable tonight, Sarah, but there really is no other way to restrain you for the moment. I don't suppose you'll want to cover up with these filthy things…" Victor picked up the corner of the musty blanket covering the bed and wrinkled his nose.

In her distressed state, Sarah had not realized how cold and damp the unheated cabin was. The prospect of the long unknown hours ahead in this miserable space made her head spin.

"I'll bring you some fresh bedding in the morning but perhaps in the meantime you might have a blanket or a jacket in the car I could get for you?" It was hard to understand how he could be so cruel and yet so solicitous at the same time.

"There's an old blanket in the back," she told him.

Alone for a few minutes, she looked around at her surroundings, wondering how she would survive her confinement here. Victor had said something about Sunday. It was only Wednesday night. Escaping was out of the question for now, especially since she had no clue where she was. She wondered whether Hunter would understand her message and would somehow manage to follow Victor here at some point.

Well, she had plenty of time to think of a way out of this mess.

Victor returned with an old wool hat and the blanket Sarah kept in the car for emergencies. Unimagined emergencies. Like this one.

Just wrapping the familiar brown plaid blanket around herself calmed her down a little.

"Put the hat on," Victor commanded her. "It will help. You lose a lot of heat through your head."

Kneeling down, he peered under the bed. "Well, thank goodness for that," he muttered and reaching with one of his long arms, he dragged something out from beneath her.

It looked like a giant white porcelain tea cup with a handle, big enough to be a water bowl for a St. Bernard. It was empty except for a dead spider.

"Chamber pot," Victor explained pushing it within her reach. "If you have to go in the night."

"Oh." She wondered how Victor had known it would be there. He left her a few minutes later, with the promise that as long as Tyler cooperated, he would return in the morning some time before noon. The lump in her throat grew bigger as she heard him close the padlock on the outside of the door. She listened carefully to the sound of the car starting up and backing out of the two lane track and finally to the fading noise as it sped off on a distant paved road.

After that the silence was complete. Sarah leaned against the cold iron frame of the headboard and stared morosely at the feeble flame of the kerosene lamp.

Tyler sat hunched in one corner of the couch, glaring at Jillian with equal parts loathing and pity. At the other end of the couch, Jillian was displaying her amazing acting ability. Physically she appeared calm and relaxed as she waited for Tyler to speak. Tyler knew that inside she was as vigilant as a mountain lion, ready to pounce.

"You people are disgusting," he finally spat out. "There was no reason to involve Sarah in this."

"There was no reason for you to involve yourself in our business," she replied serenely. "If you'd kept your nose out of our affairs, it would never have come to this."

They both jumped as the telephone rang loudly. Without breaking her eye contact with Tyler, Jillian picked up the receiver.

"No, I'm sorry he can't come to the phone right now. This is a rather late hour to be calling, you know...okay, I'll give him the message."

"Who was that?" Tyler asked.

"Someone named Hunter Adams wanted to ask you some questions about the inn. But I think he's going to have to wing it without your help." She smiled warmly at him and Tyler had the chilling realization that he had no idea how she really felt about him.

Hunter. Hopefully Hunter was a wild card they didn't know was in the deck.

"So who is he?"

"Who? Hunter? He's the cook at the inn. Took my job when I came here. I guess he's going to have be more than a cook for the next few days." He was racking his brains, trying to remember if he'd ever mentioned Hunter's name to Victor or Jillian.

"Have I ever met him?" she asked, all shining innocence.

"No." Tyler folded his arms across his chest and stared at her defiantly. The best thing he could do was keep his mouth shut at this point and think.

He had known something was up as soon as he had staggered in from his trip to Syracuse. Victor had come down on him heavily about taking off like that and repeatedly asked him where he had gone that was so important and then sent him off to a three hour rehearsal which had lasted well past midnight. In the morning, during the Goddard College performance his cell phone had mysteriously disappeared from his jacket pocket. By the afternoon he realized that the keys to the Subaru were gone also.

Before he could even begin to question anybody about these missing items, acute exhaustion had overtaken him, the kind of heavy sleepiness he associated with being drugged. As he passed out on top of his bed, the thought occurred to him that someone must have slipped something into his food at lunch.

When he awoke well after dark with a blinding headache he was sure of it. The overhead light in the bedroom had been turned on and it hurt his eyes to look at it. When he sat up he came to the disturbing realization that he was stark naked. The clothes he had been wearing were neatly folded on top of the dresser. His shoes were nowhere to be seen.

As he sat there trying to regain his bearings, he had a horrible sinking feeling that he had been physically violated during the time he had slept. His mouth was as dry as Death Valley and had an acrid taste to it. He tried to remember what he had planned to do before he fell asleep and then he remembered that he had promised to get Sarah's car back to the inn. She was probably rip shit at him by now.

Stumbling across the room, he had barely pulled his pants on when Jillian burst in. "Well, the sleeping prince awakes!" she said jovially. "We were beginning to worry about you."

Tyler tried to retort but his tongue felt too thick to speak. "Would you bring me a glass of water?" he whispered.

"Why don't you just come down to the kitchen with me where your dinner has been waiting for hours? I'll get you something to drink there."

As she linked her elbow through his, he noticed that she was not dressed in her usual leotard and jeans. Instead she was wearing a short, formfitting black dress made of some shiny synthetic material, with string straps and a low–cut neckline. Beneath the dress she wore tights that glittered with metallic silver threads. Her usual clogs were replaced by black high heeled shoes.

He tried to read the time on his watch but his vision was blurry and would not focus. "What time is it?" he croaked as she guided him through the doorway and into the hall.

"A little after ten, I think. The perfect time for an intimate supper for two." She squeezed his arm affectionately.

Even through the fog lodged in his brain he knew something was up. "I have to go. Take Sarah's car back," he mumbled. His feet felt like clumsy blocks of wood as she led him down the stairs.

"Oh, don't you worry about that. Victor's taken it back for you. Now let's get some water down that parched throat of yours." Without releasing her hold on him, she filled a tall glass with water from the kitchen sink and held it up to his lips.

Angered by all her solicitous gestures, he pulled his arm away from her and took the glass of water himself. As he gulped the water down, the numbness in his lips and tongue began to disappear. On his second glass, his thoughts began to clear. Victor had taken the car back? There was something awfully suspicious going on here.

Turning from the sink, he saw that the table was set with an antique lace cloth and embroidered napkins. Tall candles cast a warm glow over crystal goblets and gleaming china.

"I wanted to welcome you back in my own way," Jillian murmured seductively. "And to apologize for how Victor treated you last night."

There was definitely something suspicious going on here. Despite his ravenous hunger, he had a feeling that anything he ate would probably knock him out again. He drank another glass of water slowly while trying to assess the situation.

He hadn't told them yet what he had found out about Emma in Syracuse. But it seemed like they already knew he had been there and what he had discovered. He should never have come back here. He should have bailed out of this theater experience while he was still ahead.

"I missed you, Tyler," Jillian was purring, completely into a Marilyn Monroe sex kitten role now. "I don't know what I'll do without you when this play is over." Still in character, she shrieked with delight as she uncorked a bottle of expensive champagne and it bubbled over onto the floor. Filling the crystal goblets, she handed one to Tyler.

"To the future," she giggled, clinking her glass against his.

He'd seen the champagne come out of the bottle so he knew it was safe to drink. But unsure of what Victor and Jillian were cooking up (literally and figuratively) and on an empty stomach as well, he was not about to consume any liquor in his usual reckless fashion. He tipped his glass up to wet his lips but did not swallow any.

He watched her circumspectly as she filled two plates with food. Some sort of fragrantly steaming meat pie and salad of multi–colored greens. When she gestured for him to sit down across from her, he moved boldly to the place she stood by and grabbed her by the hips.

Thinking he was coming on to her, she leaned back against him and ground her pelvis against his.

Burying his face in the back of her neck he whispered into her ear, "Switch seats with me. For good luck."

She laughed and shrugged her shoulders. "I hope I get lucky later," she remarked, sliding away from him so he could sit down at the plate she had set for herself.

With a flush of relief that warmed his whole body, he proceeded to fill the empty cavern inside of him. They ate in silence; Tyler shoveling huge mouthfuls of food into his mouth, Jillian picking daintily at hers. As he ate, he reasoned they would not want him drugged all the time; tomorrow they had an afternoon rehearsal in Burlington at the University of Vermont and a performance there in the evening. He would not be able to function if he felt as dopey as he did tonight.

Jillian drank most of the champagne and became quite talkative. Tyler responded in monosyllables; what he really wanted to do was get away from her, make a few phone calls. He wanted to go back to his room and check his laptop; see if anything was missing.

Instead he ended up on the living room couch pretending to watch an old Cary Grant movie on PBS while Jillian massaged his feet. He was entertaining thoughts of asking her to go to bed with him and then tying her to the bed for some kinky foreplay and escaping. His plan was nearly formulated when the telephone on the side table rang.

It was Victor. Telling him that he had kidnapped Sarah. And that her welfare for the next four days was all up to Tyler.

So now he sat here seething on the couch, trying to figure out if there was any way to outwit the sleazy old fox. He didn't like being beaten at his own game by Victor. He didn't want to have to become another one of his life–size marionettes. He wondered if Jillian knew where he was keeping Sarah. Maybe he could get it out of her somehow. But, no, she was as good at scamming as her teacher. Maybe better.

Jillian yawned and stretched. He could see her bare thighs above the elasticized lace at the top of her sparkly stockings. For a brief second she spread her legs a little bit so that he could also see that she wore no underpants. Then she stood up and crossed to the television set. She picked up a video tape and popped it into the VCR below.

"Victor wanted me to show you this before he got back," she explained as she fumbled with the controls. "He thought it might help you understand your position a little bit better." She smiled to herself at her own choice of words.

She sat down next to him on the couch, moving her body as close to his as possible. The warmth of her flesh against him invaded his privacy and left him no space to be alone with his thoughts. Before he could protest, she had pointed the remote at the TV and pressed play.

It was a close up of a man's and a woman's genitals while they were having intercourse, a penis sliding in and out of a vagina. As Tyler wondered for a second if Jillian thought this would turn him on, the camera panned out to show the whole bodies of the "lovers." Tyler felt the room begin to spin and his dinner rising up into his throat. The two people fucking their brains out on film were himself and Jillian in his own bed upstairs.

Blinded by anger and shame, he struggled to his feet, pushing Jillian away from him. With amazing strength, she gripped him by the arm and pushed him back down onto the couch. As he fought to regain his footing, he saw that the scene on the TV had changed to a view of Jillian spread–eagled on the bed with Tyler's face buried in her crotch.

"You traitorous bitch!" He struck out at her wildly, the back of his palm colliding with her cheek.

"If you hurt me Tyler, you'll never see Sarah again," she hissed violently in his ear. "Victor will make sure of that."

He was holding her by the wrists, his breath coming hard and hot in her face as he tried to get a grip on his raging temper. The situation had spiraled way out of his control now. Not only was Victor pulling the strings, he had them looped around Tyler's neck in a hangman's noose.

Jillian was crouched over him, waiting him out, on guard for his next move. He released his hold on her and pushed her away from him as he stood up.

"I'm going to my room," he said.

"Victor will want to talk to you when he gets here." A red mark was rising on her cheek where he had struck her. A run was snaking down the thigh of one of her glittering stockings.

"Fine. He knows where to find me." He left the room, but the video soundtrack of Jillian moaning her way to a climax continued to mock him as he walked down the hall and climbed the stairs.

CHAPTER SIXTEEN

Hunter was exhausted by dawn. He had paced away several hours of the night trying to figure out what was going on and what he was going to do about it. Sarah had left with Victor and now Victor was holding her hostage somewhere. Sarah did not know where she was. She had told him to follow Victor, probably meaning that he would lead Hunter to the place he was keeping Sarah.

He had not been able to get through to Tyler which was not surprising.

Hunter was on his own, trying to put together a puzzle when he didn't even know where or what the pieces were. Tyler was the private investigator; Hunter didn't know the first thing about following someone. As he walked up and down the hall, for a few minutes he let himself wish desperately that he was in his backyard in Berkeley, getting high with a few old friends, listening to music, making plans to travel around the world.

The sound of Kashi crying out in her sleep brought him back to the present. He hadn't known anything about babies either and he'd figured that one out. But, shit, what was he going to do with Kashi for the next few days? He had to find a bartender and a babysitter before he could try to find Sarah.

A beam of light flashing across Kashi's darkened bedroom had him at the window in two seconds. Sarah's car had just pulled into the parking lot. Luckily, Hunter hadn't had the forethought to turn out the outside lights; Sarah usually took care of that along with locking up. Victor was clearly illuminated as he climbed out of the Subaru and shut the door. He looked around to see if anyone was watching him and then took off at a fast pace down the road towards the center of the village.

Hunter took the stairs two at a time and slid out the front door with the stealth of a snake. The cool night air wrapped itself like tentacles around his nearly naked body; he was wearing only his boxer shorts. Instead of using the sidewalk, he stuck to the dark shadows of the lawns. The wet grass numbed his bare feet, but he did not have to go far.

He heard a motor start up in what sounded like the parking lot of the town hall, a few buildings away. He ducked into the bushes a few seconds before the car made a wide circle around the empty lot, its headlights sweeping over the lawn he had just been running across. He watched as Victor pulled out into the road and drove past him, the lone street light illuminating the car just enough for him to make out that it was a Land Rover in a deep blue color.

Well, at least he knew what he was supposed to be following.

Limbs shivering and teeth chattering, he sprinted back to the inn. Wrapping himself in a knitted granny–square afghan from the downstairs living room, he sat down behind the front desk, beneath the single wall lamp that Sarah left on at night. It cast a dim golden glow over the lobby and helped guests find their way to the bottom of the stairs safely. He stared glumly at the list of emergency phone numbers, trying to decide who to call and what to do.

He jumped as the fax machine behind him suddenly whirred into motion, slowly regurgitating a sheet of paper. He picked it up and read, “Tyler, Any news or clues in Syracuse? Keep me posted. L.”

Lucy, the journalist from London. She was worth a try. He looked at the clock, quickly calculating the time in England with the speed of an experienced world traveler. Eight in the morning. She was probably getting ready to leave for work.

Flipping the fax over, he began writing at a furious pace. Two minutes later, he watched the machine transmit his fax to a number in London.

Sarah awoke with a start. She had not realized she had fallen asleep but the gray light coming through the filthy glass panes of the sagging double–hung window indicated that it must be day. A glance at her wristwatch told her it was nearly nine o'clock. She had actually slept for four or five hours on that smelly, decrepit bed.

After Victor left, it had taken hours before exhaustion had overcome the fear and despair she felt. She had been dreaming about visiting her grandmother in the repossessed family mansion she had heard about in her childhood. In the dream she had been walking in a beautiful garden on a warm, sunny day. Now she wished she had never woken up, her dream world had been much more pleasant than the harsh reality of her current situation.

Closing her eyes, she tried to find her way back to the safe, happy place she had been visiting. But the nagging stiffness in her neck and shoulders could not be ignored, nor could the sharp pain in her lower back or the numbness of her cold feet. She tried to find a more comfortable position but her handcuffed wrist restricted her movement. Sometime in the night she had given up being squeamish about what she might be sharing the mattress with. Now she curled up into a semi–fetal position and adjusted the wool blanket so that it covered her feet.

Sleep was the only way to get through this. She wondered when Victor would show up again.

It was nearly noon by the time Hunter had strapped Kashi into her car seat and started up the engine. He had very few ideas on what he should be doing but he knew that trying to contact Tyler was a good place to start. He could make the visit to Double Phoenix seem perfectly innocent. Sarah had been called off on an emergency and since he couldn't reach Tyler by phone, he had decided to look him up because he had some important questions to ask him about how to do certain things at the inn.

But when he arrived at Double Phoenix, the place seemed eerily deserted. The only car in the yard was the rusty station wagon Tyler had borrowed a few times to come to the inn. As he put Kashi in the baby backpack and slipped his shoulders into the straps, he was aware of the stillness that surrounded them. Kashi cooed and kicked in anticipation, she always loved riding on Hunter's back while he walked.

He tried the door of the theater first but surprisingly it was locked. After knocking loudly on the door of Victor's farmhouse and calling hello several times, he discovered that it was locked up also. He began to get a sick feeling in his already knotted stomach. Where was everybody? Something very weird was going on here.

Moving on to the students' cottages, he was relieved to find that not all these doors were locked and the ones he peeked into seemed totally lived in. Beds had been left unmade, clothes were strewn on floors, a light had been left on in a bathroom. He finally found his answer in what appeared to be a communal kitchen/dining room. A schedule had been graphed out on a chalk board that indicated that the entire troupe had left at 11:30 for the University of Vermont in Burlington to set up and rehearse during the afternoon for an evening performance at 7:30.

Helping himself to an apple from a bowl on the table, he sat down on a bench to do a few time calculations in his head. The performance took two hours, breaking down the set and packing up would take at least another hour, the ride back from Burlington was an hour and a half. That meant they would not be back until midnight. Which meant if Victor was to check on Sarah, it would not be until then.

Of course, Victor probably wouldn't hang around while the crew packed up. Which meant he might conceivably be back by eleven.

He shuddered and stopped eating as he contemplated all the hours Sarah was spending somewhere trapped and alone.

As he stepped out of the building into the weak warmth of the October sun, it occurred to him that Victor might very well be keeping Sarah right here on the grounds. Slowly he turned in a circle, trying to decide where he could possibly be holding her where no one would know. An attic or a basement. Or somewhere in the theater.

The only building with an attic or basement was the farmhouse. Was it possible that Victor would be keeping Sarah in the same building that Tyler was staying in? A central location where anybody might hear her if she shouted? He didn't think so. But perhaps there were some old outbuildings in the woods nearby.

He walked along the edge of the property, following the tree line, peering into the thick forest that surrounded the open acreage but he saw nothing. He followed a path that led around a small pond and then meandered through the woods and came out on a nearby dirt road. By this time Kashi had nodded off to sleep against his shoulder and he knew it was time to head back to the inn.

He wondered when Lucy would call him back.

Sarah watched in despair as the rays of the setting sun cast a filtered orange light through the filthy west window of the room. Around nine in the morning Victor had arrived with the supplies for her internment, which included a grocery bag of food, a jug of water, a down sleeping bag, two pillows and a couple of fat paperback books. He had also brought another set of handcuffs to lengthen her tether to the iron bed frame. She had managed to convince him to manacle her by the ankle to one of the legs at the foot of the bed so that she would have more mobility and coordination for things like lighting the lamp at night or using the chamber pot.

Again he had been accommodating but frosty. Without comment, he emptied the chamber pot and refilled the lamp. She heard him rummaging in the other room and then he returned with a couple of chipped china plates and teacups as well as some dull–looking silverware. He told her that he would not be back until very late that evening and possibly not until the next day to check on her. And then he left.

Since then she had eaten a couple of peanut butter and jelly sandwiches and read several chapters of Cold Mountain. Now she dreaded the return of night. Putting the book down, she stood up and did several stretches to alleviate the stiffness that was plaguing her shackled body. As she tried to move her tethered leg around she felt the bed frame give a little. With a sharp tug, she realized the bed would move with her if she leaned forward and walked. She dragged it six feet across the wide floorboards so that she could see out the window.

Between trees which were now nearly bare of foliage she could see down a slope to a body of water which was reflecting the pinks and oranges of the autumn sunset. A pond or a lake, she presumed. She tried to speculate where she could possibly be. She tried to remember what time they had left the inn and what time they had arrived here. She was certainly not more than half an hour from home. Which meant that she was not even as far as Double Phoenix.

She still could not imagine how Victor had come to have access to this shack in the woods. Looking over her shoulder at the closet behind her, she was suddenly determined to find out. Making a wide circle with the bed, she dragged it back to the nightstand, lit the kerosene lamp and moved slowly on to the closet.

"So, son, suppose you tell me what's really going on."

Startled, Hunter looked up from where he was garnishing a couple of grilled swordfish dinners with sprigs of parsley. Red was standing at the entrance to the kitchen, letting the doors swing shut behind him. As far as Hunter knew, Red had never been inside the kitchen of the inn before. He rarely deviated from the path between the outside door and his usual barstool.

"About what?" Hunter asked, continuing to work as Red scratched his bushy beard and scrutinized him.

"Well, you did a good job of covering your bases, you've got Clyde out there bartending and Ruby's working the dining room. It all looks pretty normal. The only thing that doesn't wash is your story."

"My story?" Hunter turned his back to Red and stirred some pan–fried potatoes on the stove to cover his nervousness.

"About where Sarah is. I've known Sarah for going on ten years now. And forty years ago I knew her mother for a few years before she died. She never knew her father. So you might be able to fool some of those other yokels out there, but you aren't fooling me." He crossed his arms and stood his ground defiantly.

Ruby blasted in backwards through the dining room doors, carrying a tray of dirty dishes. Hunter had been surprised when Ruby had appeared this afternoon in answer to his call for help. In her mid–fifties and built like a fire truck, Ruby had a thick mane of long hair which was more gray than any other color and wore an ankle length Indian print skirt and several crystals hanging from cords around her neck. She was not what he had expected but he felt right at home with her.

Neither he nor Red spoke until Ruby had picked up the swordfish dinners and swept back out to the other room, her full skirt almost catching in the door behind her. Hunter pulled the next order off the clip and studied it. "So what's your point, Red?"

"My point is that I know, and so do plenty of other people in this town, that Sarah doesn't have a brother in Seattle. Sarah doesn't have a brother at all."

Hunter could feel his cheeks burning as he turned away again. "That's what she told me when she called from the airport. All I'm telling you is what she told me."

"Well, I also know Sarah wouldn't bail out on this place during foliage high season unless something really serious came up." Despite a few beers, Red was seeing through the situation with taciturn Yankee shrewdness.

"So obviously something serious did come up." Hunter wished Red would leave. He was not a good liar and did not know how far he could go with this.

He slammed a couple of bowls onto the counter and began filling them with chili from a big pot on the stove.

"Look, I'm just worried about her that's all. You tell me that this is just some silly fib and that she's fine and I'll leave you alone."

Hunter felt fear constrict his chest and for a moment he could not breathe. He wanted to tell the truth to Red but he could not. He was too righteous; he would probably go straight to the local police and Hunter knew this could not be solved that way. For a few days, Victor had to be lulled into believing his plan was working, so that Hunter could get the chance to follow him to where he was keeping Sarah.

"I don't know if she's fine." He tried to clear the frog in his throat. "But I hope she is."

"She's not involved in one of Tyler's crazy investigations, is she? I thought he'd given that up for this new acting career of his." Red came forward and leaned against the counter. He was clearly not going to go away until he had an answer he liked.

"Uh, well, actually, yes." It wasn't even a lie. "She is involved in something Tyler's been secretly working on." Hunter gave a long sigh of relief. "And that's why I'm really not allowed to talk about it. You understand, don't you?" He winked at Red conspiratorially.

"Oh. Sure. I won't say anything to anybody." Red was instantly contrite and slightly embarrassed. "But somebody else is going to see through that brother in Seattle story soon enough so you might want to change that a little. I was just worried about her that's all. She's not doing anything dangerous, is she?"

"Dangerous?" Hunter let his guard slip for a just a minute. "I don't know, Red. And I'm worried about her too."

Red slammed his fist on the counter. "Damn that Tyler," he muttered before returning to his usual stoic façade. "Well, sorry to bother you," he went on as he backed out the door. "Like I said, I can keep my mouth shut. But let me know if you need any help."

It was after ten thirty by the time Hunter finished in the kitchen and he felt like his ass was seriously dragging. He knew he should hop in the car and race off to Double Phoenix and try to track Victor's movements but he didn't feel energetic or alert enough. And besides, he had to close up the inn and then there was Kashi.

Depressed, he helped himself to a locally brewed ale and threw another log on the fire in the lounge. But he had too much on his mind to sit and socialize with anybody tonight. Beer in hand, he wandered out to the front desk to once more contemplate who he could call to help him out. The message light on the answering machine was blinking. Hoping for a miracle, he rewound the tape and played it back.

"Hunter, Lucy Brookstone here," chirped a British-accented voice. "I've landed in Boston just now, must be around 9pm your time. I'm hoping to catch the last flight up to Burlington and rent a car there. With a good road map I should be seeing you around 1am. So leave a light on for me."

Spinning the office chair around a few times, Hunter gave a whoop of delight. Help was on her way.

CHAPTER SEVENTEEN

"So now we wait."

Hunter shifted his body so that his back rested against the passenger door of the rented Geo and so that he could see Lucy while they talked. Behind them, Kashi ate Cheerios out of a plastic bowl and tugged at the restraining straps of her car seat.

Since Lucy's arrival in the middle of the night, the petite redhead had been an efficient ball of energy. Barely five foot two, with a sturdy build and a fair, freckled complexion, it was her fluffy cloud of strawberry blonde hair that caught people's attention and captivated their imagination. It floated around her head and down to her shoulders like the nimbus of a saint, bringing to mind Venus de Milo or Queen Guenevere.

More like the Little Mermaid, Hunter had finally decided as he had towered over her when he answered the door the night before. As he studied her now, sitting behind the steering wheel of the car, he realized that if Lucy cut off her hair, her appearance would become completely average, an inconspicuous slip of a woman. Her effervescent personality would become her most distinctive feature.

"You can see the gray in it, can't you, and you're wondering how old I am," she teased him. Her blue eyes stopped watching the end of the road to meet his for a brief second before she took up her vigil again.

"I don't see any gray in it and I won't ask your age if you won't ask mine." He guessed she was in her early thirties but he knew her small size and youthful hairstyle were deceptive. She could be anywhere between twenty–five and forty–five and her clothes did nothing to date her either. She wore snug brown jeans and a short green plaid wool jacket. Hunter usually hated plaids, but he had to admit the jacket looked great on her.

"You should be looking at the highway, not me. Victor could drive by any minute now."

They were parked on the dirt road that Hunter had discovered the day before on his walk through the woods surrounding Double Phoenix. When they had arrived, shortly after dawn, he had sprinted down the path and back just to make sure that the Land Rover was there.

"It's not that far away; if we roll down the window we can probably hear him when he starts the engine." The chilly early morning air filled the car as he lowered his window. "Well, that ought to wake us up."

Lucy had made the insurmountable task of following Victor seem like a piece of cake, laying it out step–by–step for him over a two a.m. snack of tea and muffins. Hunter didn't know why he couldn't have figured it out himself. But anyway it was a lot easier to spend hours sitting in the car with someone else to talk to besides an infant. Especially a fascinating and savvy journalist like Lucy.

"I want to get the goods on this bugger," she had told him. "I've been following this deal from the London end of things and it stinks of something very rotten. I'm ready to blow this bastard's cover wide open and this may be it all takes."

Sipping their respective tea and coffee from Styrofoam cups, they shared stories about their global travels and college experiences, moving on to near escapes from dangerous situations, of which Lucy had a much larger number than Hunter did. She was involved in relating a long and involved tale about being caught in a bombing raid in a Bosnian village when Hunter suddenly held up his hand.

"Listen."

They could just hear the sound of a car engine running in the near distance. A few minutes later, the Land Rover flew by on the main road through East Jordan, heading west. Seconds later Lucy had turned the corner and was following it, leaving a safe span of highway between the two vehicles.

They tracked him for about five miles until he turned into the parking lot of a small supermarket at the crossroad to Jordan Center. Lucy drove past the supermarket and pulled into a self–service gas station which was diagonally across the intersection. Hunter hopped out to put a few dollars of gas in the car, at the same time keeping an eye on Victor's vehicle. After paying for the gas, he made a big show of washing all the windows in the Geo, much to Kashi's delight. She craned her head to watch him as he moved around all four sides of the car, dragging the squeegee slowly across each piece of glass, his heart pounding with excitement, wondering if Victor had spotted them yet.

"Here he comes," Lucy announced, starting the engine.

Hunter leaped back into his seat as Victor loaded a bag of groceries into the Land Rover and then climbed in himself. He made a left hand turn onto the crossroad and sped off.

"What are you waiting for?" Hunter asked impatiently, drumming his fingers on the dashboard. "We don't want to lose him."

"And we don't want him to see us either. We've got to give him a little space. Okay, now we're going." Lucy pulled out carefully into the right hand lane, still a little unsure of herself when driving on the opposite side of the road.

It was hard to keep Victor in sight on the winding country highway but every now and then they would catch a glimpse of him several hundred feet ahead of them. "It's to our advantage," Lucy assured Hunter.

"This way he won't really see us, but we'll see him if he slows down to make a turn."

They drove on in silence, the tension mounting inside the little car as the miles passed. They seemed to be driving farther and farther from civilization. The few houses on the road were far apart from each other and not very prosperous looking. Finally they had the fleeting impression of a blinking red taillight as Victor made a swift left hand turn onto a dirt road.

Lucy passed the turnoff at a slow steady speed. "Walker Lake Road East," Hunter read from the green signpost on the corner. More reassuring was the yellow highway sign below which said "No Outlet."

"That's good for us," Lucy assured him. "That means we don't have to worry about him turning onto another road from here. It effectively limits the scope of the neighborhood we have to search. But it also means that we can't take a chance of following him in there with the car.

"So what do we do now?" Hunter glanced back at Kashi. The hum of the engine had had its usual effect on her and she was mercifully asleep. It was a shame to waste a minute of that time.

"Well, if you think you can be discreet, you can try your luck on foot. Or we can wait until we see Victor leave and then drive in." She pulled off onto the shoulder of the road and swung a U–turn.

"Actually I've had some experience with this kind of discretion," Hunter remarked cryptically. He tucked his ponytail up under a baseball cap and pulled on his denim jacket. "Let me scope it out. I can't stand waiting around."

He loped off down the dirt road, keeping close to the trees, ready to duck into the dense foliage at the first sound of a vehicle. Within a few moments he passed a deserted bungalow and then another. They were clearly summer cottages, well–maintained but boarded up for the season now. He walked around to the backyard of one of them and discovered that it had a grassy lawn that sloped down to a body of water. Moving closer he realized that it was the narrow end of what opened up into an expansive lake.

Walker Lake. The name suddenly rang a bell for him and he broke into a cold sweat as dread and expectation washed over him.

Back on the road he continued at a more cautious pace. The road seemed to head away from the lake for a stretch as it passed around a steep hillside. There were two or three long driveways that negotiated their way up the hill on their route to the lakefront properties on the other side but he chose not to investigate those for the time being. Picking up his pace, he hurried on. As the road made its way closer to the shoreline again, he came upon several more cottages, all identical in design but personalized by paint and trimmings, and all uninhabited on this cloudy autumn day.

He stopped in his tracks, however, as he saw smoke curling from a chimney at the end of the row of houses. It was the last dwelling on the dirt lane, which swept around a circular cul–de–sac a few hundred yards beyond it. Moving more vigilantly, he approached, noting that, although the yard was mowed and there were still lawn chairs on the porch, there was no car parked in the driveway.

With his heart pounding in his ears, he watched the cottage for several minutes before finally approaching it. He had already decided while observing it that it was highly unlikely that this was where Victor would be keeping Sarah, the most obvious reason being that the Land Rover was nowhere in sight. But if someone was home who lived here, they might have seen or heard something suspicious in the neighborhood.

When no one responded to his pounding on the door, he peered through a few of the windows. From what he could see of the interior, it was funky but cheerful. The remains of a single cup of coffee and one plate with crumbs on it led him to believe that whoever lived here probably lived alone.

The fact that there was actually an inhabitant on this lonely dead end road, made him feel a little lighter. He wasn't sure why, but it meant there was somewhere to run for help if necessary or someone to hear a scream in the middle of the night. He headed back the way he'd come, knowing that his destination was one of the long unpaved drives he had passed on the steep hill.

Having isolated this fact, he pushed aside his pressing desire to continue his pursuit alone and began hiking his way back to the car. He was almost to the end of the road when he heard the hum of an engine and the crunch of tires on gravel behind him. Without hesitating to look over his shoulder, he dove into the underbrush, burrowing deep into the wet fallen leaves. He felt the dampness of the ground seeping through the denim of his jeans as, face to the earth, he watched the wheels of the Land Rover pass ten feet from where he lay. He thanked whatever god was watching over him that he had not been walking by the open lawns of the two cottages when he'd heard Victor coming.

Hunter closed his eyes and listened to Victor slow down before pulling out onto the main road and heading back toward East Jordan. He wondered where Lucy had parked the car and whether Kashi was still asleep. Suddenly he did not want to involve them in this human treasure hunt, especially not Kashi. He wished she was back at the inn, napping safely in her own crib instead of out here with him trying to elude a man who was probably a two–time murderer.

It was not the wetness of the cold ground against his clothes and skin that caused him to shudder violently. Standing up quickly, he brushed off the leaves and sticks and stepped back onto the road. He broke into a run and then stopped abruptly as he saw the green Geo turning the corner and driving towards him.

"What if he comes back because he forgot something?" he gasped as he flung open the car door and threw himself into the passenger seat.

"We'll take that risk," Lucy replied. "Remember that he has no idea that Sarah communicated his name to you or that she indicated you should follow him. Right now he thinks he's home free."

The thought was only slightly comforting. "There are three driveways off to the left," Hunter told her, still trying to catch his breath. "He went up one of those, I don't know which one."

Lucy flashed him a grin of approval. "Nice work, Watson."

She nosed the Geo into the first of the turnoffs. It moved slowly up the steep incline, crested the hill and came down the other side to a large log house situated right on the water's edge. It was built in the sprawling Adirondack "cottage" style with a long covered porch that was connected by a short boardwalk to a wooden dock extending into the lake. Forest green shutters were securely shut over each window – the house had definitely been closed down for the season.

"This looks like something Victor might own," Lucy commented. "Let's give it a look–see."

Kashi was still sleeping peacefully so Hunter felt okay about leaving her alone in the car for a few minutes. They circled the building, looking for an entrance. There was a door on the porch and one next to the driveway. Both had been tightly boarded up with thick sheets of plywood. They could not find any other way in.

Depressed and desperate, Hunter raised his hands to his mouth and shouted Sarah's name several times. The only response was the shrill chirping of a couple of chipmunks warning their relatives about the presence of humans.

They drove back to the road in silence. The second driveway had a chain across it so they bypassed it for the moment.

"Hmm, I don't think the Geo can negotiate this one," Lucy remarked coming to a stop a few feet into the third and last turn off. Large rocks and sizeable tree branches had turned the final driveway into a rugged track that could only be managed by four–wheel drive vehicles. Like a Land Rover.

"I'll go," Hunter said, his heartbeat speeding up again.

"Let me come with you," Lucy offered quickly.

They gazed at each other in silence for a few seconds each trying to second guess what the other was thinking.

"Okay, I'll stay with the baby," Lucy said finally. "But yell if you need help. And if you're not back in fifteen minutes, I'm coming to find you."

Using her free leg to kick off the down sleeping bag, Sarah sipped the steaming Styrofoam cup of coffee that Victor had left her and stared at the gray light coming through the dirty window.

Another day in paradise. Sleep being the ultimate escape hatch, she hadn't even been awake yet when Victor arrived. He had not commented on the tracks the bed had left on the floor as she dragged it around the room last night, she wasn't sure if he had even noticed. Their conversation had been abrupt; she had managed to convince him that she needed to call the inn this evening or people might start trying to find a way to contact her and realize that her Seattle story did not hold water. He had said he would be back around six with the cell phone and the change of clothes she had asked for. When she asked him how Tyler was doing, his only reply was, "You're still getting fed, aren't you?"

Reaching under the mattress, she pulled out the results of the previous evening's investigation. Her prize for an hour of dragging, contorting, stretching and sweating was a theater program, yellowed with age, from a summer stock company in Canada. She had found it in a piece of expensive luggage shoved into the back corner of the curtained closet. The plastic identification tag attached to the handle of the suitcase was empty; when she opened the suitcase she found it contained an unfolded jumble of high–priced women's clothes with designer labels. There were a few pairs of delicate sandals, a couple of lacy bras, a long silk scarf with gold metallic threads woven throughout, but nothing personal to identify the owner. She began searching the pockets of the garments and finally found her treasure hidden in a wrinkled linen jacket that had apparently been balled up and shoved, inside out, into a corner of the suitcase.

It had been hard to read in the dim light given off by the kerosene lamp but like a flea on a mangy dog, the name Victor Nesbitt had jumped out at her, as had the name of Jillian Fox.

Now, in the light of day, she took the time to peruse the program more carefully. The play had been Midsummer Night's Dream. Victor had had the leading role of Lysander, Jillian had been Titania, queen of the fairies. In the back there were photographs of the actors and short biographies of them.

The picture of Victor made her catch her breath. It showed a handsome young man with light hair and deep dimples. Round faced and snub nosed, his wide grin exuded an open innocence. If this was Victor twenty years ago, he had certainly changed. In fact, the longer she studied his features, she was sure there was no way the actor smiling at her from the page could be Victor.

Sarah's brow furrowed as she frowned, trying to understand the implications of what she had just discovered. She flipped a few pages until she found Jillian's picture. Never having seen Jillian except on stage, it was hard to compare how she looked now to two decades ago. She certainly hadn't aged much, that was for sure. The woman she had seen in the theater hadn't looked like she was pushing forty, at least not under her theatrical makeup.

Jillian's biography didn't tell her anything she didn't already know, so she returned to read about Victor. His history was as improbable as his picture. Raised by foster parents in a small town in Saskatchewan, he left home at sixteen and joined a traveling circus company. It was during a stint in Toronto that he auditioned for the director of a local summer stock company who saw his raw talent and saved him from the life of a circus roustabout. He had won a full scholarship to train as an actor at the Theater Arts Academy of Toronto and since then had played dozens of roles in serious theater productions.

Raised by foster parents in a small town in Saskatchewan....Sarah's mind ran wildly through a string of bizarre possibilities as she quickly scanned the photographs and names of the other actors in the play, finally making her way to the director and crew. These were shorter blurbs without pictures. She read over their unfamiliar names before embarking on their undistinguished histories. She stopped short when she came to the phrase, "Hailing from across the border in northern Vermont..."

The assistant director, Claude Ledoux, was from northern Vermont. Just a coincidence or did it mean anything?

She closed her eyes, dizzy from the new ideas and information swirling around inside her brain. She wished there was some way to get the old program to Tyler. He might be able to make more sense of it. She would just have to hold on to it so that she could show it to him if she ever got out of this godforsaken jam he had gotten her into.

As she got up off the bed to tuck the evidence securely under the mattress, there was a rapping noise at the window and someone spoke her name. She gave an involuntary scream. A man's face was pressed against the dirty panes, peering in at her, violating her sense of privacy, rescuing her from her forced isolation.

Five minutes later she was wrapped tightly in Hunter's arms while they each took turns laughing and crying from relief. Between the two of them they had managed to force open the old, double hung window. Hunter had boosted himself onto the sill and then slithered through the eighteen–inch opening.

He did not seem put off by how grimy and unwashed Sarah had become over the last few days. Instead he squeezed her against his chest and stroked her tangled hair. Her words tumbled over themselves as, between gulps and gasps, she told him the story of her imprisonment.

Suddenly she pulled away from him and asked anxiously, "Where's Kashi?"

"She's fine," he assured her. "Lucy's watching her in the car. And I bet she's wondering what happened to me by now." He eyed the window opening, not looking forward to sliding back through it so soon.

"Lucy?" Sarah realized that in her excitement she had not asked Hunter for the details of how exactly he had managed to get there. "Lucy who?"

Hunter grinned as he extracted himself from her embrace and stood up. "Lucy from London. Tyler's friend Lucy. Apparently she wants to nail this bastard as much as he does. She came as soon as I called. "

Sarah's jaw dropped. "All the way from England, just like that?"

Hunter nodded. "And thank God she did. I couldn't have found you without her." He knelt down to examine where the other end of the handcuffs was locked onto the iron frame of the bed. "Hmmm, looks like we'll need a hacksaw to get you free. Think you can stand another couple of hours here?"

"Another couple of hours? You don't get it, do you?" A note of desperation crept into her voice. "If Victor came back and found me gone, he would make sure that something really bad would happen to Tyler. And besides the fact that he knows where I live and what I do – he'd make sure something even worse happened to me." Sarah clasped her hands together to try and prevent them from trembling. "He's not your typical cold–hearted scoundrel; he's calculating and manipulative, working toward his own evil purpose."

Her hand slid under the mattress while she spoke. "I think Tyler has found something out that Victor really doesn't want anyone to know and this may have something to do with it." She handed him the wrinkled theater program. "Give this to Lucy. And get it to Tyler somehow."

Hunter shook his head and stood his ground. "You're crazy if you think I'm leaving you out here, lady. If he's that evil, you might not even still be alive when I get back here with that hacksaw."

"Don't be ridiculous! He's not going to kill me. He needs me alive at least until Sunday night so that he can blackmail Tyler to keep acting in that stupid play of his. Look, as long as somebody knows where he's hidden me, I'm safe. Even if Tyler gets out of line and Victor decides to stop feeding me, I'm not going to die now because you know where I am."

A shadow passed across Hunter's face. Very slowly he sat down next to her again. "I don't know about that," he said in a sad, serious voice. "I have to tell you something you probably don't know."

"You mean like where I am?" she demanded. "By the way, where am I, anyway?"

"You're on Walker Lake. And behind the house is an old, falling–down garage. The kind with old–fashioned wooden barn doors that open in the middle? When I was circling this place, I peeked inside there first." He stopped talking as though he wasn't sure what to say next.

"So what's in there? A dozen skeletons?" Sarah laughed nervously.

"No. Underneath a couple of old black tarpaulins is a red rental car with Massachusetts license plates."

"Oh, no. You're kidding. It's the one you and Miles drove up from Boston in?" Sarah sank into a fearful silence. Walker Lake, of course. That was where they had found Miles's body floating. "Well, then we've got him, right?"

Hunter grimaced. "Not while he's got you. What is this thing you want me to get to Tyler anyway?" He looked in confusion at the little booklet she was still holding out to him.

"It's an old theater program." Sarah's mind was moving rapidly now. "You know, I may be trapped but I could still be the bait. Hunter, I need you to find out who this property belongs to."

"How the hell am I going to do that?" he grumbled. "Want me to see if somebody left an old telephone bill lying around in the other room?"

"Well, there might be something out there with a name on it. I've searched this room the best I could while dragging a bed around behind me and didn't find anything. But also you can just go to the town hall and ask to see the property maps. They're public domain."

Hunter's blank stare told her he had no experience at all with that sort of project. Sarah suddenly saw the bags beneath his bloodshot eyes and the sagging of his jaw muscles. She may have spent most of the last thirty–six hours sleeping and thinking, but he was exhausted. Not only had he been running the inn and taking care of Kashi, but he'd done some first class detective work as well. She could not expect much more of him, but there was so little time to waste here.

"Anybody home?"

An intelligent freckled face surrounded by a froth of fluffy hair appeared at the open window. A sharp–eyed gaze quickly assessed the entire situation and finally met Sarah's own appraising eyes. The two women smiled cautiously as they checked each other out. Lucy noted the close physical proximity of Hunter to Sarah, whom she had thought was Tyler's girlfriend. Sarah noticed how short but capable looking Lucy was.

"You must be Sarah. Lucy Brookstone here. "She held out a hand and then waved it instead. "And it looks like you could use some help."

CHAPTER EIGHTEEN

Tyler stood in the darkness of the wings, waiting for his cue to go on stage. The concealing half–light of the backstage recesses was the only place he had felt almost alone for the last two days. Everyone's attention was directed toward whatever scene was happening, when their next entrance was, or what line they would have to say. Tracy was in the lighting booth in the back of the theater and Victor was seated in the last row. If he was going to find a time to escape, this would be it.

Except for the fact that his absence would be instantly and enormously noticed as soon as he missed his next cue.

Since Victor had returned from kidnapping Sarah, Tyler had been under constant surveillance. Victor had apparently gathered the entire troupe together and told them that Tyler was on the verge of a nervous breakdown and might try to run away again, like he had after last Sunday's performance. He convinced them all that it was in the best interest of the production for one or two of them to be with Tyler every minute of the day, monitoring his behavior, alerting Victor to any deviant conduct at all.

Up to that point Tyler had not realized how deeply Victor's students were under his spell. Tyler could not persuade any of them that Victor was full of shit and had ulterior motives here. Gabriel was his best hope; his understudy for the part of Azzolino still wanted desperately to have a chance to prove his stuff. Tyler hoped that he might be able to find the crack in Gabriel's blind faithfulness to Victor by playing on his desire to have a starring role.

His greatest fear was that, even if he played by all of Victor's damn rules, the last performance of "The Abdication" would come and go and then so would Victor and Jillian, straight to New Zealand, without releasing Sarah. Of course, if he could convince someone in a position of authority that Victor needed to be stopped, then he could easily be arrested when he got off the plane in Los Angeles or Auckland and probably be forced to tell where Sarah was hidden. But truthfully, knowing what he did now, Tyler didn't trust that Victor would keep him alive after Sunday night when he was no longer needed.

Tyler was going to have to do something desperate in the next forty–eight hours. If he could just figure out what and how.

"You're on!" hissed Paloma, poking him in the back. He had not realized she had been standing in the shadows behind him all this time. He had never really been alone at all.

Taking a deep breath, he squared his shoulders, lifted his head and strode on to the stage. He was instantly transformed into an authoritative figure, at one with himself and God, not showing any signs of the helpless trapped robot that the actor behind the role had become.

At the end of the play, Tyler was escorted back to the men's dressing room by Tony and Marcus who were under Victor's orders not to let him out of their sight. Tyler could sense how the attitude of the two younger men had changed towards him in the last few days. Awe and respect had been replaced by disdain and pity, combined with the annoyance of the inconvenience he was causing everybody.

Although they had never really been overly friendly towards Tyler, now they pointedly ignored him, shouting around him to each other as they removed their stage make–up and costumes. A few other actors moved in and out of the room and Phoebe also quietly appeared to make sure the costumes were properly hung up and put away.

There was enough activity in the small, overheated dressing room that nobody heard the commotion in the hallway until it was right outside the door.

"What do you mean he can't sign my damn program?"

It was a familiar voice but Tyler couldn't quite place it.

"How else am I going to prove to everybody back in West Jordan that I actually came here and saw him? This is a big event in my life, mister. I don't go out to the thee–ate–ter very often. Now don't go wrecking the experience for me. Let me in there."

Red. He had actually gotten off his bar stool for a night and come to see Tyler's performance. Tyler was touched that the old man had broken his nightly routine for him. "Somebody better let him in for a minute," he remarked as casually as he could. "Or this could be some very bad publicity."

Tony and Marcus looked at each other trying to decide what to do as the arguing voices in the hall became louder and more aggressive.

"Okay. But just for a minute," Marcus warned. "And don't try anything funny."

Tyler held back all the scathing comebacks that popped into his mind as Tony opened the dressing room door. The next moment Red burst into the room, his presence larger than usual in the cramped space. He was wearing a blindingly orange hunter's cap and an old wool jacket in the traditional black and red check of north woodsmen; he smelled strongly of wood smoke.

"Hey, Red, old buddy! What a great surprise!" Tyler forced his voice to be loud and jovial.

"Jesus, it's like you're already some goddamn famous movie star or something the way these people protect you, Tyler. You'd think I was breaking into Fort

Knox." Red glared at Gabriel who had been guarding the other side of the door.

"Yeah, they do treat me like gold, don't they? They all think I'm pretty special around here." Tyler flashed a phony smile at all of his fellow actors who stood watching him with frowns on their faces and their arms crossed.

"Well, sign this damn thing so that I can prove I was really here." He gruffly shoved a program in front of Tyler's face. "I know I've got a pen here somewhere," he said in a loud mumble, shoving both of his large callused hands into his jacket pockets.

At that instant there was a shriek from the hallway and then a feminine voice screamed for help. Gabriel flew down the corridor and for a few seconds all eyes were riveted on the open doorway, including Tyler's. But his gaze was abruptly redirected to meet Red's pale blue eyes as the big man pressed a tightly folded packet into Tyler's hand.

There was no chance to be shocked. By the time anyone glanced back at Tyler, he was accepting a pen from Red and staring out the door like everyone else.

"I swear it ran under my skirt and up my leg!" The woman had a breathy voice with a strong southern accent.

"Well, I'm sure you scared it away by now, ma'am." Gabriel's reply dripped with innocent sarcasm. Most of the men in the room suppressed their grins.

"Are you sure?"

"I don't see it anywhere. You can put your skirt back down now, ma'am." Almost as a unit, all the male bodies in the dressing room, except for Tyler and Red, moved towards the door for a better look.

"They found her, she's okay," Red muttered under his breath to Tyler.

For a second, Tyler thought he was referring to the woman in the hall before he realized Red was talking about Sarah. His whole body suddenly began to tingle with a mixture of fear and relief.

"What's she doing back here anyway?" Marcus was asking loudly. "You're not supposed to be backstage."

"I'm looking for my father," the woman protested. "He came back here to get an autograph from a friend. But he's kind of old and he gets lost sometimes."

So it was more than a convenient coincidence that the woman had attracted their attention.

"Here, sign it right here," Red said loudly, opening the program and pointing to where something was already written.

Tyler scribbled frantically as he read the tiny printed words. "Leave tomorrow night right after the show. Do what you have to." He quickly shut the program and handed it back to Red.

"He's in here, lady," Marcus told her. "And I'd say he's ready to go."

A petite figure appeared in the doorway holding a long full skirt away from her ankles. She was wearing a floppy velvet hat that concealed most of her hair and freckled face.

"Oh, there you are, Dad," she drawled. "It's time to go home now."

Already stunned by Red's involvement, Tyler was now rendered completely speechless.

"Oh, you must be Dad's friend, Tyler." She flashed him a big smile and extended her hand. "I'm Melinda, his daughter from Georgia." Beneath the floppy brim of her hat, her eyes warned him not to give himself away. "You did just fine tonight," she said patting his hand confidently, "and I'm sure you'll be great tomorrow night too. Let's go, Dad."

"Nice to meet you finally, Melinda," Tyler managed to blurt out as Lucy slipped her little arm through Red's elbow and led him out into the hall.

Lucy was here. In Vermont.

Tyler shoved his hand into the pocket of his jeans. His fingers closed around the packet Red had given him. Now he had to figure out how he was going to get a private moment to find out what it was.

Victor had made sure that someone was with Tyler every minute of the day and night. For the few moments he might be mercifully left alone in his room, he knew they had the video camera installed in the attic to survey him with. The only time he felt he was truly alone was when he went into the bathroom but even then someone was usually posted outside the door, waiting for him, making sure he didn't do something "insane" like try to leave the house alone.

He sat on the toilet and pulled the rubber bands off of what he now saw was a wad of paper folded up very small. He quietly unfolded a photo copy of what appeared to be a couple of pages from a theater program. Two names and pictures were circled and Lucy had made comments in the margins.

Next to the first photograph she had written, "Does this look like the Victor we all know and despise?"

Tyler had to agree that it was incredibly unlikely that the Victor Nesbitt in the picture could have aged into the man he knew. He scanned quickly to her next comment which referred to the assistant director, Claude Ledoux. The phrase "hailing from Northern Vermont" was underlined in his biography.

Lucy's notes were brief and little cryptic. "The owner of a certain piece of property on Walker Lake – Claude Ledoux – died of liver failure 1975. According to archives of local paper, his son, also named Claude. High school dropout, worked with a circus in Canada, moved on to theater work – died in car crash in Quebec in the late 70's. 3 months later Victor Nesbitt and Jillian Fox opened a theater school in London."

An arrow pointed to the back of the page. He read on. "Your friend Red went to high school with Claude

Ledoux, junior. Says the Ledouxes were dirt poor, Claude was an unfriendly, scrawny, unathletic kid whom everyone poked fun at. Red thought he saw Claude in the liquor store last month. He has come to the same conclusion that I have."

A sharp rapping on the bathroom door made Tyler leap to his feet. "Whatcha doing in there, nutcase?" Tracy's mocking voice asked loudly.

Without bothering to reply, Tyler flushed the toilet and folded the papers up as small as they had originally been. He had not finished reading everything but he had read enough to understand the implications of this new scenario.

As he flung open the door and stalked down the hallway to his bedroom, he also realized that at last he knew the true meaning of the name "Double Phoenix."

He stayed awake most of the night, tossing and turning in the dark, putting together a chain of events from all the information he now knew, trying to formulate a plan of action for the next night. He wasn't sure if someone was coming to pick him up or if he was just supposed to clear out, but he had to be ready for either event. He was not even sure where he was supposed to be going. But it didn't matter. Lucy knew where Sarah was and Victor had no hold over him anymore.

He spent a good deal of time marveling over how Lucy had magically materialized and how quickly she had done so much footwork. He spent some more time remembering the excitement and compatibility of their days and nights together in London.

He did not fall asleep until the gray light of dawn was seeping in around the edges of the curtains.

Sarah had spent most of the night awake also. Hunter had crept through the window after midnight with a backpack full of comforts. While she drank warm soup from a thermos, he had unbraided her hair and carefully brushed three days' worth of tangles out of it. Then he rebraided it for her and tucked it back under her hat so Victor would not notice. She wore the hat continually; in her sedentary condition, fighting off the chill of the unheated cabin was becoming her greatest battle. Hunter massaged her feet and then tucked them under his shirt to warm them with his body heat. But when he climbed under the down sleeping bag and wrapped himself around her, his own exhaustion overcame him and he was asleep almost instantly.

Sarah lay awake, thankful for his constant caring presence but still wary of the possibility of a surprise appearance from Victor. She thought about Lucy and how she seemed to be driven in the same hyper, obsessive way that Tyler was. She wondered if Lucy and Tyler had been lovers and then, after a brief second's reflection, she knew they had. A few weeks ago that might have bothered her; now it didn't matter anymore.

All that mattered right now was that Lucy had a plan. By tomorrow at this time, it would all be over and Sarah would be out of here.

In the darkness before dawn, she gently woke Hunter from his dreamless sleep. Together they carefully picked up the bits of leaves and dirt that had come in with him from his walk through the woods and then she kissed him goodbye.

"Be careful," she whispered.

"Be brave," was his reply.

She almost believed she was no longer afraid, but her heart pounded heavily in her chest until she heard the distant sound of an engine starting. Then she thought about the red rental car hidden in the broken down garage a few hundred feet away and terror swept through her veins, returning the chill to her blood.

Now she knew that Victor had killed before. She hoped that tonight would be soon enough to keep him from doing it again.

As the lights went out at the end of the first act, Tyler felt his stomach tightening into a tense knot. In the next hour he had to tie up some very important loose ends and if things did not go smoothly, well, then he was up shit's creek. And the first thing he had to do might very well be the hardest.

As they moved offstage in the semi–darkness, he grabbed hold of Jillian's elbow. "I need to see you alone," he murmured into her ear. "Come and find me when you've changed your costume."

The house lights came back up and she turned questioningly to him, a crooked smile playing on her lips. Tyler had no idea what was on her mind at this point but he didn't care. He had resisted her overtures for days now, sickened and disgusted by her. Now he flashed her his most seductive look and squeezed her arm.

"I'll be waiting outside the men's dressing room," he said quietly. "But hurry, there isn't much time."

She tilted her head to one side, doing a quick study of his face. Raising his eyebrows, he licked his lips and grinned. With a shrug of her shoulders, she did a dramatic stage turn, her cape arcing around her as she swept off down the hall.

He would have to wait until the house lights blinked, telling the audience the play would begin again in five minutes. He was banking on the fact that, except to give a few affirming words of encouragement, Victor rarely came back stage during intermission. He preferred to move up to the balcony of the lighting booth and watch the crowd, listening to their reactions and comments about the performance.

Sweat was drenching him from every pore. His palms were clammy, his brow dripped. Beneath his robes, his tee shirt stuck to his chest. In the dressing room he carefully pressed dry towels against his face; he did not want to have to reapply his makeup. It was not just his nerves that were causing him to perspire. Instead of just a pair of boxers, he had his jeans on under his cardinal's costume. He did not want to make his getaway in yards of flaming red cloth.

Stepping out into the hall, he glanced towards the hooks on the wall making sure his leather bomber jacket was visible and within easy reach.

Marcus lounged against the frame of the open back door to the theater, letting the night air cool his body while he kept an eye on Tyler. He wore his disdain and boredom like an extra costume.

The rustle of taffeta and netting preceded Jillian's appearance around the corner. Her masculine attire of the first act had been replaced by the beautiful and revealing gown that she wore during the second half of the play.

"Let's find some place more private," Tyler moved down the hall towards the storage room for props and costumes.

With a supercilious nod of her head, Jillian indicated to Marcus that she would take over the perpetual watch on Tyler now. She followed him into the darkened storeroom where he was fumbling for the pull chain of the ceiling light bulb.

In the unforgiving seventy–five watts of brightness that illuminated the racks of vintage clothing and glittering fabrics meant only for stage use, Tyler turned to face Jillian.

Unsure of what was coming, she sat down on an old steamer trunk and let the shiny golden material of her full–skirted gown spread out around her.

"We don't have much time, you know," she murmured smiling. "What's up?"

Tyler took a deep breath. "I know who you are," he said.

She threw back her head and laughed. "So what? Do you think that changes anything now?"

Her answer was not what he had expected and it knocked some of the wind out of his sails, just as she had known it would.

"Once we found out that you'd gone to Syracuse, we knew you were too smart not to figure it out. Why do you think Victor kidnapped Sarah?"

"Aren't you afraid someone else will figure it out? There are a few people in Syracuse who know your secret now too." He was lying but he had only a few minutes to blow her socks off.

"It's not going to matter in a few days anyhow." She was keeping an almost sneering grin plastered on her lips while she spoke. "But that's something you don't know about, Mr. Investigative Journalist."

Her contemptuous taunt was mockingly reminiscent of Sarah. Tyler felt an uncontrollable surge of anger building inside of him, forcing his words out with the power of a river swelled in spring by the melting mountain snows.

"Well, maybe you ought to take those two tickets to New Zealand and leave with your sister tonight!" he spat out triumphantly, watching the scornful expression freeze on her face. "You see, I know a hell of a lot more than you think I do. And in fact, I know a hell of a lot more than you do. Emma."

Her eyes narrowed at the sound of the name but, actress that she was, she did not flinch.

Through a slit in the side of his red robes, he shoved his hand into the pocket of his jeans and pulled out the compactly folded program that Red had passed to him the night before. "You're not the first phoenix to rise again gloriously from the ashes of another to begin a new life." Tyler's voice came out in a hoarse whisper as he unfolded the brittle paper. "Take a look at who your Victor really is."

He started to hand her the program and then thought better of it. Instead he came over and held it in front of her face. Even with her mask of pancake and powder, Tyler could see her growing pale.

"This is bullshit," she hissed. "Something you contrived. You can't prove anything."

"What did he say that convinced you to help him to drown the real Jillian? That it was really you he loved but that you'd both be happier with Jillian's money?"

"She fell overboard! She drowned herself! I had nothing to do with it." She stood up now and began pacing the room, her old anxiety over the incident beginning to surface again.

"So Victor talked you into assuming the ultimate acting role of a lifetime. To actually become another person. Just like he had."

"Don't be ridiculous. Victor's a director, not an actor." They both twitched as the lights in the building flickered, indicating that the show was about to start in a few minutes.

"You're damn right he's a director. And you're just an actor in his biggest play ever." He grabbed her by the wrists to make her stop pacing and so that he could confront with a few more facts. "Did you know that Jillian couldn't have any children? Did you know that she had progressive cancer and that without any heirs, Victor would be penniless when she died? Only if there were any children, would he become the executor of their estate until the children came of age. Why do you think he really wanted to move you to Vermont and have babies? Because he loved you? Christ, he can't even get it up unless he watches a video of you doing it with someone else!"

With a lightning quick motion, she jerked her hand free of his grasp and smacked him across the face. Tears were streaming down her cheeks leaving long black trails of eye makeup in their wake. "Our relationship is bigger than that," she whispered. "You have no idea."

"He's using you, Emma. Just like he uses everyone, only in a much grander way. He murdered Miles, he let his wife drown, he even killed himself so that he could become someone else. Do you think after you've given him a baby, the passport to his financial security, that he won't find a way to get rid of you too?"

A loud rapping on the storeroom door made them both momentarily stop breathing. "Jillian! Tyler! Second act starts in one minute!"

"We have to go," she said desperately, trying to staunch the tears with her fingertips as she moved towards the door.

"No, listen to me." Tyler grabbed her by the shoulders and spun her around. "The shit is going to hit the fan tonight. You take those Air New Zealand tickets and then you and Phoebe, or Sybil or whatever the hell your sister's name is, you get out of here. Go to the other side of the world. Get out from under Victor's spell. Start a new life. You can become Emma again. Say you got rescued in the Mediterranean by a Greek freighter and you've been working on a ship ever since. You can make it believable – you're excellent actress. Why don't you try acting like yourself again?"

Before she could reply, the door was flung open by an anxious and irate Paloma. "We need you both on stage now to open the second act. Now!" She stood in the doorway holding a clipboard against her chest with one arm and pointing down the hall with the other.

Jillian/Emma took a deep breath as Tyler released his hold on her. "You go," she whispered. "You've got the first line."

He walked away from her with long, swift strides, heading for the already darkened stage where the audience awaited his last performance as Azzolino.

After his first scene was over, Tyler headed for the lighting booth. The last two nights he had been firmly escorted there by Gabriel so that Tracy could keep him "company" during this section of the play that proceeded without him.

Tracy, Victor's henchman who had come from London with him, was an unpredictable loose end. He obviously was being paid off to keep his mouth shut and Victor kept him around so he that he could keep an eye on him. But now that all the muck on the bottom of this muddy pond was floating to the surface, which side would he be on?

Tyler knew Tracy would do anything in his power to protect Victor so that he could continue blackmailing him for enough money to support his passion for Ferraris and expensive electronic equipment.

Through the open window of the lighting booth, Tracy was watching the scene on stage, his hand on a preset dimmer switch, waiting for his cue. As Tyler stood in the doorway, he noticed that the key to the booth, which was attached to Tracy's key ring, was still in the lock on the door.

When it was time for him to return to the stage for his next scene, Tyler slipped silently out of the booth and quietly shut the door. Cupping the hanging keys so that they wouldn't make any noise, Tyler turned the key in the lock and then swiftly pocketed the whole ring. By the time he had reached the bottom of the stairs, he could barely contain his gleeful satisfaction. Not only had he taken care of the threat presented by Tracy, he now had the keys to the kingdom. And the car too.

The last scene of the play, where Azzolino and Christina confess their love to each other and then let go of it, was charged with extra emotion. Tyler knew that Jillian/Emma had the skill to push real life away and completely become whatever character she was playing.

But when she uttered the lines, "Is this my purpose in life? To abdicate everything?", her eyes filled with tears and Tyler knew that at that moment, she was not Christina thinking about giving up her crown and her love for the cardinal. She was Emma, thinking about giving up her charade as Jillian and her life with Victor.

Despite all her remorseless behavior, he felt a momentary twinge of compassion for her.

This was quickly replaced by the nervous anticipation that had been building up in him all night. In the next few minutes he was about to make one of the most daring moves of his life.

At the end of the play, he was alone on stage as the lights came down. For the few seconds it took him to get off the stage, the theater remained in blackness. Then the lights came up for the curtain call. The minor characters came out first to take their bows. Tyler usually stopped offstage just past the curtains to wait for his own turn to come out at the end. Christina would come from the other side and meet him halfway.

Tonight instead, while the actors were preoccupied with the audience's appreciation of their performances, Tyler just kept moving. He undid his costume as he crossed the backstage area. When he reached the hall, he let the red robe fall to the floor and broke into a run, grabbing his jacket off a hook and cradling it in his arms as he ran. His sneakers were shoved into the sleeves; he knew he could not get far in the cloth slippers he was wearing.

The night air hit him like a pan of cold water, waking him to the realization that he had no idea what was supposed to happen next. He sprinted towards the parking lot; he could at least speed to the inn in the Ferrari before anyone caught up with him.

As he reached the parking lot, a pair of headlights flashed once at him and a motor came humming to life. A small car he had never seen before pulled up next to him. He opened the passenger door and hurled himself inside.

CHAPTER NINETEEN

"So where are we going?"

Tyler tossed his sneakers to the floor and shrugged his way into his jacket as Hunter guided the car down the dark ribbon of road that led away from Double Phoenix. After the initial few minutes of hooting and whistling and laughing with relief, a taut silence had settled over the two of them, filling the darkness of the car with the appropriate apprehension.

"Walker Lake. To Sarah."

"So we get Sarah and then where do we go? Certainly not back to the inn." The inn would be the first place that Victor would come hunting for them.

"Not exactly. First of all, we don't rescue Sarah. Yet. This is Lucy's plan," Hunter added hastily. "The idea is to bait Victor into showing up and then forcing him to show his hand."

Tyler exhaled slowly, not sure how to respond to Lucy's idea. His gut feeling was just to get Sarah and then hide out until all the hoopla blew over. But he knew Lucy was right. They knew too much about Victor now to think he would ever let them get away with it. It was time to flush the fox out of his hole.

"So what makes you think he'll go to Sarah now?" he asked.

"Two reasons. One, because he knows you would never run away if it would put her life in danger so you must know where she is. He'll be going there as fast as possible to see if Sarah is still there. And to look for you." Hunter had turned off the main highway and was guiding the car down a dirt road now. "Two – and believe me, man, I have a hard time saying this – because if you're gone, he has no more use for her."

Tyler felt his blood temperature drop several degrees. "Look, I don't want to do this if it's going to put Sarah's life in danger."

Hunter snorted derisively in a way Tyler had never heard before. "You should have thought of that a few weeks ago, bubba," he replied scornfully. "But after this adventure is over, you won't have to worry about Sarah anymore. If you ever did worry."

Tyler suppressed his old–fashioned urge to put his fist in Hunter's self–righteous face. He was glad the darkness hid the fire in his face and eyes, but he was unable to disguise the hostility in his voice. "So I guess that means you two have more than just a working relationship now."

"Oh, our relationship works just fine. But this is not the time or place, Tyler." Hunter had turned the car into a steep driveway overhung with close branches and strewn with a thick carpet of fallen leaves. "I think we ought to put that discussion on hold for another hour, when we have less important things to do."

The headlights of the car illuminated a large house with a wraparound porch and shuttered windows, as well as the dark rippling surface of the lake behind it. Hunter stopped the car and turned the engine off.

"Is this where he's keeping her?" Tyler asked in bewilderment.

"Nope. This is where we catch the next ferry to purgatory." Hunter was already out of the car and shining a powerful flashlight at the dock. "So grab those oars in the back seat, sailor, and follow me."

There was no sound but the rhythmic dipping of the oars as the rowboat glided through the black waters of Walker Lake. "It's just the next place," Hunter murmured quietly. "The dock is falling apart, it probably hasn't been repaired in twenty years, so watch your step."

"Where is Lucy right now?" Tyler asked as he shined the flashlight in the direction Hunter was rowing. He could see the sagging wooden structure they were headed for; the end of the dock had collapsed beneath the surface of the water, the rest of it looked rotten and waterlogged.

"She's up at the cabin with Sarah. When I left them, they were trying to figure out if she could hide in this funky closet where she's been setting up a recording system." Hunter used one oar to steer the boat into position beside the portion of the dock that was still above water.

"She's hiding in a closet?" Tyler was not yet comprehending the situation.

"We felt like somebody needed to be in there with Sarah no matter what happened. You know, like in case you couldn't get out or we didn't get back here for some reason. Now hop out and get your ass up there. I've got a feeling that Victor'll be here in no time."

Tyler grabbed hold of a rickety piling and leaped up onto the dock. He noticed there was another dinghy tied up to it about ten feet away. Through the trees he could see a small square of dim yellow light. "Is that it?" he asked, but when he turned back to Hunter, he was already rowing the boat away.

"What the hell – where are you going?" he called after him.

"The path is right behind you. Hurry!"

He couldn't argue with Hunter's non–sequitur response. Scanning the trees with the flashlight, he found the footpath and moved quickly through the woods. He hated being part of someone else's plan. He wished he knew what the hell was going on.

He reached the cabin minutes later and played his beam of light over the walls. The door was padlocked from the outside, obviously just the way that Victor had left it. As he moved around the perimeter of the building, he could hear the low murmur of female voices inside. Rounding the corner he could see a feeble square of light on the underbrush in front of him coming through a dirty window.

Peeking through the nearest pane, he could see Lucy standing at the foot of the iron–framed bed on which Sarah was sitting. He watched as Sarah doubled over and Lucy lifted the back of Sarah's sweater and attached something with masking tape to her back. Lucy wore a plaid wool jacket and had her fiery hair stuffed up inside of a black beret. Sarah looked like a gypsy in layers of mismatched clothing – long skirts, several sweaters, a wool scarf, gloves and hat. A down sleeping bag lay loosely across her lap. He was mostly relieved to see that she looked none the worst for her ordeal.

His heart pounded and his brain reeled as he dealt with a barrage of mixed emotions regarding these two women. It was as if the two sides of his life were meeting; the steadfast homebody and the adventuresome risk–taker. He doubted if Sarah would ever forgive him for this incident; if Lucy had been the one held hostage she would have considered it just another feather of experience in the cap of life.

Taking a deep breath to steady himself, he rapped loudly on the window.

Both women looked up at him and froze in position, trying to assess if the visitor in the darkness outside was ally or adversary.

Tyler pushed up on the rotted sash of the old double–hung and stuck his head through the opening. "G'day, mates."

"Tyler, you dickhead!" Lucy greeted him with a laugh. "Get your blue–blooded American ass in here, quick!"

"Nice mouth, as usual, Lucy," he remarked, throwing his leg over the splintery sill and rolling into the room. Lucy was at his side in an instant, picking up the wet leaves and dirt he had brought in with him and tossing them back outside. She pulled the window closed, leaving a narrow, barely noticeable, crack open at the bottom. It certainly didn't change the temperature in the damp and chilly cabin.

Then she threw her arms around him and squeezed hard. "Last person you expected to see and the last place I expected to be," she murmured affectionately.

Over her shoulder Tyler caught a glimpse of Sarah's face running the gamut of emotions as she watched him. Extricating himself from Lucy's hug, he crossed the small room to the iron bed. Kneeling on the floor beside Sarah, he could see the expression in her eyes go from a mix of hurt and anger to sadness and guilt and then back again.

"Sarah, I'm so sorry–" he began.

"Don't. Not now." She held up a gloved hand. "He's a wicked bastard and I hate him as much as you do. So first let's do this thing together and then I can get around to hating you too." One side of her mouth turned up in half of a grin.

Before Tyler could reply, Lucy broke in. "Sorry, guys, but your touching reunion will have to wait until later. We may only have a few minutes until Victor shows. Now get up off your knees, Tyler, so I can show you what we need you to do."

Pushy broad, Tyler thought to himself as he tried not to smile at the diminutive dynamo giving him orders.

Seven minutes later, he was crouched in a filthy corner of the other room, hidden behind an antique refrigerator, holding his breath as Victor unlocked the padlock on the door just a few feet away. On the other side of the wall, Sarah had dimmed the kerosene lamp down to a faint flicker and was feigning sleep; Lucy was concealed behind the ragged curtain of the clothes closet.

Although he had rarely been more frightened in his life, Tyler got a satisfying thrill from the knowledge that Victor, the Houdini of modern crime, had no idea that he was walking into a trap.

Victor did not linger at all in the kitchen where Tyler was hiding but moved quickly and self–assuredly into the bedroom. The smell of burning kerosene became more pervasive as Victor turned up the flame of the lamp.

Then came the sound of objects being thrown hastily and angrily into a plastic grocery bag.

In the next room Sarah was drenched in a cold sweat as she tried to act as though she was awakening from a sound sleep and suspected nothing was wrong. She was not used to this kind of subterfuge; she hoped she could pull it off.

"Victor?" she yawned. "What are you doing here? I didn't think you were coming back tonight." She had never spoken in such a pleasant voice to him before. She hoped he would put it down to having just awoken.

"I hope you didn't expect that your boyfriend really cared about your life that much. Because apparently he doesn't." Victor's voice had a cruel edge to it that Sarah had not heard before.

"What do you mean? What are you talking about?" This time the actual fright she was feeling made her tone sound just right. She realized that Victor was frenetically clearing away all the supplies he had brought for her, throwing paperback novels in the same bag as apples and peanut butter.

"He couldn't play by the rules. He disappeared after the show tonight. The devious bastard." This last part was muttered under his breath.

"He what?" It hit Sarah in a sudden flash what Victor was doing. He was planning to leave her in the cabin to die, taking away her food and water and the few creature comforts he had allowed her to have. Even though she knew she was safe, her anger at his unthinkable actions heated up her blood with the force of a forest fire. At the thought of what might have been, hot tears began to run down her cheeks.

"He obviously doesn't love you enough to save you from slow death by starvation. I should have realized as much when he began fucking my wife every night. Too bad there isn't a VCR here – I've got a few videos you might like to see."

Sarah's already flushed cheeks deepened in color. On the other side of the wall, Tyler was nearly blinded by rage and clenched his fists, trying to stay focused.

"You're not really going to leave me here to die, are you? It's not fair. I haven't done anything to you!" Sarah's wail was real; she was outraged at the injustice he had planned to perpetrate.

"You must know by now, Sarah, that life is not fair. I'll take that sleeping bag now, if you don't mind." Victor stood there, looming over her, impatient to be finished and gone.

Sarah froze. She could not give him the sleeping bag. It was time to move on to Phase Two. She took a deep breath and forced herself to be calm.

"Well, you should know better than most people that life isn't fair. Especially not to orphans from Saskatchewan." Still a little shaky, she managed to come across clear and confident.

Poised as always, Victor hesitated only a few seconds before rising to the bait. "So Tyler has done more homework than I expected he had. But I can't say that life hasn't been fair to me."

"But, I wasn't talking about you. I was referring to the real Victor Nesbitt."

There was only the slightest pause before Victor laughed harshly. "I don't know what the hell you're talking about. Now just give me the sleeping bag and that good cashmere scarf of mine that you have around your neck so that I can be on my way."

"I think you know exactly what I'm talking about, Claude Ledoux." As she spoke, she squirmed beneath the sleeping bag, making a few adjustments just in case he should make a dive for the bag.

"Claude Ledoux! I worked with him in Canada. He's been dead for years." Victor began to pace a little nervously, trying to assess the extent of what Sarah knew. "How could Tyler possibly know anything about Claude Ledoux?"

"Now why would you bother to keep up this charade with someone whom you're about to murder?" she asked, ignoring his question. "Did you play these kinds of games with Miles Romano before you drowned him in the lake?"

Victor snorted derisively as he advanced on her. "Your imagination has definitely run away with itself these last few days. You should be able to keep yourself totally entertained once you reach a state of dehydrated delirium." With a swift motion he pulled the sleeping bag off her lap and began pushing it into a sack. "Of course, you may die of exposure first. You're going to have to give me most of those clothes you're wearing as well. It wouldn't do for your body to be discovered ten years from now with the remains of Jillian Fox's English wool long underwear still on it."

Sarah was almost enjoying herself now, knowing that her ordeal was nearly over. She forced herself to be appear duly horrified at Victor's suggestion that she strip off her outer layers in order to give back Jillian's long johns as she continued.

"Well, here's a question I've been thinking about in all my free time here. Was it worth murdering your own father to inherit this falling down piece–of–shit house?"

She and Lucy had only speculated about that one. But even in the dim light of the oil lamp she could tell by the expression on Victor's usually controlled features that this was uncharted territory, never before crossed.

"So that makes three people so far that you've done away with because they got in your way. Am I really only the fourth? Or are there others?"

She had allowed a taunting tone to creep into her voice. It was just enough to push Victor over the edge. "I'll take that scarf now," he said unevenly. Before she realized what he was doing, he had reached out with both hands for the loose ends of the scarf that was wound around her neck. Instead of unwinding it, he began to pull the ends in opposite directions.

Gasping, she tried to grab for the scarf but it was too late. The luxurious fibers were tightening around her throat and beginning to cut off her air supply.

"Tyler!" She tried to shout but her voice came out as a thin squeak.

"Your boyfriend wouldn't help you if he could hear you," Victor sneered, ducking as Sarah's fingernails lashed out at his face. "Now that he's tasted Jillian's juicy cunt, I'm sure he's lost his taste for yours."

From somewhere behind him came a war cry of rage. Victor turned around, caught off guard just long enough for Tyler to lunge at him and knock him to the ground. As Victor's hands involuntarily released the scarf that was strangling Sarah, Tyler got his own choke hold on Victor's neck.

"You sick bastard! What do you know about integrity? You've never saved anyone's skin but your own," Tyler shouted at him, tightening his own grip on Victor's bare neck as Victor twisted and flailed beneath him, trying to toss him off. "Well, now it's time for you to play Truth or Consequences. I want to hear you admit that it was your wife that you drowned last summer in the Mediterranean, not a swim team champion from Syracuse named Emma Erickson."

Sarah, who had collapsed on the bed and was slowly unwinding the offensive scarf, looked down at them in amazement. Somehow she had missed out on learning that important piece of the puzzle.

Victor did not respond to Tyler's accusation. Instead he became perfectly still on the floor beneath Tyler, who, with his hands locked around Victor's neck, was straddling his chest like a race horse jockey. Tyler was sweating and trembling; Victor, even in his trapped position seemed cool and controlled.

"Say it, Victor. Say you killed your real wife because she had cancer and could never have any children which would leave you penniless when she died. Say that you installed a great actress with an uncanny resemblance to your wife in her place, a great actress with good reproductive organs, I might add. I'm sure you planned to do away with her as well when the heirs to your future were born. You ruthless son of a bitch."

Victor still said nothing. He remained steely–eyed and immobile which only served to infuriate Tyler even more.

"But you've acquired a skill for this sort of thing over your lifetime, haven't you? It wasn't the first time you'd knocked off someone who wasn't really dead. You'd done it to yourself years before, so triumphantly that you couldn't imagine that it wouldn't work again. And to prove your point you came back to settle down in the hometown of dead, good–for–nothing Claude Ledoux, so you could pat yourself on the back on how successfully you had put this life behind you. You just hadn't counted on unimportant Emma's life ever catching up with you until Miles showed up in your theater one –"

With a sudden karate–like movement, Victor twisted his body, sat up and flipped Tyler off of him. As Tyler went sprawling on the dirty pine planks of the floor, Victor loomed over him, pointing a small pistol with hands that were still surprisingly steady.

"Get up, Mackenzie."

Tyler stared at him, dazed, wondering where the pistol had come from, wondering whether Lucy's "plan" could cover this unforeseen turn of events.

"I said get up. Now."

With his eyes riveted to the gun, Tyler began to move slowly to his feet. Somewhere to his right he heard a small cough and then a voice said in a near whisper, "Drop it right there, Victor."

Out of the corner of one eye he saw Sarah using both hands to shakily train a handgun on Victor who had not even bothered to look over at her. Tyler had not known about this part of the event, but he could guess why the women had kept it secret from him. "She's got a gun, Victor," he warned. "You better do as she says."

With lightning speed Victor glanced at Sarah. "What the hell–" he muttered angrily, and then with one long step he was beside Tyler and had the cold metal of the pistol pressed against Tyler's temple.

"Don't do anything stupid, Sarah," Victor warned. "I'm sure I could put a bullet through Tyler's head faster than you could hit me."

For a few tense seconds, they all remained frozen in this bizarre standoff. Then, still keeping his gun against Tyler's forehead, Victor stepped behind Tyler and threw an arm across his chest. Using Tyler as a body shield, he began backing towards the door.

"Go ahead, shoot me now, Sarah," Victor taunted as he backed all the way out of the cabin, pulling Tyler along in front of him.

Outside a cold rain bordering on sleet had begun to fall. The chilling wetness of it against his face and head brought Tyler out of his numb disbelief at how the situation had turned out. Somehow Victor was running the show again and now, in order to save his own life, Tyler would have to play along with him.

"Padlock that door," Victor ordered him. Tyler did as he was told. He knew it didn't matter; Sarah and

Lucy could still escape. He was glad now that Lucy had remained hidden. At least Sarah was not alone.

"Now walk down that path in front of me and I swear to God, one stray move and I will not hesitate to shoot you." Victor kept his stranglehold on Tyler as together they stumbled through the dark towards the dim outline of Victor's Land Rover.

"There's a tree down here. Step over it. Don't try anything funny. Okay, here's the car. Now open the passenger side door." Tyler lifted the door handle, trying to decide when the best moment to bolt would be. The interior light went on inside the Land Rover. "Now move over into the driver's seat. You're going to drive."

He couldn't be serious. But as Tyler scrambled over the stick shift, he realized that Victor had no option. There was no way he himself could drive and keep a gun pointed at Tyler. Well, at least this would give Tyler a chance at some sort of control.

"The key's in the ignition." Tyler could feel the end of the firing end of the pistol pressed against his Adam's apple now. He wondered exactly what Victor had in mind for him.

Rain water ran down his forehead and off the end of his nose as he put his foot on the clutch and turned the key. As the engine roared to life, the inside of the car was suddenly flooded with bright light that came from behind. For an instant Tyler thought that something had exploded and that very possibly that something was his own head. Then the light flashed on and off a few times and he realized it was the headlights of a vehicle parked behind them.

"What the fuck," said Victor. "I never did ask you how the hell you got here. Who's your accomplice?"

"You shoot me now, Victor, your ass is grass," Tyler said, relief warming his chilled body and spirit. "The police are on their way, if that's not them already." He was making it up now but it was definitely the only way to go. "The best thing for you to do is run for it alone."

He dared a glance in Victor's direction. In the flash of the headlights, he could tell by the expression in the other man's eyes that he was becoming a little unstrung.

"Hah, good try. But not without you, I don't. If that's the police, you're my passport out of here. Open your door." Victor nudged hard against Tyler's throat with the barrel end of the gun.

"Don't be ridiculous. I'll just slow you d–down." Tyler coughed a little as the gun pressed harder against his esophagus. "Okay, okay. Where are we going? Back to the house?"

"No. Past the house. Down to the lake."

"The lake? What lake?" Tyler asked, feigning ignorance, trying to figure out how he could work this to his advantage. He remembered the other boat at the dock. But Victor couldn't possibly know about it. And if things had gone the way Tyler thought they had, the boat would be gone by now.

"Get out of the car, Mackenzie, or do I have to blow a hole in one of your arms to get my point across?" Victor's voice was hoarse and unreasoning now.

"You've watched too many John Wayne movies," Tyler remarked as he threw the car door open, knowing that his offhand comment would rankle a theater highbrow like Victor.

The headlights of the car behind them continued to flash on and off as Tyler and Victor moved slowly back up the path. Their way was illuminated until they had passed by the house and crested the hill and were heading down towards the pond. Tyler did not know what Hunter was planning, but he prayed that he had something more in mind.

"Here shine this torch on the path." Victor shoved a flashlight into Tyler's hand.

"Torch. You can give up the British bullshit game now. Claude. We call them flashlights in America." Tyler knew it was not smart to taunt him, but holding the solid roundness of the flashlight in his hand gave him the beginnings of a small sense of empowerment.

"Shut up. And don't even think about turning it off and making a run for it. I've got another torch in my pocket."

Sure you do, Tyler thought to himself, but the possibility brought him down a few notches.

"Okay. There's the old dock. Now shine the light off to the right. There should be a brown tarpaulin covering a rowboat. Damn. Where is it?"

Tyler moved the beam of light back and forth across the bank, letting it finally come to rest on a pile of plastic tossed into the underbrush. "That looks like your tarp there but I don't see any boat."

"Damn. Damn. Damn." As Victor muttered angrily to himself, it seemed as if the freezing precipitation falling from the sky began to pick up in intensity. "Shine that light towards the end of the dock."

As the icy rain from above hit the warmer waters below, a fog began to rise off the surface of the lake. Tyler pointed the flashlight in the direction of the crumbling dock but it was becoming increasingly harder to see more than a few feet.

"We'll have to move closer to see anything," he said to Victor as a plan started to form in his mind. Without waiting for a reply, he moved forward. Victor stayed closed behind him.

The old wooden planks of the dock were not only rotting; they were very slippery now as well. Unfortunately Victor held onto Tyler tightly and kept the gun in the small of his back. If one of them fell, they both would go down. Tyler knew he might have a chance if he turned off the flashlight and jumped into the water but that was a last resort.

"Do you see anything tied up to the end there?" Victor growled, his mouth very close to Tyler's ear.

"We'll have to move closer but there are a couple of boards missing here." It was obvious to both of them that Tyler could not step over the empty space in front of him if Victor kept his tight grip on his arm. "Loosen up on me, buddy, okay? I'll step over and then you come over."

"One false move and you're a dead man, Mackenzie," Victor warned.

"What movie did you pick that line up from, Victor?" Tyler's legs were long enough to span the gap in the dock without actually jumping across. As Victor followed him, Tyler quickly played the beam across the water. "Oh, yeah, I see your rowboat now."

He hoped the faint pinpoint of light he was seeing down the shoreline was what he thought it was.

"Where?" demanded Victor.

Suddenly the dock was as brilliant as midday, lit from behind them by a powerful blinding beacon. "Police!" shouted an authoritative voice. 'Drop your weapon and put your hands above your head! Now!"

The circle of light was staggeringly bright; it hurt Tyler's eyes to look at it. "You're cooked, Victor," he said, trying not to sound too triumphant.

"Never." Moving the pistol up to Tyler's temple, Victor whirled around so that Tyler was between him and the blazing spotlight, creating a human shield of safety for himself. Beneath their combined weight, the rotten boards groaned and made splintering sounds.

"Turn off that light or I shoot this man in the head!" Victor shouted at his unseen assailants.

Still awash in the eye–piercing glare, Tyler was able to discreetly turn off the flashlight he was holding. "He means it. Do what he says!" Tyler called. "It's okay!"

As suddenly as the dock had become bright, it was now pitched into an equally blinding darkness, made even more so by the flashbulb effect left by the giant light. Pulsating circles of glowing color, those magic tricks of the retina, gave Tyler the momentary disorientation he needed.

Bouncing forcefully, he heard more than he felt the disintegrating wood beneath his feet giving way. As Victor began to lose his footing, Tyler used the loss of balance to his own advantage. With one fluid motion, he pushed Victor backward and leaped forward himself.

His shoe touched the dock and immediately slid off the icy surface. Behind him he heard a wayward gunshot and then a muffled splash. Desperate, he threw his upper body forward, tossing the flashlight aside. The side of his face and the palms of his hands landed on the rough wood at the same time his toes hit the water. Ignoring the splinters in his skin, he painfully clawed his way to safety.

Breathing heavily, he began to crawl the length of the dock back towards the shore line. His voice came out in a ragged whisper. "Hunter, are you there?"

"Over here. Are you alright?" He heard hesitant footsteps coming towards him in the dark and then the welcoming human contact of Hunter's knee colliding with his face. "Sorry. You okay? You're not shot, are you?" It was hard to believe the fearful boyish voice speaking to him was the same one that had just boomed so loudly behind the spotlight a few moments before.

"I'm fine. But turn that light on again quickly. Shine it on the lake."

A second later the powerful light once more illuminated the watery landscape, displaying the smoke–like puffs of fog that rose from the choppy surface which was pockmarked by the sharply falling rain. There was no sign of Victor at all, not in the water or on the dock.

"Where is he? Do you think he drowned?" Hunter's tone was awesome and hushed.

"I don't know. Shit. I don't know." As Tyler reached for the big battery operated light, his hands were shaking visibly. Stressed, freezing and probably in shock, he turned the beam towards the shoreline. Up one side and then down the other, he searched the woods for a sign that Victor had managed to swim through the frigid water and climb out onto the steep banks.

"I don't know," he repeated. "But if he did drown, then he got what he deserved."

In the distance they could hear the approaching wail of a police siren. On the other side of the hill behind them, the sky was eerily lit by the repeated flash of blue lights.

"Lucy and Sarah?" Tyler asked, tilting his head towards the siren, suddenly too exhausted to finish the question.

Hunter nodded. For a moment they both stared dazedly at the empty dock and the dark waters beyond it. Then they headed slowly up the path that led to the cabin and the cars and the inquiries that undoubtedly lay in wait for them.

CHAPTER TWENTY

"They've been up there a long time," Lucy remarked as she pulled her sweater over her head. Tying it around her waist, she resumed her perch on the end of the kitchen counter where Hunter was chopping vegetables. "It gets hot in here, doesn't it? So what do you think is going to happen?"

"With Sarah and Tyler? Seems inevitable to me." Hunter reached for a large stainless steel stockpot that hung on a hook above the stove. He dropped it onto a burner with a loud, purposeful clanging that said volumes more than his words.

"You think it's over then?"

"I sure as hell hope so." With a sweeping gesture, Hunter dumped the contents of the cutting board into the pot.

"And just supposing it's not..."

He stopped what he was doing and turned to face her. Lucy was baiting him, but it was the way she talked to everybody, always trying to force their hidden feelings to the surface. Just in case it made a good story.

"You mean if they decide to take another shot at it? Then I guess I'm out of here. Back to California."

"Just like that? You and Kashi? Or just you alone?" Lucy nabbed a slice of carrot and popped it into her mouth, grinning at him.

His stomach gave a sudden sickening lurch in response to her questions. "You are diabolical, you know that, don't you? Well, I don't have to tell you anything, you nosy girl reporter. I wouldn't want to see my words in print in the London Times."

"Oh, please, don't act so juvenile." She purposely used the word knowing it would keep him on edge. "Nobody in London would be interested in reading about you when I can feed them miles of copy about Victor and Jillian. Especially if neither of them ever turn up."

Hunter did not reply. His mind was busy exploring the various combinations of possibilities in his own life that depended on the outcome of Tyler and Sarah's confrontation. He had promised himself he would not think about the future until he had a reason to and Lucy was forcing him to deal with it before he was ready.

"Do you ever think about going back to college?" she asked.

"Lucy, you're a pit bull," he said, shaking his head. "Yes, I think about it."

"I've forgotten. What was it you were studying?"

"Horticulture."

"Oh, yes. You like to grow things. Now let me guess what it is you like to grow best." Although he was not looking at her, Hunter could hear the mischief in her voice.

"Broccoli."

"Of course, there's a big market for that in California these days, isn't there? Isn't that where they've legalized broccoli for medicinal purposes? Must be a lot of competition among growers. Have some of them actually been able to come above ground?"

"Lucy–" Hunter's tone was merry but threatening. "Give it a rest."

"Okay, okay. But it would be a great story." Lucy pulled a small notebook out of the back pocket of her jeans and quickly jotted a few thoughts down. "If I left your name out of–"

"There is nothing to write about. I haven't lived in California for nearly two years! Why don't you go pick on someone your own size!" He tossed a potato at her which she deftly caught with her left hand. "Or you can help me peel these potatoes."

Sarah was exhausted. Now that she was home and could let down her defense mechanisms, the days of confinement in an unheated cabin were finally taking their toll on her. The fact that they had not gotten out of the police station until nearly dawn had not helped much either. She felt like she was on the verge of coming down with a serious cold, but she could not give in to it yet. There was still some serious business that needed dealing with.

She and Tyler sat at opposite ends of the couch from each other, as estranged as they had ever been in their entire relationship. Nobody had gotten more than a few hours of sleep, especially not after Hunter had picked up Kashi from Jennifer's house where Jennifer and her mother had been babysitting Kashi overnight.

Sarah knew Tyler had been annoyed by the amount of attention she paid to the baby she hadn't seen in three days, but she didn't care anymore about what annoyed Tyler. She would not even consider talking to him alone until Kashi went down for her afternoon nap.

"This poor baby has already lost her first caretaker. She needs to know this one is not going to leave her stranded," was Sarah's explanation despite the fact that Kashi did not seem the worse for wear after three days without Sarah.

All Sarah wanted to do now was get this confrontation with Tyler over as fast as possible. She had already expressed her revulsion over Tyler's sexual relationship with Jillian/Emma and Victor's claim that he had video tapes of it.

Tyler's defensive response had been that he knew she and Hunter had been going at it in his own bed, that he had slept with Jillian because he was hurting and jealous. By the time he was finished, he had almost convinced himself of his own innocence.

"What I don't understand," she said, finally forcing herself to look at him, "is why you told her to run. Why did you help her to get away? She was nearly as guilty as he was."

"I don't think so," Tyler replied, not about to back down. "She was actually the biggest victim of all. I don't believe she had any idea when she went sailing in the Mediterranean with the two of them that Victor had any plans beyond a lascivious ménage–a–trois. I think he talked her into impersonating his dead wife. Maybe he blackmailed her into it with the threat of blame for the murder, at the same time convincing her that her life would be more rewarding as Jillian Fox than as Emma Erickson, who was just worthless white trash from Buffalo.

"He knew what a chameleon she was; on stage she could be anybody, she was completely open to suggestion. She was the perfect opportunity for him and she looked remarkably like Jillian who, with her life threatening cancers and lack of reproductive organs was rapidly becoming worthless to him. No matter what anyone else says, I believe he was using Emma for his own personal gain. I think she deserves a chance to start her life over."

Suddenly in desperate need of a beer, he stood up and headed for the refrigerator in the next room. "And I hope that she and her sister are on their way to New Zealand right now," he continued loudly. "And that they get through customs and get lost in some Down Under city before the police figure out where they've gone."

"But she drugged you and set you up, she used you!" Sarah argued when he returned with an open bottle. "She was his assistant, aiding and abetting him in crime! How can you just let her get away with it?"

"She needs a fresh start." But he knew Sarah was right. Emma had not been a total innocent when she went to London to enroll in Victor's school. The depraved part of Victor had recognized a kindred soul in the uninhibited American girl who was not offended by any obscene act he had asked her to perform in his tasteless videos. The fact that she was infatuated with him and highly suggestible had made his controlling dominance all that much easier.

"So really you've involved yourself, you know. Knowingly aiding the escape of a wanted criminal."

"Sarah."

"Okay, okay, I won't go there. But I just hope you aren't deluding yourself with the idea that you're a hero in this situation. You might have solved a mystery but I don't see how any justice has been done yet." Sarah's sharp, pointed words drove themselves like a stake into his heart. She was right. In the end, what good had he really done?

Hopefully Victor was dead at the bottom of Walker Lake. But it would take hours of diving and dredging to ascertain that fact. Tyler suspected that somehow, once again, Victor had managed to get away. At least this time the world was on to him. IF he was alive, he would not be able to hide forever.

Tyler upended his beer. After not drinking anything for several days, it was nectar to his taste buds, cold and delicious. "So," he said. "What happens now?"

"Meaning?" Sarah's cold tone covered the dread she was feeling.

"Us. You and me."

The deep sigh she gave said it all. "You can't stay here anymore, Tyler. You know that, don't you?"

Much as he had known the words were coming, he had not wanted to hear her say them. They could not look at each other now. He picked at the label of his beer bottle, one of his bare feet tapping nervously on the floor. "So what does that mean; that your California drifter boy is moving in?"

"For now. We'll see." The tremor in her voice revealed the emotion that she was feeling.

"How long do you think that will last?" he asked bitterly.

"It doesn't matter. Probably not that long. But that's not the point." To her dismay, a fat tear began working its way out of her left eye. She dashed it away angrily. "The point is, you and I can't live together anymore. Our agendas are way too different. My priorities are not your priorities, and vice versa."

Annoyed that he could not conceal the emotion that he too was feeling, he decided to lay all his cards down. "You're right, Sarah. But the truth is, I may be an asshole, but I still love you. As much as ever."

Sarah cut him off. "Come on, Tyler. You must know by now there's more to living together than just being in love." More big tears were streaming down her cheeks now. "I'm sorry. It's just over for now. You have to go." She covered her face with her hands in a feeble attempt to keep her grief to herself.

She waited until she heard the empty bottle slam down on the coffee table and the door close behind him. Then she cried.

Lucy found Tyler sitting at the bar in the darkened lounge. He had two empty bottles in front of him and was working on a third.

Without turning on the lights, she climbed onto the stool next to him. "Bad news?"

"Not news. Just bad. Nothing I didn't expect."

"Sorry, old chum. So what are your plans?" As always, Lucy was appropriately sympathetic but ready to move on.

"I have none. Right now I've lost everything I had going for me. I'm not an actor, not a cook, not a journalist, not even a boyfriend." Tyler stared morosely into space.

"Sounds like you're doing a bang–up job of feeling really sorry for yourself." Lucy helped herself to a mouthful of Tyler's beer. "That's not like you. Besides, I think you're wrong."

"About what?"

"Once a journalist, always a journalist. Why don't you come back to London with me for a while? Get some background for the blistering expose of Victor Nesbitt you're going to write for the American press." She acted very nonchalant, as though the idea had just occurred to her.

Tyler slowly turned his bloodshot gaze on her. "You mean it, Lulu?"

"Of course, I mean it. You know you're a damn good writer. You just get distracted so easily. You need someone to keep you on course while you get your sails up again. "

"You're doing this just because you feel sorry for me, right?"

"Because I'm your friend, damn it." She gave him a hearty slap on the back. And then, even though they were alone in the empty lounge, she leaned over and whispered conspiratorially in his ear. "And because I, for one, can't walk away from opportunity. I've been waiting for her to throw you out for years."

Despite himself, Tyler realized he was grinning. "Oh, come on, you don't really mean that."

"Don't hurt my feelings, Tyler! You're making fun of me when I've just bared my soul to you!" She punched him in the shoulder. "Now I'm going to call the airline to see if there's space on my flight tonight. You better stop drinking and start packing."

When Hunter finally caught up with her, Sarah was sitting on the edge of the bed in Kashi's bedroom, watching the baby sleep in her crib. "Watching the grass grow?" he teased.

"No, that's your favorite pastime, not mine." She was surprised she could joke with him the way she was feeling.

"Oooh, below the belt. Hey, I've got something to show you." He sat down next to her and retrieved a small green daypack from beneath the bed. Unzipping the front pocket, he pulled out a small flat pouch. He handed it to her. "Open it."

Peering inside, she recognized the blue color of an American passport and some papers in a ziplock bag. The passport revealed a smiling picture of Miles Romano. In the plastic bag was a Nigerian birth certificate and adoption papers.

"Where did you find these?" she asked in amazement.

"Right where I knew they would be. Under the seat of the rental car in the shed at Walker Lake. I picked up the backpack the first time Lucy and I went out there." Slipping an arm around her shoulder, he pulled her close to him.

"So what now?" she asked, her eyes were still skimming the adoption papers, the words a blur of legalese.

"I think a trip to Ohio is in order, don't you? Maybe next week, after foliage season is officially over, you can close the inn down for a few days."

Ohio. To see Miles' parents. About Kashi. She did not have to speak her thoughts and fears aloud. He knew what she was thinking. "What do you think they'll say?" she whispered.

Hunter shrugged. "Only one way to find out."

So many things to worry about. Tyler was way in the back of her mind now. "Hunter, are you ready for this? I mean, I know I am. But you're young and a traveler; are you really prepared to settle down and have responsibilities?"

Hunter shrugged again. "Only one way to find out."

"I mean, what if this doesn't work out for us? What if you decide to go back to California and finish college? What happens to Kashi then?"

"Well, she stays with you, of course, until I'm ready to come back and be with you guys again. I don't know, Sarah! How can we know what's going to happen unless we give it a chance?"

He was right. Tucking the papers back into the plastic bag, she stood up. "I better go put these in a safe place," she said.

"Wait, don't go yet." He grabbed her arm. "Tyler's in there packing," he explained in answer to her questioning look. "He's off to London with Lucy tonight."

"He is?" She sat down heavily on the bed, suddenly overwhelmed by the upheaval of events in her life.

"That's good, isn't it? I mean, he's leaving because you asked him to, right?"

She nodded, unable to speak.

Hunter wrapped his arms around her and pulled her close to him. "Stay here with me for a while," he murmured. "We can start working on Kashi's baby brother."

"Don't be ridiculous!" she laughed as she let herself fall backwards onto the pillow with him.

"Why?" He was already undoing her jeans. "Because we aren't ready to have a baby or because the inn opens for dinner in less than an hour?"

"Fuck dinner," she said, pulling his shirt over his head. "Life is too short."

ABOUT THE AUTHOR

A lifelong lover of travel, mysteries and creative expression, Marilinne Cooper has always enjoyed the escapist pleasure of combining her passions in a good story. She lives in the White Mountains of New Hampshire and is also a freelance copywriting professional. To learn more, visit marilinnecooper.com.

ALSO BY MARILINNE COOPER

Night Heron
Butterfly Tattoo
Blue Moon
Double Phoenix
Dead Reckoning
Snake Island
Windfall
Catnip Jazz
Second Wind

Jamaican Draw

Made in United States
North Haven, CT
10 November 2022

26563334R00153